Decorating
SCHEMES

Decorating
SCHEMES

Deadly Décor Mysteries

Book 2

Ginny Aiken

Revell

Grand Rapids, Michigan

Published by Fleming H. Revell
a division of Baker Publishing Group
P.O. Box 6287, Grand Rapids, MI 49516-6287
www.revellbooks.com

Printed in the United States of America

Library of Congress Cataloging-in-Publication Data
Aiken, Ginny.
    Decorating schemes / Ginny Aiken.
        p.   cm.— (Deadly decor mysteries ; bk. 2)
    Includes bibliographical references.
    ISBN 0-8007-3045-3 (pbk.)
    1. Women interior decorators—Fiction. 2. Teenagers—Crimes against—
Fiction. I. Title.
PS3551.I339D43 2006
813'.54—dc22   2005026358

Published in association with the literary agency of Alive Communications, Inc., 7680 Goddard Street, Suite 200, Colorado Springs, Colorado 80920.

Before I formed you in the womb I knew you,
before you were born I set you apart.

Jeremiah 1:5

1

Wilmont, Washington

Stripping is not the best way for a woman to earn her living. I mean, really. To start out with, the clothes you have to wear are nothing to write home about, and then look at what it does to your skin. All those caustic chemicals ruin your hands. At least I'm the kind who wouldn't be caught dead at a nail salon; the cost of manicure upkeep would rival the federal deficit.

As an interior designer and new owner of a major auction house, I come in contact with more than my share of old pieces that need nips and tweaks if not complete face-lifts. For that, I have to rely on those nasty stripping compounds. And don't even think about the all-natural or organic kind. They just don't do the job as well or as fast.

That leads me to my other problem. No matter what kind of gloves I use or how fast I work, they always wind up melted before I finish the fix to the furniture's finish.

That's what my newest pair had started to do when the phone rang in the workshop at the warehouse.

"Norwalk & Farrell's Auctions, Haley Farrell speaking."

"Hi, Haley." The fudgy voice was more than familiar. Before I could respond, Noreen Daventry continued. "I hope I didn't catch you at a bad time."

For my gooey gloves, and the phone, no time would be good. The gloves were done for, and I'd have to douse the receiver with stripper to rid it of the rubbery mess, then hope and pray that it too wouldn't succumb to the chemical. But I couldn't tell one of the richest women on the West Coast I was too busy to talk to her.

"It's never a bad time for a chat with you, Noreen."

"That's very kind, Haley." A hint of humor underscored Noreen's voice, a clear reminder that we know more about each other than either likes.

"Since you're in such a benevolent mood," she went on, "this should be a good time to ask you a favor."

Groan. "Sure. What do you need?"

"I don't need anything. But I do have friends whose home is in dire need of your talents."

Now she was playing my kind of tune. "Really? What's their problem?"

"Oh, no problem. Just a house that hasn't been touched in the last . . . oh, I guess it must be fifteen years now. They're newlyweds, and Dr. Marshall would like to offer his darling new bride the chance to make the house hers."

"Dr. Marshall . . . do you mean Stewart Marshall, the plastic surgeon?"

"You know Stew, then."

"No, but I do read newspapers."

"Then you already know this job would be very lucrative for you. And I've raved about your work to Deedee, the new Mrs. Marshall. They'd like you to come over as soon as possible—this evening, even—to take a good look at their place and give them your expert opinion. They like what you did with my new home."

Noreen bought a white-elephant money pit almost a year ago at the first auction I ran after my inheritance cleared probate. I worked like a horse to finish the redesign in time for her to move in this spring. She's been in the home a mere eight weeks now and has already hosted six social-column-worthy bashes.

"I'm glad." I checked every surface for paper and pen or pencil but found none. Besides, my hands were in no condition to touch anything. "Tell you what. I . . . ah . . . have a minor mess to clear up here, and then I'll call you back."

A throaty laugh flowed over the connection. "Hope you're not in trouble with the law again."

The nerve of the woman! I haven't been in trouble with the law.

Never.

Not really.

They just jumped to judgment a few months back and thought I'd committed a crime that anyone with a shred of brain matter would know I never could have done. But I had to hold my tongue if I wanted to land the job—not a piece of cake for me.

"Um . . . er . . . no. Nothing like that. I just need to take care of some ah . . . paperwork—" paper towels might do the job "—to give the Marshalls my complete attention."

Another chuckle tested my patience, so I sent a quick prayer heavenward.

"I'll be waiting for your call, then," Noreen said. "Oh, and by the way. You might as well know ahead of time. The Marshalls decided to hire Dutch too."

This time I couldn't keep the groan to myself.

Noreen laughed harder. "That's what I thought. I suppose I should warn Deedee that fireworks will be a daily thing when her general contractor and interior designer come face-to-face."

What could I say? Dutch Merrill and I don't see eye to eye on much. Actually, we don't see eye to eye on anything, as we discovered during the months we were forced to work together on Noreen's remodel.

Well, I'll admit his work at Noreen's place was outstanding.

A tantrum wouldn't do; I had to get a grip.

I had no choice but to play nice. "You're right. The Fourth of July has nothing on us. But we did do a good job on the Gerrity mansion. You haven't stopped raving about your new home, and the Wilmont Historical Society feels that although we didn't necessarily restore the mansion to its original glory, we didn't hurt its architectural or historical integrity either."

"You've a point there. Even if you did fight like cats and dogs the whole time, you and Dutch somehow worked a miracle. The house looks fabulous, you both came in under budget, and you even finished three weeks ahead of schedule." She paused. Then, "But you have to agree, your spats did add much-needed of comic relief to a dreary process."

Oh yeah. A woman always likes to hear she's become entertainment fodder for the obscenely wealthy. *Dignity, Haley. Shoot for dignity.*

"Don't worry, Noreen. Dutch and I can work just as well for the Marshalls as we did for you. Now, if you don't mind, I do have to get back to this mess—I mean, to the matter I have to clear up."

With still more of Noreen's laughter ringing in my ear, I ran to the bathroom next to the office in the warehouse, scraped the mushy remains of rubber gloves off my hands, and made use of my favorite bank-busting but essential moisture cleanser. The thick, creamy lather soothed my itchy hands, and the lukewarm water felt like a balm.

Was I ready to face off against Dutch Merrill again?

His handsome image materialized in my head. Yeah, he's a hunk, and he can fix a crumbled wall five hundred ways to Sunday, but his questionable reputation still cloaks him like green stuff does month-old leftovers. Then there's that embarrassing moment we shared a year ago.

"Aargh!" The mere memory of that humiliating episode made me squeeze the tube of super-duper megarich cream with a hair more oomph than necessary.

"How long is it going to hover in the back of my mind,

Lord?" As I wiped up goo and waited for a heavenly response, I spied my cowardly gray eyes in the mirror.

Bummer. Time to fess up. It'll hover as long as I keep dredging it up, as long as I yank it back every time I dump it on God's lap.

I glared at my image in the mirror. "Hey, lady! Cut me some slack here. I'm still rusty at this faith thing, you know."

The whole faith thing isn't as easy as I'd like it to be. Once upon a time, I was an innocent preacher's kid who only heard and saw the good side of the world. Then, as a young adult, my world crashed down on me thanks to a brutal, godless thug.

Then the criminal justice system failed me, so I turned away from the God I believed also failed me. Now, after almost five years of hard-won partial healing, I know I have a ways to go before trust and faith become the easy default setting for my gun-shy gray matter again.

I turned from the mirror, hairbrush in hand. Since I am blessed with a mane of uncivilized hair, the frequent application of brush to locks is required. I yanked and muttered on my way to the desk, hoping my lecture sank in, if by no other means than through the pores on my stinging scalp.

"Good grief, Haley Farrell." Maybe the lecture would give my attitude a healthy adjustment. "You're an interior designer with an insanely successful auction house on the side, not a bottom-sucking catfish. You have a job to do, and your job description does *not* include mental muck dredging—"

"Dredging, Miss Haley?"

"Aack!" I jumped about a mile in the air. "Ozzie! You scared the stuffing out of me. You done already? When'd you get back?"

My partner, the meek, mild, and mousy Ozzie Krieger, stood in the open doorway to the office, the usual frown on his basset-hound face. He'd gone to appraise an estate early this morning, and I hadn't expected him back until midafternoon.

Ozzie's wrinkles deepened. "Already? It took me hours to count, identify, and catalog all those Lladros, Hummels, Dresden lace figurines, and even more unsigned shepherds and shepherdesses of questionable pedigree. It's precisely 4:30 according to my pocket watch."

"It's 4:30?" Where had the time gone? "Oh, oh, oh, oh, oh! Gotta run. I'm supposed to set up an appointment with a potential new client for later this evening, and I can't show up in these awful rags."

Ozzie took a good look and wrinkled his nose—the one part of his face not otherwise creased. "Yes, indeed, miss, you do look a fright."

No matter how much I beg, wheedle, or nag, Ozzie refuses to call me by my first name. I'm the majority partner in the business and therefore, in his fuddy-duddy, Victorian mind, require formal address. I'll never get used to it, but I try not to object anymore.

"Gee, thanks. I really needed confirmation."

"Just speaking the truth, miss, as I vowed I'd do when we signed the documents."

Ozzie has a blot or two in his past. When I offered him the partnership, he refused an equal share. He agreed to a 40 percent stake but insisted our lawyer add verbiage as to his commitment to honesty at all times; in all matters, in every way, form or fashion; beyond a shadow of a doubt; forever and ever; till death do us part—you get the picture.

"Yeah, okay. I know how you value honesty, and I appreciate it. But I have to run. I'd love to land this job, even though I'll have to work with Dutch again."

Ozzie donned a knowing smile.

I squirmed.

"You two do charge the air with more power than a badly wired lamp," he said. "But you also make a lovely couple indeed."

"Couple! You're nuts, Ozzie. The guy's a menace, and I only put up with him because I wanted Noreen's job. And I want to do the Marshalls' house now. They already hired him, so I'm stuck working with the . . . the . . . oh, you know what a pain he is."

Ozzie's droopy features lit up with more animation than I'd ever seen on him. "I don't know, Miss Haley. There is much to be said for that certain effervescence between a man and a woman—"

I clapped my hands over my ears. "No way! I won't listen to one more word. Gotta go."

With that, I ran out to the parking lot, jumped into my trusty Honda Civic, looped the handless gizmo for my cell phone over my head, and pulled out into the street in front of the warehouse. Thankfully, the traffic was light.

A quick call to Noreen gained me the phone number and directions to the Marshall home. Another short call set up a meeting with Deedee Marshall for the evening. But when my new potential client mentioned that Dutch would meet us there, the memory of my indignity returned with a vengeance.

I didn't want to come face-to-face with him—ever.

I stopped at a red light. As I waited dread grew to elephantine proportions. I really, really didn't want to see Dutch Merrill again. But as the old Rolling Stones song says, you can't always get what you want.

"Aargh!" I smacked my forehead against the steering wheel. The man was something else. The last time that song came to mind was back when he was sure I'd murdered Marge Norwalk and he wanted me jailed.

I wanted nothing to do with Dutch. But I wouldn't get what I wanted, at least not when it came to him. And I wanted the Marshall job.

The light turned green, traffic remained light, and I made it home in record time. At the Wilmont River Church's manse, I ran up the porch steps, gave Midas, my demanding golden retriever, his obligatory ear scratch, scooped clean clothes from closet and drawers, and flew to the shower. But once I found myself under the soothing, warm spray, my reluctance grew.

One way or another I would have to get over my Dutch phobia. I couldn't handle the gargantuan task on my own, but I knew God alone could move mountains, create worlds, heal hearts. Surely he could . . . oh, I don't know . . . maybe he could turn Dutch into a golden retriever of a man.

You know, friendly, always happy, quick to cooperate,
eager to please.

I stepped out of the shower, and Midas, the real deal,
stood at the door to my room. His fluffy golden tail thwacked
either side of the door frame, his goofy grin spanned from
ear to ear, and his beggar's brown eyes beseeched, invited
me to play, conveyed his certainty that I was the best thing
since faux-finish glaze in five-gallon cans.

A vision of Dutch's face popped in between Midas's
long, wavy-haired ears, and I laughed. Okay. The idiotic
image went a long way to ease my dread. The next time
the forceful, opinionated, argumentative, stubborn, good-
looking contractor gave me a hard time, all I had to do was
click back to this image, and my perspective on whatever
grief he was dishing would improve.

I snagged my portfolio, where I keep a ring of paint-
color chips, a wide assortment of sample fabrics, a few
pieces of wood with different stains, and catalogs from
my favorite to-the-trades furniture manufacturers, then
hurried out only to have to dash back inside for my camera and hundred-foot-long tape measure. Can't do much
without those.

Then I drove to the Marshalls' ritzy address. Massive
brick columns flanked open wrought-iron gates. Since the
gates hung ajar, and Deedee Marshall knew I was on my
way, I went right on through. After what seemed like a
miles-long drive up the side of the hill, I spotted the house.

Three stories of redbrick Georgian formality loomed at the end of the circular white gravel drive.

I pulled to a stop in the small, rectangular parking spot to the right of the mansion. Awestruck, I gathered my paraphernalia and headed to the house.

Black double doors wore identical brass knockers polished not so long ago—no fingerprints marred the rich gleam. Before I used one, the right-side door opened to reveal a tall, slender blonde in head-to-toe pink silk. She was maybe thirty—no less than twenty years younger than Dr. Marshall—and wore a welcoming smile with all the pink.

"You must be Haley," she said, her voice a soft and breathy echo of Marilyn Monroe. "I'm Deedee. Come on in."

When she stepped aside, I caught my first glimpse of exquisite antique mahogany, gleaming marble, a vast gilded Victorian mirror that must have cost more than the land the manse and church sit on, and the most exquisite old Turkish Oushak rug I've ever seen.

"I don't understand." I turned another circle in the cavernous foyer. "You don't need my help. This is the most beautiful place I've ever seen."

Deedee wrinkled her nose. "Stew's ex was into antiques, but I don't like them. I like contemporary styles. And I, like, can't stand these serious colors."

"Okay." Wait till my nemesis heard Deedee's description of this magnificence. Dutch and I nearly came to verbal blows when he thought I harbored evil intentions for a Carrara marble fireplace mantel in Noreen's new mansion.

"So tell me, Deedee. Where would you like me to start? I have my camera, and I'd like some pictures to start to put together a design concept for you."

"Oh, that's so cool! Let me show you the back patio." She trotted off down the center hallway, and I followed, practically drooling at the beauty I recorded with my camera along the way—these were for me. I fought to keep my attention on the trophy wife's words.

"Stew and I want to knock down the back wall of the kitchen and dinette area so we can put full-length windows in its place."

Deedee stepped into the large kitchen with 1980s décor, then pointed to the farm-style door a bit left of center. My digital camera did its thing.

Then, with a twist of her delicate, acrylic-nailed, pink-manicured hand, Deedee turned the doorknob. "Let's go outside so you can see our killer view—"

Her blood-curdling shriek put an end to her words.

The Marshalls have a killer view, all right. But the killer view had nothing to do with the girl who lay sprawled in the middle of said patio's concrete floor, her body's lower half drenched in bright red blood.

I screamed too.

2

What is it with big old mansions, dead bodies, and me?

When my throat hurt too much for even one more scream and my body shook too hard to stay upright, I leaned against the brick wall of the Marshall home.

A kaleidoscope of images clicked through my mind. About a year ago, I walked out of another Puget Sound–area mansion and found my mentor's corpse under a monstrous rhododendron. Today's bloody body didn't have even a shrub to provide it a decent shroud, but the pool of blood looked the same. It had the same sick, sweet stench, and its life was just as gone as Marge's had been last year. It brought back horrible memories.

Don't ask how I knew the girl was dead even from a distance of fifteen feet. I can't put it into words, but trust me. Once you see someone who died a wretched, bloody death, you can never forget it.

And that brought me back to my original question. Why did I have to find yet another corpse at yet another huge, expensive house I was about to redesign?

Then the stupidity of my thoughts hit me. I can only blame it on shock. None of that mattered. Someone had died, and something had to be done about it.

A male spit out an expletive. The familiar voice brought me around. "What are you—"

"*You* again?"

"Yeah, Dutch Merrill. It's me again. The Marshalls told Noreen they wanted me to redesign their home. I came to meet Deedee, she brought me out here, and this is what I found. Want to make something of it?"

"No. I want to call the cops."

I closed my eyes and sagged against the wall again, camera still in hand, portfolio at my feet. "Please do." My voice shook; all of me did. "We just walked out here seconds ago. I was too stunned to do more than scream."

When he didn't come back at me with some smart dig, I cracked an eyelid and saw his expression soften. He pulled out his cell phone, hit a button—gotta wonder about a guy with the PD on speed dial—then gave a terse, urgent description of our situation.

I stayed propped against the wall for what felt like a lifetime. I felt too shaky to attempt any movement. How could I move, think, come up with a design plan for a client?

Only then did I remember Deedee Marshall. She sat in a plaid-cushioned redwood chair, face pale, expression grim, eyes fixed straight ahead, about a foot above the body on her patio floor. She looked . . . I don't know . . . fierce? No, that wasn't right. What I read as ferocity was the most impressive display of self-control I'd ever seen. Where everything inside me pushed me toward an emotional edge, Deedee managed to keep from falling apart with great dignity.

I was impressed and felt the birth of admiration for the pretty blonde.

"Deedee?" I said. "Are you all right?"

Slowly she faced me. "All right?" Her voice came out wispier than ever. "Did you just ask me if I'm all right?"

With every syllable, the wispy voice became shriller, sharper, harsher.

I nodded.

She surged to her feet. "How can you ask if I'm all right when I just found this . . . this person in my house like . . . like this?"

By the end of her question, her whole body quivered with tension. Her cover-girl face had regained the color it earlier lost; it now looked redder than the enamel on a Japanese tansu chest.

At least I wasn't the only one rattled out of her wits.

The snap of Dutch's phone echoed in the unnatural silence. I jerked as though stuck by a staple gun.

"I can understand how you feel," I told my maybe client. "It was a shock—still is." I allowed myself a nanosecond glance at the body, then shuddered. "Dutch called the police."

"Oh." She shook her head and looked around the patio. When she saw him, her lips widened a fraction into a tight smile, that control back in place. "I didn't know you'd arrived. I expected you earlier, right around when . . . ah . . . she . . . ."

Deedee looked at me with vacant eyes, and I realized she'd forgotten my name. I supplied it, then added, with a hint of sarcasm, "Imagine that. You missed his arrival. He does have a gift for sneaking up on people."

Dutch glared. "Got caught in traffic on I-5. Everyone does. I've told you many times, Haley, I don't sneak, but I also don't barge in, and there's a world of difference between barging in and arriving."

I rolled my eyes. "You also have a talent for showing up at the most unfortunate moment—"

I swallowed the rest of my words when a smirk tipped the corners of Dutch's mouth and a twinkle spiced up his green eyes. I winced.

"Is that any way to refer to my very heroic rescue?" he asked.

I can't believe I set myself up for that one. I scrambled for a change of subject, but my mind refused to turn to any but the obvious, hideous one. "Do you know her, Deedee?"

Deedee started, darted a look at the corpse, then gave a single, tight shake of her blond head. "No."

"Then you wouldn't know why she came here to die, would you?"

The firm, musical voice that uttered the question was way too familiar. I turned to greet Detective Lila Tsu of the Wilmont Police Department.

"Guess we'll be seeing each other a bit again," I said in a rueful voice. "At least you don't have to ask me all the dumb stuff about who I am and where I live this time."

"*This* time?" Deedee squeaked, her alarm almost comical.

Almost.

Ms. Tsu gave an unreadable look from where she knelt at the corpse's side. "Miss Farrell and I have had occasion to meet."

"You mean she's a crook?" Deedee's voice could've shattered Waterford crystal.

"Maybe not a killer," Dutch said.

"Not then," Ms. Tsu said, her fingers on the corpse's slender wrist.

"Hey! That's not fair. You both know I'm not a killer." I rounded on Dutch. "Besides, you're the one with the slippery-slope history."

"You killed someone?" Deedee asked in horror. Then she faced Dutch. "You build stuff that slips?"

The detective, upright again, gave a discreet cough. "Children, children," she said, wry humor in her voice. "Let's not rehash ancient history. There's a dead girl on the ground, and although I'm only too familiar with the bizarre reactions people have to violence, we have to find out what happened here."

I arched a brow and grinned. "We?"

Lila Tsu's eyes opened a fraction wider. Since unpleasant history had brought us together in the past, I knew her well enough to catch that minimal response.

"It was just a figure of speech," she said. "Don't read anything into it. I . . . meant my officers, who are right now gathering evidence in the house and out front. They'll be here soon. Keep in mind, you're again at the scene of an . . . unexplained death."

"Seems to me," Dutch ventured, "that Haley was pretty helpful to you last year."

The petite Asian policewoman drew herself up to her full height. "Haley's knowledge of decorative antiques did come in handy in the end. But that's in the past. This is now. Do any of you know her?"

"Because the hair's so long and it's all over her face, I haven't had a good look at her features," I said. I picked up my portfolio, unzipped it to drop my camera inside, and took another look at the girl. "I can always move some of the hair aside so we can see—"

"There she goes again," Dutch muttered, "messing with evidence."

Before I had a chance to refute his scurrilous accusation—I never messed with evidence; I just happened to land on some—Lila spoke again, her competent, professional voice back in full force.

"That's enough, Mr. Merrill. Don't accuse her, and you, Haley, don't snipe. Just because he caught you in a number of awkward situations doesn't mean you should lose perspective here. And you know better than to disturb the scene, not to mention leave fingerprints that might prove troublesome like the last time. I'll move her hair so you can look at her."

The detective set her ultrachic square black leather purse on the redwood patio table to our left and then knelt by the girl again. She moved a cloak of auburn hair to one side, and I saw the straight nose with a light dusting of brown-sugar freckles over a now colorless mouth. The features looked strained, perhaps contorted by pain at the time of death.

I also saw that she wasn't yet out of her teens, as I'd suspected. How tragic.

"I've never seen her," I said around the knot in my throat.

Lila glanced at Deedee. "How about you, Mrs. Marshall?"

As if she'd been forced awake from a deep sleep, Deedee looked from the dead girl to the detective.

"Ah . . . no." She shook her head—hard.

"And you, Mr. Merrill?"

A deep frown etched parallel lines between the contractor's thick, straight brows. He clamped his lips and exhaled a short, harsh breath. "There's something familiar about her . . . I can't put my finger on it, but I feel as if I know her. I don't *think* I've seen her before. I don't get to know a lot of kids—don't meet too many of them in my line of work."

Lila crossed back to the patio table and withdrew the familiar notebook and silver pen from her purse. She'd flashed them each time she interrogated me last year. With a graceful, smoothing glide of her hand down the straight-cut thigh of her white linen pants, she sat in one of the redwood chairs, crossed her right leg over her left, then turned her gaze on Dutch.

I read the look loud and clear. I'd hated being on the receiving end of it. I almost felt sorry for him.

"Not even the children of the homeowners who hire you?"

"When I renovate an existing home, the family often moves in with relatives or into a short-term-lease place to avoid the chaos and stay out of my crew's way." He ran a hand through his thick, dark hair. "New construction? Well, there's no one there. It's usually the husband or the wife who comes out to check the progress. But you could be right and she might belong to a family I've worked for."

Lila's pen caught the diffuse light of the sunset and reflected a soft shade of crimson as she scribbled in her notebook. I didn't look forward to her use of the writing implement when she questioned me.

"Ah . . . since you're busy with him," I said, "do you think I could go home now? I mean, if you have questions for me, you know where to find me."

I heard sirens in the distance. I knew what was coming, and I also knew I didn't have the stomach to stand by while a medical examiner and crime scene investigators did their thing.

Lila turned, and our gazes locked. "You know better than to think it's a matter of *if* I have questions for you. I'll have them, and soon. By the way, Tyler says hello."

"I'll see him tomorrow."

Tyler Colby runs the martial arts studio where the detective and I both practice. Once upon a time, he vouched for each of us to the other. He also pitted us in a sparring match that lasted longer than any I've ever witnessed. It ended in a draw.

His word still counted with me; I hoped it did with her.

"So can I? Go home, that is."

Voices approached from somewhere around the right side of the Marshall mansion. I shot a panicked look at Lila, who cocked her head sideways, gave me a strange look, then nodded. "I do know where I can find you. You and your beautiful golden."

I smiled. "Midas is a heartthrob, isn't he?"

"Still dateless but for a canine?"

"I know no better."

I heard a snicker, and when I looked away from the detective, I saw another familiar face. This one belonged to a blue-uniformed man.

"Is that the best you can do?" he asked.

"Is there a reason you have to go out of your way to bug me? Oh, I get it. You're stuck back in sixth grade."

The cop roared with laughter. "Yeah, I guess I did 'bug' you, didn't I?"

"Yes, Christopher Dylan Thomas. A big, fat, hairy spider in my desk is the kind of bug that's kind of hard to forget. But I'd think you'd have forgotten by now. Especially with all the pranks you played over the years."

His eyes crinkled at the corners when he smiled—he'd turned out quite well, in a blond, blue-eyed, California surfer way. Still, a woman had to cling to her dignity, even in the face of so much masculine beauty.

He crossed his arms. "I did forget all about it, but you reminded me that time you called to report a break-in."

"You were a pain that time too. The least you can do is be a gentleman and not annoy the daylights out of a woman every time you talk to her. Especially during an emergency."

"But it's so much fun to 'bug' you." He narrowed his gaze. "Hey! Are you about to barf? With your stomach and how you keep getting mixed up in homicides, I'd bet you're having buckets of fun. Get it? Buckets?"

"Ahem!" Lila did not look amused. "Please resume the nostalgia some other time. Officer Thomas, you and the guys might enjoy gallows humor, but remember, you have a job to do. And, Haley? Expect my call."

Chris's ears reddened, but he shot straight to attention, nodded, then hurried off toward the body.

I arched a brow. "Quite an effect you have. As opposed to my lack thereof."

"I keep a tight rein on my crime scene investigations. I'm good at my job, and I want to continue that way."

"You know, you've told me that a time or twenty. I got the picture then, so I think I'm going to leave you to your job. That you do so well, you know."

Lila frowned.

Dutch snorted.

I glared.

"One of these days," he said, "that mouth of yours isn't going to get you out of the trouble it got you into in the first place."

I winced. "Okay. So this is where I take my foot out of my mouth and creep away into the sunset."

With measured but hurried footsteps, I made my escape. As my trusty portfolio slapped my thigh, I mentally kicked myself for my verbal blunders. When I gave up on that futile endeavor, I went for wisdom. "Lord? Why did you give me a mouth with a life of its own?"

While my trusty Honda started right up, God didn't respond as easily.

It figures. Nothing good comes easy.

At the manse I parked the car in the driveway and ran inside. "I'm sorry I'm so late," I told my dad, "but you'll never believe what happened."

He set down his newspaper, laid his half-moon reading glasses on top, then smiled. "Try me, honey."

I collapsed into my late mother's rocker, a maple piece that holds treasured memories. "I told you earlier that I was going to meet with a potential client this evening."

"Mmm . . ."

"Well, I did, but that's when things went really, really bad. We found a dead body on her patio."

"You did *what*?"

"You heard me. Deedee Marshall went to show me her patio, since she and her husband want to knock down the whole back wall of their house to take advantage of the view of Lake Union, and when we got there, we found a teenager collapsed in a sea of blood."

He closed his eyes. His lips moved in silent prayer. A moment later he asked, "What happened?"

"Hmm . . . You know? I can't really say. I know people don't just bleed for no reason. But I don't know if she was in an accident or . . ."

I met his gaze. "I don't know why I feel this way, but I'm pretty sure it wasn't an accident."

"You said it. People don't just bleed to death. Something made the girl bleed. And there are only two logical possibilities. If you say it didn't appear to be the result of an accident, then I'd have to say you can't be too far off in your way of thinking."

"I know. But I don't want it to be."

"What, Haley? What is it you don't want it to be?"

Of course, Dad knew what I wanted to avoid. He knew how hard it was for me to find Marge Norwalk, the woman who helped me through the roughest moments in my life, dead in a pool of her own blood. Dad also knew, better than anyone, how I'd avoided dealing with the aftermath of the attack I suffered nearly five years ago now.

The look on his face told me I wasn't about to get away with a dodge, be it cutesy or funny or cowardly in any way. I'd come too far in the last year to backslide now.

"I don't want it to be, but I'm pretty sure I stumbled on another murder."

3

After Dad made me put my greatest fear into words, I finally broke down and cried. He let my tears pour. Then, when my sobs began to ease, he sat in the armchair at my side. I reached for his hand.

"I'm sorry I'm so chicken, but thanks."

"I understand why you're hesitant," he said, a gentle smile on his face. "But you don't have to be. Remember God's words to Joshua."

I gave him a crooked smile. "Be strong and of a good courage; be not afraid, neither be thou dismayed: for the LORD thy God is with thee whithersoever thou goest."

"Wow! And in the King James, no less."

"Mrs. Merchant didn't like what she called newfangled versions, remember? Not even for third-grade Sunday schoolers."

"She was good though. I'm impressed that you remember."

"I remember the verse, but I don't remember to do what it says—not often enough."

"The life of faith isn't easy, honey. It's tough to bring your will to the cross of Christ and accept the Father's will in its place. We humans want to know what we're getting into ahead of time, and we like to control our days. But that's not what God calls us to do."

"I know. It's that part where we're called to be a living sacrifice to God and the part about the regular renewing of our minds that trip me up all the time."

"That's what gets us all, the day-after-day part. That's why the Christian life is a walk we take with the heavenly Father. We pick it up every morning we spend down here. Meeting Jesus is only the first step on that walk."

I sighed. "I think I need to put in some knee time. Karate Chop Cop will be after me soon enough, and I have to fortify myself."

"That's an awful name for such a lovely young woman." Dad gave me a crooked smile. "I'm very proud of you though. You've made great progress in one year."

"What can I say? I went backward when I should have stood firm. Now I'm going forward at a snail's pace. And even though it's not in such a dramatic lurch, I seem to fall back all the time. I'm getting whiplash from the zigzag jolts."

"But you haven't denied the Lord again. And that's a tremendous accomplishment. Trust him, honey. He won't fail you."

For a moment the bad memories threatened to return, but as I went up the stairs, I whispered, "Be not afraid . . ."

I crawled into bed with Dad's resounding amen in my mind.

Early the next morning, while I hovered in that woozy stage between wakefulness and sleep, I heard a car door slam outside and footsteps on the front porch.

Midas went ballistic.

I dragged myself upright and walked to the window. I groaned.

"Be right there," I called out.

At the front door, I greeted homicide detective Lila Tsu. "Come on in."

She tipped her head in a slight nod. "How are you?"

I pointed her to the white-cotton slipcovered sofa. "Fine, if you don't consider walking out onto a dead body a problem."

"I do, and that's why I asked. This *is* the second time I've dealt with you after you've done it."

Lila's rose-colored suit looked great against the white slipcover on the sofa—and on her. My pajamas left me at a disadvantage.

"I'm sure you're not here to check out my mental state. I expected you sometime last night."

"It was a long one." She pulled out her silver pen and that familiar notebook from her chic square purse. "Why don't you tell me about yesterday afternoon, starting with your call to Deedee Marshall."

I related everything I remembered. I even told her about Noreen's call. Then, when I got to the part where Deedee threw open the patio door, my voice quit. Nothing more came out.

"That's when you went to the patio, right?"

Thank goodness for the detective's much-vaunted talent for her job. Her question forced me to focus and function. "Yes."

"I realize this will be hard, but I need you to tell me exactly what you saw."

I squeezed my eyes shut. This was where I hadn't wanted to go. "The ocean view's amazing there. And yesterday afternoon was beautiful. Everything looked crisp, fresh-starched, and ironed. But I couldn't miss the . . . the body. It was just there. On the patio floor. In all the blood."

"Could you tell me how the furniture was arranged?"

"I didn't notice any until I looked for Deedee. And that was after Dutch got there. Hmm . . . let me think. Four redwood chairs with green, tan, and brown plaid cushions. Oh, and the table. The round table was in the middle of the chairs."

"You're sure Dutch Merrill wasn't there when you arrived?"

"He wasn't on the street in front of the property, he wasn't on the long drive up to the house, he wasn't on the front lawn, and he wasn't in the foyer, hall, or kitchen either. That's all I saw of the Marshalls' place."

"How did he come out onto the patio?"

"What do you mean?"

"From which direction did he come?"

I noticed her precise manner of speech. "He came out the kitchen door."

"Do you know how he entered the house?"

"Never thought to ask, but I would imagine the Marshalls have some kind of help. Maybe whoever it is let him in."

Lila narrowed her almond eyes. "Have you spoken with Mr. Merrill since yesterday afternoon?"

I shook my head and pointed at my Betty Boop pajamas. "You woke me up."

"Did you two compare notes?"

"What, are you nuts? We didn't compare anything."

"I'm as sane as ever. It's just interesting—and somewhat alarming—that you explained Dutch's arrival the same way he did."

"Give me a break. I was just being logical—something you've never accused me of being."

"Exactly. That's why I have to wonder how you came up with the same information Mr. Merrill gave me."

"Why? Did you expect the guy to leap over tall buildings to get from the front to the back of the house?"

She tightened her lips at my flip response. "Could he have hidden somewhere nearby?"

"Don't you think it'd be a little hard for a six-foot-plus guy to hide in a couple of rosebushes?"

Lila shrugged. She returned her pen and notebook to the black purse, snapped the bag shut, and stood. She turned to leave, but I'd reached the end of my rope. I erupted to my feet and tried but failed to keep the sarcasm out of my words.

"I know how serious you are about your job, but don't you think you can tell me something about the girl? What you've learned?"

The detective faced me but didn't speak.

I pressed on. "I mean, just from your questions, and that you asked them in the first place, I know she didn't just bleed to death from a paper cut."

"The sarcasm is superfluous. But yes. You're right. It was not a wholly natural death."

Her clear, intent gaze zeroed in on me. I recalled the many times she'd put me under her investigative microscope the year before. I didn't get a good feeling.

"So what you're saying—"

"What I'm saying, Haley, is that I have a multitude of questions about Dutch Merrill and Katherine Cecilia Richardson's unexplained and untimely death."

"Go for it."

"Did Dutch give you the girl's name yesterday?"

"Of course not. You were there when he said she looked familiar, but he didn't know from where." I didn't like the way this conversation was going. "Does this mean he does know her?"

"He knows the family."

I took a sharp breath. Things didn't look good for the guy. "How . . . ?"

"Business and personal."

Lila's clipped response gave me a weird feeling. "Something tells me there's trouble in *that* paradise."

She fixed her dark eyes on me. "Bad blood."

"And you're wondering if that bad blood might've led him to . . ."

Lila nodded.

"Hmm. . . ."

"That's all you have to say, Ms. Farrell?"

"So we're back to the Ms. Farrell. The girl must have been murdered."

"It's not official yet. But what is certain is that a healthy fourteen-year-old girl, the daughter of someone toward whom Dutch harbored ill will, hemorrhaged vaginally on the back patio of a home Dutch is about to remodel."

My breathing grew shallow. Chills returned. Bile churned up my throat. "She hemorrhaged vaginally?"

"Preliminary results show that KC Richardson gave birth shortly before she bled to death on the Marshalls' back patio. Nobody knew she was pregnant. Not even her boyfriend." Lila's eyelids lowered, turning her eyes into angry balls of jet. "Who fathered KC's child?"

I gave a vague wave. That didn't matter so much. Something else mattered much, much more.

I opened my mouth to set free the words I eked out from the deepest corner of my heart. "Where's . . . KC's . . . child?"

Lila's dark eyes reflected my distress. "I don't know, but I have to, and soon enough I will."

A shot of grief made it hard to breathe. "It's horrible. A child gave birth to another child, and now one's dead and the other . . ."

"That's the reality of my job. No one wins, not even when I succeed."

"How do you handle it?"

"How do you manage your demons?"

I laughed without humor. "Don't forget our sparring match."

"My question was rhetorical, Haley. I know how you cope with life's horrors. Tyler wasn't that far off when he said you and I have a lot in common. If nothing else, we both take out our stress on punching bags, bricks and boards, or equally trained martial artists."

I studied her for a long moment. "Hey, did you ever get that new pup you wanted?"

"I've been too busy to even look for one."

"Midas's mom had a new litter. You asked me to tell you when he had siblings. Do you want the breeder's phone number?"

The longing on her face caught me by surprise. It made her more human than I'd seen her before.

"Oh, I don't know," she said. "I work such long hours that I doubt I can give the poor baby the attention it needs." She glanced down at the floor. "I'll have to pass. Maybe when things are calmer at the department—"

"Are you telling me you figure the crazies are going give you and your giant Smurfs a break sometime soon?"

Her smile curved up only one side of her mouth. "A girl can always hope."

"Yeah, sure, and someday my prince will come on some enchanted evening, and we'll climb every mountain with a lonely goatherd in a surrey with a fringe on the top."

By the time I finished my wacko spiel, Lila's smile had

evened out, and her expression told me loud and clear she doubted my sanity. But I knew I was right, so I went on.

"You're never going to clean up all the swill fallen humans spew around. So then what? Are you ready to go through life without a golden to make you crazy in that special goldenish way? Uh-uh. That's too easy."

"You are crazy."

"Certifiable, but you still need a dog. There's just something way real about walking around the neighborhood with a doggy-doo bag in hand. Housebreaking makes you look beyond all the other junk."

Did I really say that? To a cop? Oh boy.

"As weird as that is, you might be on to something there. Okay."

"Okay, what? That housebreaking's a pill? That poop scooping stinks—for real? Or that you'll call about a pup?"

"That a puppy will probably do me good, which is what you said without coming right out and saying it. I'm guilty of tunnel vision."

"I'll say. And I'm awfully glad I found the light at the end of your tunnel. Hard to believe though it might be, I almost feel sorry for Dutch. You're a formidable enemy."

"I'm not Dutch's enemy any more than I was yours. It's my job to find out the truth."

"That's not how I saw it."

"Sometimes things aren't as they seem."

I tilted my head to study her. "Maybe you'll remember that the next time you insist Dutch killed that girl."

"I haven't said he killed her, just that he might have had

something to do with her unexplained death. Do you have evidence he didn't?"

"No, and I'm not saying he's innocent either. I'm just echoing you. This situation may not be as it first appears. There's probably a truckload of muck you have to rake up before you find the truth. At least, that's what happened to me last year."

"Crime's not clean and neat, Haley."

"Never thought it was." I headed for the kitchen, where I keep the dog breeder's info. "That's why you need a pooch to keep you sane."

Lila didn't answer. I came back to the living room, neon-orange sticky note in hand. "Here you go. Don't wait too long though. The Gold Dust Kennel has a great reputation, and their pups sell fast. You need a dog to own you in the worst way."

She chuckled. "That's the truth, isn't it? They own you more than you own them."

"Good luck."

"Thanks, and if you hear anything or if Dutch tells you anything that might help, please give me a call."

"Did you forget already how I hounded you last year with every idea I got and each maybe-clue I found? Of course I'll call you if I think of anything."

The detective stopped at the front door. "I almost forgot. I'll need your camera—you did take pictures at the Marshalls', didn't you?"

"I did. But why would you want pictures of antiques, a kitchen wall, and an old back door?"

"I don't want them for their own sake, but you might have caught something important when you took the shots."

"Great," I muttered on my way to my portfolio. "Now I'm going to have to get a disposable until you let me spring this one back out of your evidentiary clutches. And I'll need to go out to the house again. I still want to do the redesign, and I'll need photos to prepare a proposal."

"I'm sure you'll manage."

"Yeah. I guess I will." I handed her the camera. "But hey! Gotta look on the bright side. At least I'm not the one you're dissecting this time."

"You're not all the way in the clear. Not yet. You were one of the first on the scene, and this is your second strange death in about a year."

"It may be the second one I uncovered, but as far as any crime I might've committed? Uh-uh. I'm still at zilch." I opened the door for Karate Chop Cop. "And you know it."

After another of her piercing looks, Lila turned and went toward her plain-vanilla unmarked car. She opened the door, tossed her purse inside, and called out, "I'll reserve comment on that until I know who did what."

"I'll be waiting for that comment."

"Don't hold your breath."

"Oh, I won't, but I could. I know you'll find I'm right."

4

After Lila left, it took me a few minutes to remember what today was.

Bummer. It was Saturday.

Now, for most people, Saturday means the weekend, that they can put in some more sack time than usual, that they can do as little or as much as they want. For me, on the other hand, Saturday means something a bit different.

Saturdays are missionary society meeting days.

I have nothing against missionaries or the church groups that support their devoted work in the trenches. My quibble is with the meetings themselves.

Last year I was named to the post of president of the Wilmont River Church's missionary society thanks to the silken bullying of a late member of the congregation. She and a bunch of others believed, and most still do, that I'm the rightful heir to my mother's favorite position now that Mom is no longer with us. I, on the other hand, know I'm as well suited to the job as Austin Powers is to the redesign of the White House.

But I'm coming around. There's nothing like the satisfaction I get when an update comes from the mission field. The missionaries we support are so grateful for our help, and they manage to accomplish so many minor miracles on a shoestring that no one—certainly not me—can be so coldhearted as to not be moved by their great faith. I'm glad my inheritance allows me to contribute more than I ever could before.

This Saturday, fresh off my grisly discovery last night, found me right back to my earlier reluctance. I didn't want to deal with fundraising schemes or Robert's Rules or the petty rivalries that mushroom between members with exasperating regularity.

I especially hate to deal with Penny Harham.

Penny, Wilmont's postal clerk, can't stand me, and she makes sure everyone knows it each time we meet. But since Penny is a pillar of Dad's congregation, she isn't someone I want to alienate, so I slave to keep the peace for the sake of Dad's sanity.

At the risk of mine.

Then I remembered the agenda I'd worked up for today's meeting. I was excited by what I learned when I researched one of my better ideas. I hoped the rest of the members shared my interest. I hurried through my shower and cut short my usual argument with Midas. He wanted to come along, but I didn't want him there to distract the membership. He's a favorite with the congregation, and even more so with the ladies of the missionary society.

With wet streamers of hair glommed onto my clean T-shirt,

I ran into the church's activity room just as the donated grandfather clock struck the last gong of nine—a good thing, since one of Penny's favorite hobbies is keeping an eagle eye on my occasional tardiness.

Ina Appleton, our hospitality chair, met me with a cup of bliss, better known as Starbucks House Blend. "Here you go, Haley. And don't let Penny get to you. She's in an especially foul mood today."

Swell. Just what I wanted to hear.

I took my place behind the lectern at the front of the room and brought down the gavel. The room fell silent, and I surveyed my . . . subjects?

Yikes! This whole presidency thing was getting to me.

I shook off the momentary imperial delusions. "Hi, everyone. I'm so glad you're here. As all of you know, I want to put together a missions trip to Indonesia. I did some reading and made a bunch of phone calls, and I'm ready to roll. Those poor, poor people are still hurting from the earthquakes and tsunami, and whatever we do to help is only a drop in the bucket, but . . ."

The meeting was a winner. Seventeen women pledged to travel to the ravaged area, and seven spouses, cell-phoned during the reading of last meeting's minutes, promised to make the trip as well. Later, during the refreshments and fellowship time, I noticed a newcomer.

I held out my hand. "Hi. I'm Haley Farrell, the pastor's daughter and president of the society. I've never seen you here before, so I'd like to take the time to welcome you."

The silver-haired woman shook my hand with a pleasant, firm grip and offered a warm smile. "Thank you, Haley. I'm Madeleine Ogleby. I moved to the area to be closer to my only daughter. She married four months ago, a local gentleman she met through business contacts. I . . . I've had a difficult pair of years, and I found I missed her too much to stay back home in Portland."

A bittersweet pang struck hard. "I can relate. I still miss my mother, and she's been gone for a couple of years."

"Oh dear," Madeleine said, her smooth brow creased, her warm clasp on my arm a comfort. "I'm so sorry to have brought up the subject. It wasn't my intention—"

"Please don't apologize. You couldn't have known. And really, I'm fine. I know Mom's with the Lord and finally out of pain. It was a blessing for her, even though Dad and I do still miss her every day."

"I understand. My late John died of cancer. It was a mercy when he entered a coma at the end."

Her tender smile rang a bell in my memory, and suddenly I knew whom she'd brought to mind. "Has anyone ever said you look a lot like Grace Kelly?"

"The actress who married the European prince?"

"That's the one."

"My goodness! That's quite a compliment. She was a lovely woman. Thank you very much, Haley. And no. No one has ever mentioned it before."

"Well, it's about time they did. And they would have if they watched the classic movies channel as much as I do. The resemblance is pretty major."

Madeleine blushed and changed the subject. We discussed the trip to Indonesia, the schedule of Sunday services, a couple of other church ministries, and the everyday details of life and shopping in Wilmont.

Then Penny made her presence known.

"Madeleine dear," the postal clerk bleated. "I see the pastor's daughter has you cornered. Do forgive the poor child. As you can imagine, we humor her—her father, you know. Go on, Haley. Go back to your little scraps of cloth and bits of wood."

The newcomer looked from Penny to me and then back to Penny again, the mildest hint of alarm in her expression. "I didn't feel cornered for a single second, Miss Harham. Haley has been most informative, and I've enjoyed our conversation more than I can express."

Twin red blotches bloomed on Penny's sallow cheeks. "Well! If it's information you want, then Haley's hardly the one to turn to. She's little more than a child. You want someone with years of experience to provide you with adequate details. Here. Why don't I—"

"My daughter is near Haley's age," Madeleine said, her position firm in spite of Penny's best efforts to drag her away. "I find Deanna quite well informed as a general rule. I also see no reason to question Haley's capabilities. Now, if you'll excuse me, Miss Harham, I'll take a minute to step into the ladies' room."

"Oh, sure, Madeleine dear," Penny said, her brownnoser's tone oilier than ever. "Let me show you—"

"No, thank you. I need no help in that department."

I spun to hide the laughter I couldn't quite snuff out, but when I crashed into roly-poly Bella Cahill, her blue eyes full of mischief, all my efforts at self-control went down the drain.

"Only Penny would get in the way of a woman with a need for speed to get to the john," the outspoken senior said.

That did it. I howled and Bella giggled. Her mane of electric royal-blue hair shook like mutant peacock plumes caught in a helicopter's drag. The shaggy cut is a self-inflicted imitation of the choppy Hollywood style she acquired on her seventieth birthday. She'd had it tinted a fierce shade of magenta, but for some strange reason, it soon faded to Pepto pink. When she got tired of that subnormal result, she decided to experiment, and these days we can't begin to guess what side of the color wheel she'll attack next.

"You're bad, Bella," I finally said.

She pulled herself up to her full height, never losing her Pillsbury Dough Boy curves, then winked. "Thank you. I'm so bad, Haley girl, that I'm hip—that's what the kids say these days, you know. And Penny's just plain nasty. So who's the snooty Nordstrom's model you were talking to?"

"Hey! That's not nice. Besides, you're the former model among us."

Bella shrugged and smoothed her white *gi*, her latest fashion statement, over her abundant middle. When she learned last year that I practice martial arts, she joined a class at Tyler's *dojo*. I suppose the *gi* is better than the neon-orange-and-red animal-print spandex bike shorts she favored for a while last summer.

"Takes one to know one, you know. So who is she?"

"Your curiosity never ceases to amaze me. But what I don't get is why you didn't just go up to her and introduce yourself. I'm sure she wouldn't have minded."

"Fine, but who is she?"

I rolled my eyes. "Her name's Madeleine Ogleby, and she moved to Wilmont a few months back to be closer to her daughter. The daughter married someone local."

"Hmm . . . I wonder who."

"All I know is that the daughter's name is Deanna." I looked back toward the restroom but saw no one in the hall, and the cracks beneath the restroom doors now showed dark. "Anyway, Madeleine seems very nice, and I think you'll like her."

"Is she into karate? Jujitsu? Or maybe she's more the kickboxing type. What do you think?"

"I thought you'd decided she was snooty and elegant. I don't agree with you, but I also doubt a woman like Madeleine is into anything more than a brisk walk with her cute pooch every morning and evening. Didn't you get a good look at her?"

"Gotcha! That's why I said she's snooty. I don't think even a single one of her perfect hairs can move."

I glanced up through my eyelashes at the obedience-challenged curls on my forehead. "Wish I could say the same about mine."

"No way. Not me."

No joke. Bella's blue mop is as far removed from Madeleine's silver French twist as avocado green Formica countertops are from dark Ubatuba granite ones. "Anyway, it's getting late, and the leaning tower of laundry is calling my name. Besides, I'd bet Dad's ready to run away from home, thanks to Midas. His Golden Majesty wasn't happy when I wouldn't bring him along."

"What your dad needs is to get back into action," Bella said. "He's a hunk, and we don't have too many of 'em our age around anymore."

Dad? A hunk?

Yeah, right. With his balding head, small paunch, and unfortunate habit of losing his reading glasses when he most needs them, my father doesn't strike me as anyone's idea of a hunk. No matter what age. But who am I to judge?

"If you say so. And you'd better get back home yourself. That demented cat of yours has probably torn the place down by now."

"Now, Haley girl. Bali H'ai is the sweetest baby. I don't understand why you're so down on her."

"Bali H'ai is sweet, and I just flew in from the sixty-ninth moon of the planet Dream On. I've been on the wrong side of one too many of her attacks, Bella. Way I see it, I'm the epitome of Christian forgiveness when it comes to your cat. Haven't you noticed how far I stay from the gray beast?"

Bella tipped up her exquisite straight nose. "You're just a feline Philippine."

"A what?"

"You know. Those Bible folks who didn't know what for."

"You mean Philistine. That's someone with no appreciation of the finer things."

She smirked. "If the Birkenstock fits . . ."

"Yeah, yeah. Fine. Just chalk it up to my love of dogs."

Bella lives in deep denial. She'll never accept that my opinion of her cat is a result of my close encounter with repulsive green slime on one ill-fated occasion, after which Bali H'ai pounced on me. Bali H'ai's extreme response that time was the same as it always is. And I'm hardly her only victim.

"Okay, Bella. Why don't you go home to your kitty cat so I can get back to my pooch?"

"Is everyone else gone?"

"Do you see anyone here besides us?"

"Nope. Which means I'm outta here."

"I'm right behind you." I locked up and went out into the crisp, late spring day, the fragrance of Puget Sound salty and fresh all around. "Beautiful day."

"It'll be open-window sleeping tonight," Bella said, her voice full of glee. "I love nothing more than a cool, breezy night. So does Bali H'ai."

Sure she does. Bali H'ai's favorite pastime is dumpster and trash can diving, which Bella facilitates when she leaves her windows open. I'd have to check the green plastic gar-

bage bin our fair hamlet provides its residents and make
sure it was firmly braced. "See ya."

"God bless you, Haley girl."

"Thanks, Bella. You too."

I hurried to the manse. I wanted nothing more than to
crawl into bed, slip my feet under Midas's warm belly, and
dive right into a great read.

Which is what I did, after I took care of the trash can and
moved the tip of the mountain of grimy clothes, but I managed to read only about a page before I fell asleep.

The ringing phone woke me up.

Muzzy-headed and fuzzy-mouthed, I said, "Hullo?"

"What did you tell that KGB-agent cop?"

"Run that by me again?"

"I said, what did you tell that KGB-agent cop?"

His dentist would put three kids through college on the
bill for cracked enamel on Dutch's gritted teeth.

Then he added, "Haley, were you sleeping? At 2:00 in
the afternoon?"

"Uh . . . no. I . . . I was . . ." My bedside clock said 2:00
p.m. Then I spotted my abandoned novel. "Oh yeah. That's
right. I was . . . I mean, I *am* reading. A really good mystery
too. You oughta pick it up. Really, you should. It's all about
a Social Security Administration something-or-other who
has to find out who's bumping off old folks to get their
monthly checks, and only those whose cases she handles.
But then her mother gets swept off her feet by a fake oil
tycoon who's so broke he only wants her pension and may
kill her for it, and the daughter's gotta make sure—"

"Stop! I'll have all the time in the world soon enough, if that crazy woman gets her way."

"What woman? Did some poor infatuated creature come on to you? Oh, I get it! It's like my book, only backwards. She's stinking rich and wants to set you up for life. That's so sick, Merrill. I get why you're so fired up."

"What are you, deaf?"

"Not yet, but I could be. Your bellows come through loud and clear."

"Then how about you tell me what you told Lila Tsu about me."

"Oh, *that* woman. I didn't tell her anything about you." Lila had done the telling by the questions she asked. "Mostly I've talked to her about my innocence. And my dog."

I thought back farther, to those horrible weeks when the detective had me pegged as her prime suspect. "Oh. Well, yeah. I have told her a couple times that you're nuts. That was when you were trying so hard to get me arrested for a murder I didn't do, but that's only the truth. You are insane."

"I should've tried a lot harder."

"Give me a break, Dutch. You know I couldn't kill a flea. Well, I can and do kill fleas. Midas takes that flea-killing pill every month, but—"

"Would you stop babbling long enough to listen to me?"

"I don't babble—"

"Yeah, you do, and I have no patience for it right now."

"What's up with right now?"

"What's up with right now is that if I don't do something

quick here, Detective Lila Tsu's gonna lock me up for good. She thinks I—"

"You killed the girl!"

"I didn't kill her!" he roared. "How could I have? I haven't seen KC since she was about six weeks old."

"So you really do know her. That puts you way ahead of the game when it comes to suspicion. Thank goodness I'm out of Lila's crosshairs this time."

"Yeah, but I'm not, and I had nothing to do with my goddaughter's death."

"Whoa! Not only do you know her, but you're also sorta kinda related to her? Oh boy. You're in trouble now, Merrill. Karate Chop Cop's gonna be all over you like gilt on French Provincial froufrou. Take it from me. Been there, done that."

"That's just it. I don't have a problem with Lila follow-ing me—that'll show her I have nothing to hide. What I do have a problem with is more negative publicity or any jail time. My business nearly died thanks to a slick con artist and the media-circus trial afterward. And you know it. I don't need anyone to lob false accusations my way. Those will just drive the last nail into my career's coffin."

"Well, Dutch, how does it feel to be on that side? How does it feel to be accused of something so hideous you'd never even think of it—not until you learn it happened? How does it feel to have everyone look at you like you're a monster?"

Silence.

"Well, Dutch Merrill? How do you like being innocent and having everyone believe you're everything but? How do you like being where you put me?"

5

He stayed silent. He'd been the most vocal of all when Lila and her dark blue Smurf crew of cops saw me as the likely killer of Marge Norwalk. I would never have hurt Marge; I loved her like a second mother, but that didn't stop the suspicion, and I was even jailed. All because Marge left me everything she owned.

"Pretty rotten," he said after a bit. "But this is different. You were there, on site, when Marge was killed. I was nowhere near the Marshalls' place yesterday. I was stuck in traffic on I-5."

"And do you have anyone who can back up your alibi?"

No response.

I went on. "That was my problem. For less than ten minutes, no one could say they'd seen me. You, on the other hand, more than likely had plenty of time to do . . . whatever you did to the girl, get back in your car, drive down I-5 one way, get off at a convenient exit, then head this way again."

"You *did* talk to the cop!"

"Why? Because I know how she'd think?" I gave a short, bitter chuckle. "Think, Dutch. I know how Lila and cops in general think because I've had more than my share of contact with them."

"I can't argue that."

He again fell silent, and since I had nothing to add, I did the same. It became the most bizarre phone nonconversation I'd ever had. I'd already awarded him the Nobel Prize for lousiest condolence call last year, and now he was the leading contender for the weirdest-performance-during-a-phone-call Oscar. The man has a gift.

I glanced at my clock. It was almost 2:18. We'd argued for only ten or fifteen minutes max. The silence had now lasted for about three minutes, and I was getting antsy.

"Ah . . . Dutch?"

"Yeah?"

"What's the deal with the heavy-breathing phone call?"

"Huh?"

"Yeah. Your last three minutes, eloquent as they've been, underwhelm me."

He muttered something I didn't quite catch—I'm glad. Then, "You're a weird one, Haley Farrell."

"Hey, you're the one who called and then sat and breathed for an eternity. If you don't have anything more constructive to say than to accuse me of accusing you, then I'm done."

His sigh sounded heavy, pain-filled. A shot of sympathy rushed through me. I knew where he stood. "Listen. I'm really sorry you've become Lila's prime suspect here. I guess there's no doubt the girl was murdered, is there?"

"She bled to death. Perfectly healthy fourteen-year-olds don't do that out of the blue, even after giving birth. Yeah, I'd say someone did something to her. Detective Tsu wasn't sure what yet, and neither am I. I just know I didn't kill a girl I held in my hands when she was barely days old."

I kept quiet.

Another heavy sigh. "She's my former partner's oldest daughter. Ron was so proud when she was born, and Lori too. They couldn't not show her off."

"You said she's your goddaughter."

"I was pretty proud too. That day in church was one of the most amazing days of my life. They were dedicating her to God, and I promised to watch over her. But . . ."

When he didn't go on, I said, "But . . . ?"

"But Ron and I didn't see business the same way. I didn't want to run things the way he did, so we argued, dissolved the partnership, and went our separate ways. Last time I saw Katherine Cecilia Richardson was two weeks after the christening."

"But you said she looked familiar when Lila moved her hair aside."

"She's a carbon copy of Lori, her mom."

"And you say things went sour between the girl's dad and you?"

"Ron came up with a scheme I couldn't stomach, and when I refused to go along with him, he didn't want to go my way either. We had words."

"Hmm . . ."

"Yeah, hmm. That's just how Detective Tsu sees it. She

figures that since my business is in trouble, while Ron is rolling in more dough than Croesus, I must have let bitterness eclipse common sense and decency and taken revenge on little KC."

"It's happened."

"Yeah, but not this time. Not to, by, or in any way because of me."

His voice rang with conviction and determination. I knew how he felt. And I told him so again. "When I speak with Lila, and I know the glamour girl's probably about to glide up onto my front porch any minute again, I can honestly say I didn't see you anywhere near the Marshall home when I got there."

"Gee, thanks. That place is acres and acres huge. You could hide Buckingham Palace *and* the Taj Mahal there, and no one would know."

"Hey, it's the best I can do."

He sighed again. "You're right. This isn't your problem—at least, it isn't if you're telling the truth."

"What would I have to gain from lying?"

"Well, if you killed KC yourself . . ."

"Now you're really reaching, Merrill. Why would I do that? I don't even know her. You at least have a connection to her, weak as it may be. That is, if you really haven't had contact with her or her family for as long as you say."

"Don't start that kind of deal. I didn't hurt KC, and I'm going to prove it. Even if it means I'll have to rehash that old mess with Ron."

"Hmm . . . seems I've heard that somewhere before. Good luck."

"Your skepticism warms my heart."

"It's better than an accusation—which is all I got from you."

"I guess I'll have to take what I can get."

"Good idea. Now, there's this really great book that's calling my name."

"Go back to your Austrian count in the IRS office."

"Not even close, but I'll let it pass. You can have the book when I'm done."

"Don't bother. I have a conviction to avoid."

The misery in his words again got to me. "I'll keep you in my prayers, Dutch. And I'm serious this time."

After another long silence, he said, "Okay. It can't hurt. See ya."

After I hung up, I leaned back against my pillows. An icy rush chilled me with the memory of everything that happened to me last year. Not only did I find Marge dead and bloodied, but I was also arrested. Those hours behind bars left an indelible stain on my mind. It rivaled the hideous moment when I was attacked five years ago.

A rapid-fire series of images flew through my head. I began to shake. Tears oozed from my eyes, and eventually sobs took over. Midas, sweetheart that he is, crawled up and nestled his head into the crook of my arm. I welcomed his warmth, but it didn't thaw me out from the grip of the memories.

We stayed like that for what seemed like hours. Soon

enough, though, Midas's bladder sounded its alarm. I headed for the kitchen, my mind on a fresh cup of java. On my way there, I detoured past the Roseville jardiniere where I keep my stash of Milky Ways. Midas is about as crazy for chocolate as I am, but the theobromine might kill him. So I keep my second vice hidden where he can't reach.

In the kitchen I let him out, then paused. What an ugly mess. A feud between business partners, a dead teenager, a missing newborn child. If only it were the movie plot it resembled so much. But I'd seen the girl. And Lila didn't know where the infant had gone.

Misery caught my heart in its vise grip.

Babies, babies, babies . . . A baby had played a part in Marge's death. Now this girl, KC Richardson, had given birth, but there was no sign of her child. Dread lodged in my gut. Where was that tiny, helpless infant? What had become of it? Was it a boy or a girl? Did it have red hair like its mother, or did it have no hair at all?

A tear rolled down my cheek, and I scooped a generous measure of Starbucks House Blend beans into the coffee grinder, whirred it to a fine grind, poured it into the filter, filled the water reservoir, then pushed the coffeemaker's on button. I picked up the coffee canister, and a sob broke free from my throat.

I watched my hands shake as if from a distance. Still, I turned to the fridge—coffee beans keep better in the cold. As I opened the door, the image of KC's lifeless body materialized before my eyes.

I moaned.

The canister fell.

Stoneware shattered, and coffee beans bounced.

I dropped to the floor to clean up the mess, but many more images, vivid and painful, filled my mind. My sobs deepened, grew more painful. My tears fell among the brown bits. The piece of broken china I reached for slipped from my unsteady fingers. I followed it on my knees. It skipped just beyond my grasp.

I gave up.

The coffeemaker chimed.

I stood, then reached for the comfort of my favorite beverage. At the table I peeled the wrapper from the Milky Way, but the thought of even one bite made my stomach heave.

The first sip of coffee scalded my tongue. The second and third went down better. "Dear God, how can you bear to see your children hurt each other like this? It's more than I can stand."

I prayed. I prayed for Dutch and KC's family, for KC and her baby, for Lila, her Smurfs, and for me.

On the heels of my heartfelt sigh, the back door burst open.

"Okay, Haley girl," Bella bellowed. "I gave ya plenty of time after the cop left, and now I'm here. I'm your secret weapon. We don't want her to know I'll be investigating." She stopped cold. Then, "What *are* you sniffing out this time?"

If anything could get me out of my funk, it'd have to be the sight of—oh, great; new hair color—greenish/bluish-headed Bella, *gi* a splendid white, all aquiver at the thought of a mystery to solve.

My watery smile wasn't enough for her to pause. "I know!" she added. "I'll bet you're investigating the disappearance of all the packages of that plant food down at Percy's Plant Planet. You know they make bombs out of fertilizer, don't you?"

"Why don't you sit and write a book, Bella? You have to have a wilder imagination than the average New York Times best-selling author."

She thought for a moment. "Nah. That's way too boring. I wanna go where the action is. Since your last case, I've done my homework. I've studied up on investigative procedures. Got me a roomful of books off the Internet, and I'm an expert now, if I do say so myself."

Last year Bella showed us just how expert she was with a canister of pepper spray. My eyes still sting and my nose still runs at the memory. "That's why you should try your hand at writing."

"Don't try to put me off. I'm not your typical old lady, you know. I know karate."

My lips twitched. Bella began to train at Tyler's *dojo* almost a year ago, but in spite of her attempts to pass the test for yellow belt, the white belt still scored her belly in two.

I had to distract her. "So have you figured out yet that the plant food's manufacturer had a fire at their production facility? That's why that lurid lime-green stuff you and Dad sprinkle on every growing thing is no longer in stores."

"No . . ." Bella looked like a kid who'd had her ice cream cone stolen. "Really?"

"Check Sunday's paper. Someone wrote a letter to the editor, and the response was published right next to the question."

Bella's blue eyes danced. "You mean they really and truly put my letter in the paper?"

"Are you Greeny Growy in Seattle?"

She preened. "What do you think?"

"That you've got a color fixation. First the pink hair, then the purple and the orange, now the bluish/greenish—"

"Turquoise, Haley girl. Southwestern Turquoise by Beauty Be Done."

I shuddered. "Okay, turquoise it is. Anyway, the greeny bit gives you away."

She bustled to the kitchen pantry door, familiar as she is with our setup. "Let me see," she muttered while she rooted through the old newspapers. Then she reared up. "Eeeuuwww! What's this moldy, wet wad of newsprint doing here?"

"That's just a running joke between Dad and Ina Appleton's granddaughter. It's yesterday's paper, so it can't be moldy. Not yet."

"It's still disgusting." She continued her search. "Oh yeah! Here it is. Hmm . . . did you cut out the section? To preserve for posterior, you know. Or did you keep it intact? At least this paper didn't get caught up in that dumb joke of the reverend's."

I chose to ignore her blooper. "It's not all that dumb.

Remember how much trouble Sandy Appleton used to be in? You know, right after her parents died."

"Oh, Haley girl. She about drove poor Ina bananas."

"Well, Dad and Ina got Sandy to apply for a paper route. She really wanted the money, so she did, and that's when she and Dad got into a fuss about where she should leave his paper."

"That doesn't explain the wetness."

"Simple. Sandy likes to throw the paper on the lawn. That way she doesn't have to get off her bike at each house and can finish sooner. Dad wants it on the porch, where it stays nice and dry."

"Ah . . . so when it rains, like it did Saturday night, you guys get soggy wood mush with black ink."

"Something like that." I wasn't about to try to explain the perfectly dry copy that always appears on the back step. Bella might suggest alien intervention or spontaneous materialization as its source. You can't predict the twists and turns of Bella's mind.

But she wasn't senile or dumb. "So what does that have to do with Sandy's getting into trouble all the time? I thought she'd stopped all that."

"She did stop. She and Dad are buddies now, and he takes her apple muffins every time he bakes. She's also a regular member of his youth group at church."

Bella looked befuddled. "All because of wet papers, huh?"

Sometimes repetition is best. "Something like that."

"Weird."

Before I could remind her of pots and kettles calling each other black, Bella plopped into a chair. "Anyway, if the plant food plant burned, and nobody's stealing the stuff to make bombs with, then what did the cop come to question you for?"

I was getting desperate. Delay tactics were the best I could come up with. "Who says she came to question me?"

"Well, she's not your best friend, Haley. What, do I look stupid or something?"

Dumb? Not exactly.

Something? Definitely.

Eccentric and then some. The aging beauty made an art of her individuality.

"Never said you were dumb."

"Then it's got to be that poor dead girl at that face-lift and tummy-tuck doctor's place."

Trust Bella to get right to the heart of the matter. I couldn't think of any other way to distract her, and I really object to lying. "The Marshalls want me to redesign their new home."

Her blue eyes grew big as Delft platters. "Oh, Haley girl. You *were* there. You saw it all."

Before I could get a word in, her glee did runneth over.

"Ooh! It's gotta be better than that. I bet you found the body. Oh, that's it. That's *it*! I just knew it. You're a born gumshoe."

"More like a clodhopper."

Bella gave an airy wave. "Pshaw! Of course not, dear. It takes one to know one. See? I figured it all out. Just like you found a way to find the body."

I grimaced. "Actually, all I did was keep an appointment with a home owner. When she went to show me her back patio, the girl was there."

Bella's expression alternated between warm empathy and fascinated horror. "Was it really awful?"

I met her gaze. "Worse."

"Oh, Haley girl. And here I've been acting like a ghoul. I'm so sorry."

"At least I'm not under suspicion . . . much."

"What do you mean 'much'? Is the cop stupid or something?"

"Thanks for the vote of confidence, but Lila Tsu is a diamond-tipped blade in the PD's workshop."

"So the girl was murdered."

"Not definitely. She bled to death."

"How'd the bleeding start?"

"Lila said the preliminary examination showed she'd just had a baby. Who knows? Maybe she didn't get proper treatment and lost too much blood."

Bella shook her head. "That's not normal. True, if she's really, really young, then childbirth could cause major tearing, but if that happened, then why would she show up on someone's patio?"

"It's Lila's job to find that out, don't you think?"

Frown lines appeared on Bella's surprisingly smooth forehead. "Something doesn't add up. A dead girl. Childbirth. A patio. And a plastic surgeon with a silicone-filled trophy wife. Where do you fit in?"

"I just told you. I went to look at the house so that I could come up with a design plan. They want to remodel the whole back of the place to take advantage of the view of Lake Union. Then the new Mrs. Marshall wants me to turn her exquisite traditional décor into some übermod museum showplace."

My neighbor didn't speak, but I could almost hear the gears crank around in her overactive head. Then she snapped her fingers. "I got it. The teen girl is the doc's daughter who's come home to daddy when she got herself in trouble. But those horrible baby sellers stole the baby right from her body and then left her to die."

"Bella! Shame on you. That's gruesome."

"Don't look at me. I'm not the one who comes up with the stuff. I saw something just like that on the late-late-late-night movie the other night. It probably happened just like that here. You don't know who's watching them shows and picking up sick ideas."

"In the first place, the girl's not the doctor's daughter. And in the second, we don't know for sure that anyone did anything to her."

I was sure, but why encourage Bella?

She took even my nonanswer and ran with it. "So who's the girl? What's her name? Where does she live? Is she a runaway? And where's the baby?"

The painful constriction struck my heart again. It all seemed to come back to my recent question for Lila. Where was KC's baby?

"The girl's KC Richardson; she must live somewhere in the Seattle area, since Dutch and her dad were partners once upon a time; and I don't know if she ran away."

"Dutch? That's the hunky construction guy I got to come and bail you out when you nearly died last year, isn't it?"

I winced—I do that a lot around Bella. *When am I going to get a grip on my mouth, Lord? What's it going to take?*

"Yes, Bella, that's Dutch."

"Poor guy. There he went to help you, and you just—"

"Let's not go there, okay?"

"Then tell me, Haley girl. Where's that KC's baby?"

I struggled with my emotions, fought for a deep breath. "I don't know, Bella. And I just can't get that thought out of my head."

Bella reached over, her face serious, full of love and concern and complete knowledge of how my psyche works. "Come on, now. Don't let it stew inside you like that. That kind of thing can make you go mad. Maybe the thought's stuck in your head because the Lord wants you to find out what happened to that child."

The memories came at me fast and hard. "I can't. I just can't go there, Bella. I'll never make it if I do."

6

Later that night I waged the sheet-and-pillow battle of my life. Since I'm not prone to insomnia, much less used to little or no sleep, I got up grouchy and irritable in the morning. Even Dad's sermon on God's faithfulness did nothing to change my mood.

The teen's death weighed on my psyche, both the conscious and unconscious side, and in defiance of Bella's advice. There wasn't much I could do about it. At least, not at home, in or out of bed, and with not much else to think about.

Monday broke no better.

Which meant I had to go back to the Marshalls' mansion.

Breakfast held no appeal for me, not even Dad's fresh-baked apple muffins, which I normally devour on sight. My lack of appetite was so unusual that it led to raised eyebrows on his part.

"Are you okay?" he asked.

Reluctant to worry him any more than I already had in the last few years, I shrugged, grinned, and said, "I'm off to slay the brontosaurus for dinner. There's a beast of a place to redecorate—according to the plastic surgeon's new wife."

"You're not happy about what she wants." It wasn't a question.

"Nope. The place is gorgeous as it is. Whoever did the décor has perfect taste and played with proportions like a master. Who knows what Deedee will really want—besides the wall of windows out the back, which isn't all that bad, since it will bring light into the dark kitchen."

"See? You already agree with her on one thing. She'll probably surprise you with her good taste."

That wasn't the impression I got from Deedee at our first meeting. But for Dad's sake, I smiled again, the edgy feeling I'd had since I dragged myself out of bed as strong as ever.

"I can always hope."

"Take a muffin with you if you're not hungry now. You can't go without food and expect to think clearly."

I wanted a muffin for breakfast about as much as I wanted a couch for lunch. "Okay. Maybe I'll get the munchies soon."

Not a chance, but why worry Dad any more?

I went to the desk in my room, called the Marshall home, and agreed to meet Deedee in an hour. Then I rummaged through my samples, chose plain, neutral swatches for the upholstery, checked to make sure I'd brought home the pieces of teak and mahogany I prefer for case goods in the design I think she wants, and pulled a catalog of ultracontemporary and midcentury modern reproduction furniture from my bookshelf.

Once I had it all packed in my portfolio, with a smattering of design projects I'd done at school to spark some ideas, I turned to my Bible and curled up on the chaise by the window. God's inspired Word seeped into me and soothed my restless heart.

This time when I got to the Marshalls' front door, I had to make use of the shiny brass door knocker. Heavy footsteps sounded their approach over the polished marble I'd admired the other day, and then the solid wooden slab opened.

"You painter lady?" asked the short, gray-haired man garbed in tails, bow tie, and big-time sulk.

Oh boy. "I'm the interior designer, if that's what you mean."

He gestured for me to enter, which I did.

"What? You no gonna paint the place?"

His accent identified him as Latin American, and his assumption told me he had no idea what it is I do. "I won't do the painting itself, sir. I'll work with Mrs. Marshall to choose the paint colors, furniture styles, rugs, drapes, and to make sure it all works well together."

He made a face when I mentioned my client. "She no Mrs. Marshall. Mrs. Marshall lady in Europe. This one . . . what you say?" He scratched his pointed chin. "I know. She a flozzy."

"A what?"

"You know. A flozzy. She no care for nothing but money, big house, and do no work. Oh, she like diamond too. Many diamond. You know. Big, flashy—like TV bimbo."

Good grief. I backed away. "I have an appointment with the floz—er . . . the lady of the house." His frown made me pause. "Please let Deedee know I'm here."

"You name?"

"Haley Farrell."

"Oh, the woman who got the rich lady's used furniture place when she got dead."

My fame travels far and wide. "Something like that. I do have an appointment with Mrs. Marshall, and I prefer for her to know I arrived on time."

"I go get—"

The rich notes of the Westminster chimes cut off his words. He turned and drew back the front door again. "Who you?"

I knew who it was. "He's the contractor. The one who's supposed to rebuild whatever he tears down."

Alarm widened the man's large, somewhat bulging eyes. "What you gonna tear?"

"He's not going to tear down anything important, Domingo. I told you already. Please believe me."

Deedee's plea bore more strength than her usual feathery fluff. But Domingo wasn't buying. Interesting. I filed the detail in my mental lock box until I had a chance to talk to the outspoken . . . what was he, the butler?

Deedee approached, her smile all sugar-and-spice bright, her inner strength impressive again. "I can't wait to get started on our project. This place is, like, depressing, you know?"

Behind me, Dutch gulped. I sent him a sympathetic look.

Deedee went on. "Let's go into the living room. It's got the most windows, so it's not as dark and dungeony as the rest of the house."

Silk drapes in warm rusty red, rich toffee cashmere upholstery, and a spectacular maroon, ivory, and black Turkish Oushak rug don't read like a dungeon to me. But what do I know? I'm just the hired help.

Once Dutch, in all his rugged splendor, was seated in a substantial toffee-toned wingback and I in a French bergère accent chair done with the most magnificent cream-colored Chinese brocade, I turned to our client.

"Aside from the wall in the kitchen that you'd like to remove, are there other structural changes we need to discuss with Dutch?"

Deedee twinkled at the builder. "That's such a cute name . . . Dutch. Do you come from . . . well, you know. Are you Dutch?"

The man looked pained. "No. My mother says she just got tired of all the Davids and Stevens and Dannys and Toms, so she said the next thing that caught her eye would be my name."

I arched a brow. "Wooden shoes and leaky dikes?"

The pained look deepened. "No. A tulip catalog."

I laughed so hard, my eyes leaked like the little Dutch boy's dike. "How . . . how could she?"

"That's what I asked."

"And she said . . . ?"

Before he could answer, Deedee offered a soulful sigh. "That's so sweet."

Dutch and I looked her way.

"Huh?" Dutch asked.

I fared no better. "What's so sweet?"

The home owner's pink-glossed lips curved into a perfectly delightful smile. "She told you that flowers brighten the world and that you came to brighten hers."

Dutch winced.

I snickered.

"I'm right, aren't I?" Deedee asked.

"Not even close." Dutch's cheeks wore a scarlet primer beneath their tan topcoat. "It's even dumber than that. She said it just sounded good."

Hard as it was to control my mirth, I turned back to the matter at hand. "You were about to tell us if you wanted more structural changes than just the back kitchen wall."

Deedee stood and smoothed the hem of her pink top over her cerise miniskirt. "I don't know how anyone can stand so many walls all around. I want them gone. Every last one."

Her slender hand pointed to all but the exterior walls. I shot a peek at Dutch. This was going to be a rocky project. Maybe not so much because of our differences, but because the home owner's tastes had already rubbed him wrong.

"That wall to your right," he said, "is load-bearing. If

we take it out, then the whole upstairs will come crashing down."

Deedee narrowed her eyes. "But it blocks the flow." She turned to me. "I watch the decorating shows. I know all about flow. I even know feng shui."

I winced. "That's nice, but in this case, there won't be much flow if the upstairs takes a seat on the downstairs."

She tapped the toe of a strappy high-heeled pink sandal. "There's just got to be a way . . ."

With an apologetic look for Dutch, I ventured, "There is something we can consider. How would you feel about columns?"

"Aren't columns kind of old-fashioned?" She wrinkled her straight nose. "You know, like those Greek things that crumbled in the ruins."

"There are columns," I answered, "and then there are columns. We can do sleek, round ones without detail at the top or bottom. That way we can use them to define the various spaces, and the upstairs stays where it belongs."

Deedee tried the idea on for size. "Sleek?"

"Yes, smooth, sleek, and uncomplicated. The perfect thing to set off your contemporary furniture. Oh, and artwork. I'm sure you want to incorporate the works of today's best talent, don't you?"

"Sure . . ." she said. "Maybe. But I'm not crazy about a bunch of weird colored paint slapped on canvas. Can we maybe get some pictures made to order? You know, like, to match the décor."

With enough money, you can buy just about anything. "I'm sure we can commission some interesting pieces."

"Ooh! Custom made just for me! How cool!"

I wasn't sure if what I heard was the chair groaning under Dutch's solid six-foot-plus frame or his heartfelt opinion of the job we were about to undertake.

I gathered courage to face him. "So, Dutch? What do you think? Is it columns for the Marshalls?"

"It's curtains for the classic Georgian architecture," he said, his jaws tight, "and columns for the Marshalls."

I breathed a mental sigh of relief. I wanted the job. Not so much for the chance to turn a magnificent old home into some kind of space-age station, but for the need to find answers to the questions in the back of my mind.

"Let me show you some of the fabrics I have." I unzipped my portfolio and withdrew the swatches. I spread them out on a walnut side table that had to be at least 250 years old. Then I held out my color chip fan.

"Here. Why don't you show me what colors grab you?"

She pushed it away. "Oh, I don't need that. I know exactly what I want. I've read that smart women always decorate their home in the colors that best show off their complexion."

Suspicion sizzled in my mind as dread dug deep into my gut.

Dutch leaned forward, placed his elbows on his knees, and laced thick, strong fingers together. "What colors would those be for you, Mrs. Marshall?"

"Oh, please, Dutch." She fluttered her fingers. "Call

me Deedee. I'm sure we're going to become good, good buddies."

Uh-oh. I saw the look of horror on Dutch's face. I turned back to Deedee.

"You were about to tell us what colors you'd like us to focus on."

"There's only one color I care about," she said. "Pink! I love pink. I want to see nothing but pink, pink, pink."

Visions of Bella's Pepto-pink hair danced in my head. Candy-sweet Deedee was every decorator's nightmare. But I still wanted access to the patio where we'd found KC.

"Okay. Pink it is." I made an effort to avoid Dutch's gaze. "With splashes of white and black to set it off."

"Pink and black sounds so sexy."

This time, even I knew the groan had nothing to do with ancient hand-tied springs. I didn't know what to say.

Turns out, I didn't have to say a thing. A bloodcurdling shriek came from somewhere toward the back and left side of the house. All three of us leaped to our feet and ran to investigate. We arrived at a many-windowed sunroom, then screeched to a halt.

Plastered against the French doors to the yard was a too-familiar feline, each of her long-fuzzed legs splayed in its own separate direction, ready for quartering, her face glued to the glass, fangs gleaming, claws embedded in the wood frame, mouth open and still emitting the inhuman sound.

"Bella!"

I should have known she'd follow me. She'd shadowed me ever since she got Dutch to help me last year. I opened the door. "Come scrape your maniac cat off the door."

Deedee gasped. "You know that—that *thing*?"

"Regrettably."

"It's *yours*?"

Now came Dutch's turn to snicker.

I glared. "No way, no how, nowhere, and not in this lifetime."

"Then how'd it get here?"

"She belongs to a neighbor—" I looked around and bellowed again—"*who used to be my friend!*"

Turquoise hair appeared next to the cat still smeared across the lower right-hand pane of the glass door. Bella snatched up her beast, tucked her under her arm, and let herself into the room. Uninvited, of course.

"No need to turn hostile, Haley girl," she grumbled. "I only came 'cause I got your back, you know."

I rolled my eyes. "You watch way too much TV, Bella."

"What do you mean? I only watch *Murder, She Wrote*, cable news, and late-night movies."

"That's what I mean. Your imagination can't handle Jessica Fletcher's escapades, your language sounds like one of the too many convicts they interview on the news, and late-night movies mean you don't get enough sleep to know what's what."

"I'm an old lady. I don't need as much sleep as you do."

"If you're just another old lady, then I'm Christopher Lowell."

"Nope," Bella said with a shake of her teal-blue shrub. "You don't do a whole lot with FMD—"

"MDF—medium density fiberboard," I corrected.

Bella shrugged. "Whatever. And you've got way more hair than Christopher does."

"Who," Deedee asked, "is *she*?"

The look on my client's face was priceless. I can relate. Bella takes some getting used to. "She's the neighbor—"

"Who owns the cat who tried to eat Haley."

"Thank you, Dutch Merrill. I really needed that."

He laughed. "It was one of your better moments."

"Ahem!" The polite cough made me want to tear my hair out.

"Hi, there, Detective Tsu." Bella's smile nearly spanned her whole head. "It's good to see you again."

Lila nodded, her eyes glued to the wiggling, wriggling, twisting, turning, and bucking creature in my neighbor's clutches. "Is that the same cat?"

I snorted. "Do you really think there could be another?"

It might have been a stumble as she walked toward the center of the sunroom, but I'm pretty sure it was a shudder that shook Lila. I know the thought of one Bali H'ai sends shocks of fear and trembling through me, never mind two.

"Hey, you!"

We all turned toward the door to the inside hall. Domingo's frown could've peeled old wallpaper without a drop of stripper.

Deedee sighed. "Oh, Domingo, I've asked you so many times to please call me Mrs. Marshall. Or you can call me

Madame. That's what proper butlers in England call the ladies of the house."

The Latin butler muttered something about flozzies, then added, "You want I bring tea, beer, Scotch, vodka, martini?"

I blinked. The walnut clock out in the hall hadn't even reached eleven. Was Deedee in the habit of imbibing alcohol? And at such an early time of day?

She blushed, but her spine straightened. "That was nasty. I'm not like that, and you know it. But we'll have to discuss it later. I need a carafe of coffee and a pot of fresh tea now, please."

On his way back out, the butler shot his mistress a malevolent glare.

"I'm so sorry," Deedee said, her Marilyn Monroe voice somewhat strained. "The man is a menace. Stew is so sweet and sentimental, and he won't fire the disrespectful creature. Domingo's been with the family for almost thirty years."

That's when I became an instant psychic: Domingo's job was toast, and he'd done the toasting himself.

"But let's sit down," the pink-garbed blonde continued. "It's nice in here. We can have our tea and coffee, talk about my new décor—"

"Mrs. Marshall," Lila said, "I'm here on police business."

Deedee's smile melted. She bit her bottom lip, and the sparkle in her eyes took a hike.

I felt for her.

"Of course," she said. "Well, then let's get on with it so we can get back to happier things, like the redesign."

Bella perched at my right on the cast-iron love seat. Bali H'ai took her owner's momentary distraction to make her escape. I seized the opportunity.

"Bella, go get your cat."

The former model pouted. "She won't hurt a thing. Bali H'ai's a shy little kitty. There's too much commotion and too many strangers here for her. I'll bet she's hiding under a bed or in a closet."

"Shredding the place is more like it."

"Haley girl! My darling wouldn't do a thing like that. She's a sweet, gentle baby."

"You can discuss the merits of your cat once I'm gone," the detective said. "I have additional questions for Mrs. Marshall, Haley, and Mr. Merrill, so it's convenient to find all of you here."

Dutch drew in a sharp breath. I slanted a look at him and took in his tight jaw, the muscle twitch in his cheek. I reached across the space between the love seat and his chair, then caught myself.

Where did that come from?

Startled by my impulse at Dutch's distress, I sat back and stole another peek at him.

Then I caught Lila's words. ". . . need to identify the prints."

"I'm sorry," I said, a furious blush hot on my face. "I missed that. Could you run it by me again?"

Karate Chop Cop gave me a puzzled look. "I said we

found footprints in the rose bed on the left side of the house. The corpse lay only a few feet away. We need to identify who made those prints."

"I never stepped off the patio," I said.

"I don't do dirt," Deedee offered.

"I wasn't here," Bella added.

Silence followed.

"Well, Mr. Merrill?" Lila prompted. "You're the only one present who hasn't denied ownership of the prints."

The anger on Dutch's face took me by surprise. Sure, he'd been mad at me last year when the police delayed the sale of the mansion where Marge was killed. He thought I'd killed her, and he'd wanted—needed—the remodeling contract. But I hadn't seen any emotion so strong, so heated, so dangerous twist his handsome features.

"That, Detective Tsu," he said, his words precise, "is because I can't. The prints are probably mine."

7

He stood. "And you know it."

Lila tipped her head in silent acknowledgement. "Then could you explain how they got there? Especially since the designer, the home owner, and the butler all say you reached the patio the conventional way."

He stood, paced. "I came for a look at the property, to get an idea how the house sits on the land, the general condition of the structure as it stands. I like to know what I'm getting into when I consider a new job."

Lila's notebook and pen came out. "And when was that?"

"In the morning. Right after I got Noreen's call."

"After the rain?"

"After the morning's shower."

"What were you doing in the rose bed?"

"I wanted to check out the foundation of the house close to the patio. Noreen told me the Marshalls want to remove the back wall of the house, and I wanted to see if I would need to rip out the slab to do it right."

Lila's expression didn't give away a hint. "Why didn't you come to the front door? It would seem the logical thing to do."

Dutch sighed and jammed his hands in the back pockets of his faded jeans. "I did go to the front door. I even banged that heavy brass knocker about ten times—you probably already lifted my fingerprints from there." One hand left a pocket to make a helpless gesture. "But nobody answered, and I figured since I'd taken the time to come, I might as well look at the foundation and the patio."

"And there was no teen here at that time."

He gave Lila a hard look. "When I returned in the evening, the pool of blood was fresh and wet. I bet the body was pretty warm too. So no. There was no one on the patio that morning."

"You didn't touch the corpse?"

"I never got close to the body. I walked out, saw what had happened, called the PD, and then you showed up—as fast as always. No one touched the girl while I was here."

Having found myself at the end of Lila's questions once too often, I took pity on Dutch. "He's right, Ms. Tsu. None of us got near her. You were the first to touch her. At least, the first I know of."

The silver pen danced over the page again. Then Lila pinned Dutch with one of her keen looks. "When was the last time you had contact with KC's father?"

Dutch closed his eyes.

I winced. His answer wasn't going to help him.

"During my trial."

"That ended only early last year."

"January."

"That's not as long ago as you first said."

He ran a hand through his thick, dark hair. "It's not as if we resumed a friendship, much less a partnership, Detective. The same subcontractor affected us both. The home owner sued me, while Ron was a witness."

"And was that contact amicable?"

"I'm sure you've read the reports by now. You know we had a shouting match in the hall outside the courtroom."

She acknowledged his words with a nod. "So you parted again on bad terms."

"You could say that."

"For the second time you came off worse after a confrontation with Mr. Richardson."

"That's right, but it doesn't mean I hatched a plan to hurt Ron, especially not through KC. It takes a lot of time and effort to try to restore a career and reputation that were raked through the mud—unfairly, I might add. I've been busy."

"Care to tell me what you argued about?"

Dutch's expression grew stormy. "Are you trying to tell me you haven't read any of the tabloid tales? They had a field day with everything we said."

"I don't read tabloids, Mr. Merrill. Please do me the favor and tell me what went on."

"Sure." The derision in his voice made clear he'd caught her nonanswer. "Ron made a crack that questioned my integrity. I reminded him that lawyers can and often do paint a picture of respectability that deceives. Anyone can hide behind that and still be crooked as a twelve-foot snake."

The detective closed her notebook. "To your credit, Mr. Merrill, you haven't tried to lie."

"I have no reason to lie. I know the footprints and the trouble between Ron and me look bad. But I don't know anything about KC. I don't know how she got here. I hadn't seen or heard anything about her since she was six weeks old."

"Again, to your credit, the Richardsons say the same thing." Lila put away her writing implements, then glided to her feet. "You understand that I'll have more questions for you."

He gave a hard, brief nod. "And I'll have more of the same answers for you. I don't know how that little girl got here, who got her pregnant, or why she bled to death."

Lila headed for the sunroom door. At my side Bella wriggled her way up to her feet. "Excuse me!"

The detective stopped, turned, and stared. "Yes?"

"What about the baby?"

A pang sliced through me, but I didn't speak.

Lila turned back to Dutch. "Yes, Mr. Merrill. What about the baby?"

"I know nothing about the baby."

I couldn't stop myself. "Someone does. Who is it, and where is the child?"

In the silence that followed Lila's quiet "I'll let myself out," a conviction took root in my heart. As tough as I knew it would be, and as potentially dicey as it could become, I also knew I couldn't just sit around and wait. Not while a baby was out there, where it might be hurt, where it could meet the same fate as this other child, the one who gave it life.

I had to find KC's child.

The aftermath of Lila's grilling was as surreal as the lead-up to it had been. At first no one moved, not for long, silent moments. I have no idea how much time went by while we sat—or stood, in Dutch and Bella's case—like statues, but then Bella's monster made a second appearance at the outside French door.

"How did that cat get back outside?" Deedee asked.

"She probably found an open window," I answered. Then to Bella I added, "You'd think the dumb cat would learn."

Bella sniffed. "Bali H'ai is anything but dumb."

"Then how come she's there—" I gestured toward the animal "—splattered up against the same glass all over again? You'd think she'd have the sense to stay inside if she wants in that bad."

The feline screeches started up again, so sharp and loud that they seemed to surround us, so I didn't catch Bella's response. It was probably for the best. She loves the ball of malice and fur.

"What she is, Haley, is talented." Dutch's wry tone went over Bella's head; she had her beast back in her arms. "That cat throws her voice so well that it almost sounded as if her screams came from inside the house."

That Bella heard. She preened. "See, Haley? I told you Bali H'ai's a special cat. Maybe I should send that David Letterman a tape. You know how he has all those special animals on all the time."

"Yeah, Bella. And the segment's called 'Stupid Pet Tricks.'"

Her smile did a 180. "Oh. Maybe not."

The feline melted in boneless splendor all over Bella's generous midsection. The owner smiled. "I don't care. She's still special. I bet she's the only centrifugal cat in the world."

"What did you call her?"

"You know, centrifugal. Like those guys with the wooden dummies."

"Ventriloquist, Bella. They're ventriloquists."

"Pshaw, Haley girl! Don't you know anything? Those ventrilocker whatsits are some thingies in the heart. My doctor checked mine out not so long ago. They work fine too."

I did some eye rolls. "Ventricular. That's something related to the ventricle, a part of the heart."

Bella lifted a shoulder, a gesture that jiggled the fluid spill of gray fur in her embrace, with no perceivable reaction from the fur.

"No big deal," Bella said. "That's just a bunch of weird words. What's the big deal is my hot-shot superstar cat."

I gave up. "Just keep a good grip on your superstar, and sit down—if you refuse to go home, that is."

Back at my side, woman and cat scooted to the farthest

reaches of the love seat. Fine. I wanted no contact with the
critter, be she talented or not. Give me Midas any day.

In the split second of silence, during which I experienced
an irrational pang of gratitude for the brief break from the
pain of tragedy Bella and her beast had offered, I heard footsteps approach. A woman's pleasant if puzzled voice called,
"Deanna? Where are you, Deanna? I just saw that policewoman drive away. What was she doing here again—"

Madeleine Ogleby fell silent in the doorway to the sunroom.

I gaped so wide that my jaw almost clipped the sisal rug
underfoot.

"Well," the newcomer said, a puzzled look on her beautiful face. "Isn't this something? I didn't know you had
company, dear. And I would never expect to find Haley
and Bella here. Have you been attending Sunday services
at the Wilmont River Church too?"

Deedee shook her head.

"I get around," Bella added with a pat to Bali H'ai.

I waved and smiled. "So Deedee is really Deanna."

"She's always had her friends call her that, but I prefer
the name my husband and I chose for our only child."

A glance at the daughter revealed her tension. Did the
new Mrs. Marshall object to the use of her given name or
did she object to Madeleine's arrival? It occurred to me that
a mother who walks right into her newlywed daughter's
home unannounced, and *that* after a move across state lines
to be closer to said daughter, might prove more like smother
than mother.

And it was way past time for us to go. I stood. "How about if I call you tomorrow, Deedee?"

She sent me a grateful look. "That sounds great. Maybe we can make a date for you to show me some fabrics with better color."

"Pink."

"Pink is in," she replied as she rose.

Domingo entered the sunroom. He lurched and staggered under the weight of a massive silver tray laden with silver serving pieces and a platter of finger sandwiches.

"Oh!" Deedee frowned. "I forgot I sent him to get refreshments. And now you're leaving. Please, take a couple of sandwiches before you go. He did go to some trouble for us."

Domingo glared at his mistress. He clunked the tray on the glass-topped cast-iron table in the far right corner of the room. "You want coffee and tea, you got coffee and tea. I know coffee and tea need sandwich too."

Everyone got it.

With a final disdainful sniff, Domingo left.

Madeleine tsk-tsked and wrapped an arm around her dismayed daughter. "I'm so sorry, dear. You didn't exaggerate, did you? He really doesn't like you."

Deedee shrugged and nibbled her bottom lip. The sudden vulnerability gave me a glimpse at yet another facet of Deedee Marshall.

She lowered her gaze to the floor. "Even though Stew divorced Sharon years before I met him, Domingo thinks I'm in the way of a reconciliation." She tossed her blond mane. "Sharon's been in Europe since the final decree. I hardly think she's pining for old times."

Deedee really was more than sugar and spice and all pink things nice. Maybe the job wouldn't be half as bad as I first thought. But we were now as welcome as fresh-killed skunk at a designer showcase home.

I stood. "Come on, Bella. We've overstayed our welcome."

My neighbor gave me the kind of "Do I really have to?" look I normally associate with my beggar dog. I jerked my head toward the door.

She pouted.

I gave her what Dad calls the hairy eyeball.

"Oh, all right." When Bella stood, Bali H'ai slithered all the way down her owner's *gi* and split to parts unknown. Bella turned to me. "Oh dear. Bali H'ai really likes it here in this awesome house."

"Get your cat so we can leave this family alone," I said through clenched teeth.

"Ever hear of herding cats?" Dutch asked, clearly amused.

I blinked—not so amused. "You're still here. I forgot."

"No one's ever accused me of being forgettable." He grinned. "I guess there's always a first time for everything."

"Yeah, well, put your ego with your troubles in an old tin can, and smile, smile, smile." What can I say? I'm addicted to old movies, songs, and books. "While you're at it, why don't you give Bella a hand with her cat so I can gather my samples?"

"Hmm . . . I have to wonder why you won't give her a hand yourself. Maybe you and the cat don't see eye to eye."

"Yeah, and maybe you like to think of yourself as my white knight. So prove it and go save me. Retrieve the hair ball. It's time this circus left town."

Bella cooed. "Now there's a thought. Do you think Bali H'ai's talents would do better at a circus than on Letterman? I could probably do some business with her in a sideshow tent. You know, 'Come and hear the ventrilocker vixen here!'"

My client and her mother eyed us with something akin to horror.

"A vixen is a fox, Bella." I hurried to the door. "It's related to a dog."

"Oh, that's right." She tossed her outrageous hair "She'll be the talking tigress instead."

Just then said tigress darted into the room, dashed between Dutch's somewhat spread legs, circled Bella's ankles, flew onto the glass table, crashed into the silver creamer, then leaped to one of the cast-iron chairs, where she perched on the tan cushion and groomed her tail.

"I'm outta here," I muttered. "They're all yours, Merrill."

As I stepped into the hall, however, the maniacal beast zipped out past me, her unnatural wails guilty of permanent damage to my eardrums.

I took another step and entered the Twilight Zone. Bali H'ai shot past me again.

Headed in the same direction.

Without going back into the room.

I blinked, shut my eyes, rubbed them hard.

"Uh . . . Haley?" Dutch asked.

"You mean I'm not seeing things?"

"Not unless we're having a mass hallucination."

"Told ya my cat was special," Bella crowed. "She's like an amoeba in biology class. You know, she's into that no-mattress-mambo kind of reproduction. She turned into two before our very eyes. Wait'll Letterman gets a load of that!"

I turned and met Dutch's gaze. "What happened?"

He shrugged and opened his mouth to speak, but before he could eke out even one word, a catfight ensued in the hall. Shrieks and yowls and wails and cries filled the air. A not inconsiderable amount of fluffy gray fur flew.

No one moved. We just stared.

Domingo came from the kitchen and muttered some unintelligible Spanish, a tall, full crystal pitcher held high over his head. Without further ado he dumped the whole thing on the fighting felines, who froze under the icy on-slaught.

"I thought you said there was only one of those crazy cats in the world," Deedee said, awe in her wispy voice.

I groaned. "Why would anyone clone that mangy mon-ster?"

"Nasty, nasty, Haley girl," Bella said. Then she turned to the twin wads of gray. "Aw . . . Bali H'ai, baby. You poor little thing. That mean man went and messed up your pretty coat. Come to Mama. I'll take care of you."

She reached down for her cat but stopped partway to the sodden fur. "Uh-oh."

I chuckled. "I'll say."

"Which one's which?" she asked, bewildered.

"Does it matter?" It didn't to me; both beasts seemed cut from the same cloth. "Unless the clone belongs to one of them."

I glanced at mother and daughter, who grimaced and shook their heads. Domingo scooted back to the kitchen, Spanish denials ripe on his lips.

I turned back to my neighbor. "Well, then, Bella, my dear, it looks like this is your lucky day. You got yourself a twofer."

Bella's blue eyes revealed her concern. "But how am I gonna tell them apart?"

"Again, does it really matter? From where I stand, it's the three of you from here on in. One for all and all for one. Instead of the three musketeers, you're the three B-keteers: Bella and Bali and Faux Bali too."

8

By the time I got home after the nightmare at the Marshall place, my head hurt worse than if I'd spent the morning swinging a rubber mallet at it. It didn't help that Bella had followed me, her 1965 vintage pink Caddy way closer to my rear bumper than I liked.

When I parked in the driveway to the manse, I didn't bother with the portfolio I'd thrown into the backseat. With a slam of the Honda's door, I gathered up my fury and marched across the street to confront the owner of Bali H'ai and now Faux Bali too.

Every ounce of frustration I'd held in for the past few days spewed into my words. "Do you realize the kind of chaos you created back there? You probably cost me the job too."

Chagrin etched twin lines between Bella's silvery eyebrows. "Oh, Haley girl, I'm so sorry. I just meant to help. I didn't want you to get hurt like the last time. I still have nightmares about that day."

Talk about nightmares. "I understand your concern, Bella, but I can take care of myself. That's why I've spent the better part of five years working out three times a week at Tyler's *dojo*. I don't need a babysitter, but I think you just might."

The hurt in Bella's blue eyes gave me pause. Oh great. That hadn't been my intention. I reached out, but she turned away.

Remorse is hard to swallow. "I'm sorry, Bella. All that's happened has upset me, and besides that, you have to admit, things got way crazy over at the Marshalls."

"Sure, they did," she said, her back toward me, her tone quiet and serious, unusual for her. "But I didn't hear anyone else snap or gripe about it."

She glanced over a shoulder. "What is wrong with you, Haley girl? I've never known you to get so nasty."

An alarm bell gave a weak clang in the back of my mind, but I threw a blanket of evasion over it. "Nothing's wrong. I'm just tired, I have a headache, and I really do want to do the Marshall job. Then there's the dead girl. And that missing baby."

"That is enough to make anyone jumpy," Bella conceded. "So why don't you go make yourself a pot of that black tar you like so much? It usually makes you all mellow. I don't know how, with all that caffeine. But I've seen it do wonders for you."

"Starbucks does have that effect on me." I doubted it would do much right then though. "I'm sorry I've been such a grouch. I'll go hibernate in my cave until I turn more human, okay?"

She raised one shoulder. "If you feel like it, maybe you can come help me figure out which cat's which after you chill."

"Oh yeah. Sure, Bella. I'll come see you, all right. But when I do, you better make sure your twin menaces are locked up tight."

Bella unlocked her front door. "Goodness gracious, you better get a move on. Catch yourself that nap. It might help—something's got to. I'll see you later."

Once her door closed, I headed home. On the way past the behemoth pink car, I glanced in and saw the whirling dervishes go at it again. By the time Bella got around to retrieving her pets, there might not be much of anything to identify.

After I grabbed my portfolio and ran inside and up to my room, the restlessness that had tortured me for days only grew worse. Anxiety knotted my stomach, while too many thoughts churned in my mind. I'd never be able to concentrate like this, so I didn't even consider the possibility of work.

After I paced back and forth in front of my bedroom window for no less than twenty-five minutes, I surrendered. It was nearly two in the afternoon, and I knew from my copy of the *dojo*'s schedule that Tyler was about to teach a class in a few minutes. What better way to relieve the tension coiled inside me than to go sweat, kick, and maybe punch a stuffed bag or two?

I grabbed a clean *gi* and drove five over the speed limit, hoping to get there before the class began. I made it too—and without a ticket.

Kickboxing was the special of the day. Tyler teaches a mongrel mix of martial arts disciplines, a blend all his own yet fully Asian. During his stint in the army, he spent three years in Korea, where he fell in love with everything oriental, especially martial arts. Once he retired from the service, he returned to the Seattle area, married an Asian American doctor, and worked his way to black belt in more disciplines than I knew existed.

He cuts a formidable figure too: tall, lean, and muscular, head shaved to a shine, dark brown skin smooth and supple. He has a warm and caring personality, his faith in Christ underscores his every thought and deed, and his intelligence and street smarts make him wiser than I like.

He knows me too well.

A fact he proved yet again.

He matched me up with one of Wilmont High's lanky basketball stars for the sparring match. When the kid yelped after I landed one especially well-placed kick, our *sensei*'s eyes glittered with something dangerous.

"Class is over," he said, then jerked his head toward the studio's office. "We have to talk."

I had no doubt whom he meant. Still, I tried to fudge my way out of it.

"Oh, sorry. I can't stay today." I hustled out to the hall, headed for the locker room for the army surplus duffel in which I carry my gear to and from lessons. "Some of the ladies in the missionary society are getting together at the church to bake cookies and cakes. One of them who's too broke to foot the bill herself won't let me pay her way, so we're having a sale to raise funds so she can join us on our trip to Indonesia—"

I quit when, bent double over the duffel, I caught a glimpse of his stony stare.

"In my office," he said.

There'd be no way to avoid Tyler's inquisition. No matter how much I wanted to. No matter how hard I tried to blab my way out.

Once inside Asian World, as many of us call his themed office, Tyler pointed to his comfy couch. "Sit."

I gave him a Heil Hitler salute.

"Knock it off, Haley. You just hurt a kid who did nothing to you in the first place. I want to know what's up with you."

"You're not my conscience, you know. I don't have to tell you anything."

"And I don't have to let you back into my place."

I glared.

He stared.

Neither of us budged.

But I knew he was right. And his steadfast stare broke through to me. I began to shake. My stomach flipped, and the tears began to pour. The images of Marge and KC clicked through my mind, their rhythm fast, steady, relentless.

Death is so final, so ugly when it's violent.

I dropped onto the couch. Tyler tossed me a box of tissues. I wiped my eyes and blew my nose, but the tears continued to fall.

"Have you talked to Lila in the last few days?" I asked.

"No. Seems she's got a couple of tough cases on her hands right now. She even called off teaching her class on Wednesday mornings."

"Well, there you have it. I did it again."

His dark brown eyes narrowed. His voice lowered and deepened. "You did what again?"

"I stumbled—what a word!—on another corpse."

"Run that by me again."

"Okay. Here's the whole scoop . . ."

I gave it to him, blow by gruesome blow, even the Bali and Faux Bali fiasco. When I was done, my eyes had dried up, but I didn't feel a whole lot better.

"You know what you got to do, don't you?"

I shrugged.

"Give it up, Haley. You messed yourself up long enough with that closed-up attitude of yours. It's too clear to me you need to go to Tedd before you fall apart again."

No great news there—the falling apart bit. I just didn't want to go through the mind-churning ordeal of spilling my guts to my shrink-turned-friend. "I'm okay. I feel way better now that I talked to you. There's no need to bother Tedd. You know how busy she is all the time."

He stared on.

Well, I hadn't really lied. I did feel better now that I wasn't bawling anymore and my nose wasn't so snotty.

But that wasn't what he meant. He knew where I was trying to go here. He refused to let me get away with it.

He held out his red phone. "Call her."

"Oh, I can't interrupt Tedd right now. She's got to be with a client."

"Call her."

"Okay. I'll call her as soon as I get home." I stood, ready to make a run for it.

"You're not going anywhere until you call her." He reached back and picked up something from his desk. With a grim smile, he jingled my car keys.

"Hey! That's against the law. You stole my keys."

"It'd also be against the law to let you go out there all messed up like this, to let you hurt someone. A couple of someones, you and someone else."

I glared.

He stared.

Finally I blinked in our little game of chicken. "Oh, all right."

The conversation with my counselor, a good friend of Tyler's wife, was short and to the point. She would meet me under the nearest Golden Arches. We'd reached a point in our relationship where we were more friends than psychologist and client. Last year, a short time after my arrest, we began to meet at McDonald's. We'd kept it up, even though these days I could afford to feed a crowd at any five-star joint, sadly, thanks to Marge's death. Tonight's meeting wouldn't be just a meal between two good friends.

I rounded on Tyler. "So. Are you happy now?"

"Satisfied, but not happy. I won't be until you're in a better place. Have you given prayer much thought?"

I sighed, exhausted, anxious, troubled. "I've done little

but. It's just that KC died in such a strange way. And no one seems to know or even care what happened to her baby. It's eating me alive."

He took the phone from my clenched fist. "Ever since your attack, you've had a thing for victims. But if you don't get some perspective, it really will eat you alive."

A detailed study of my Birkenstocked feet became wildly appealing.

Tyler went on. "You know you have to keep the date with Tedd."

"Yes," I whispered.

"And you know just as well that it's Lila's job, not yours, to find out what happened to the teen and her baby."

"Yeah, but—"

"No buts, Haley. Let Lila do her job."

"The baby's missing, Ty. Why doesn't anyone get it? It's so little, has no way to protect itself. I have to make sure it doesn't get hurt. That it doesn't die too."

"You don't have to do anything but go see Tedd."

I took a deep breath, squared my shoulders. "Fine. But if she doesn't agree with you, you'll have to get off my case."

"She'll agree."

"Not if you don't call her ahead of time."

"You know I wouldn't do that."

"I'm not so sure. You always think you know everything."

"Nowhere near everything. I just know you."

"Gee, thanks." I could talk circles around us both until

we dropped from exhaustion or boredom, but nothing I said would change his mind.

Nor would it change the facts.

I needed to see Tedd.

"Okay, *sensei*. You win this round. I'll go eat burgers with Tedd. And I'll let Lila do her job—I'd like to see me try to stop her."

He smiled for the first time. "The two of you are well matched."

"You should know."

"That was one of the most instructive moments of my teaching career. I learned way more than I think either one of you did. I now know you and Lila better than I did before I pitted you in that match."

"Don't go doing me any more favors."

"Ah . . . but that's just it. You haven't figured out yet what a favor I did you. Someday you and Lila are going to be the best of friends."

"I doubt Karate Chop Cop would like to hear that."

"I've told her more times than I can count."

I crossed to the office door. "Lucky her. I know how it feels to have Tyler Colby pound away at you with something."

He chuckled. "Watch your driving while you're at it, girl. You have a lead foot when something's not right with you."

"Never had an accident, daddy-o."

"There's always—"

"A first time for everything." I grinned. Dutch had said the same thing only a short while ago. "And this is the time

for me to split. Give me the kid's phone number, will you?
I need to apologize to him."

"Now you sound more like yourself. But you still need
to—"

"I know, I know. I'm on my way. I'll give Tedd your
love."

"Tell her Sarah says hi."

"Your wife needs to get out more often. Between her
doctor's hours and your sweet little Mei Li, Sarah's become
a phantom figure."

"She's thinking about going part-time."

"Really?"

"Yeah. Morning sickness is getting to her this time."

I spun and poked a finger into his rock-hard chest. "You rat!
You didn't say a thing. Congratulations! When's she due?"

We chatted about the soon-to-come little Colby while I
went out into the hall to retrieve my duffel bag. Then, when
I reached the front door to the studio, Tyler held his arms
outstretched. I walked into his warm hug.

A sob hitched in my throat. "You're a good friend, *sensei*.
The best."

"I love you too, sister. The Lord tells us to love and care
for each other, and you're an easy one to love. Even with that
hard head of yours doing a number on me all the time."

My chuckle died on another sob. "Hard head? Look
who's talking!"

"Ah . . . get out of here!" His gentle shove got me to the
door. "Be careful, and be blessed with the Father's love,
Haley."

"You too, Ty. And thanks again."

Since I had an hour to kill, I drove to the end of my favorite cul-de-sac at the north end of Wilmont, parked, and
walked out onto the beach. This part of the Puget Sound's
shoreline was covered with rocks, smooth silver-gray stones
I loved to touch, even collect. One never knew where in
the world they'd started their trip here. I always let my
imagination run with the possibilities.

But today nothing came to my mind. Nothing but the
tragedy of a dead teen and her missing child. And memories
of Marge, a friend I still missed too much.

I did need to see Tedd. The ache inside had grown too
great.

About a half hour after I found a boulder to sit on, my
cell phone rang.

"Hello?"

"It's Lila Tsu, Haley."

"Okay. To what do I owe this rare honor?"

"Not much of an honor. I just called to let you know you
can stop by the station and pick up your camera. We're
keeping the memory chip, of course, but there's no need
to bag one more thing in the evidence room. It's crowded
enough as it is."

"You know? That's got to be one of the most interesting
places around. I can just imagine all the different stuff you
have in there."

"You'd be surprised. It looks more like a strange grocery
store with shelves full of brown cardboard boxes."

I couldn't quite call up that image. "Bummer. You just shot down one of my favorite cop show illusions."

Silence. Then, "You do realize, don't you, that this is real life as opposed to a TV show?"

"Of course I realize that. Your jail cell was way too real to mistake. I just thought producers generally try to keep their shows as close to reality as possible."

"One would think, but when it comes to law enforcement, fiction is far more interesting than reality."

"Too bad."

I fell silent, and Lila didn't speak either. This was a strange call. It reminded me of the earlier one with Dutch. In spite of Tyler's crazy prediction about a potential friendship between the detective and me, I wasn't used to chatting with homicide detectives while watching the Puget Sound's waves lap the shoreline. Nor sharing deep, meaningful silences either.

"No, really," I said. "Why did you feel the need to call me on my cell? You could have left me a message on my home phone."

Her sigh came over the air waves loud and clear. "I really shouldn't do this, but I knew you'd want to know. I also knew you'd start bugging me soon enough and wouldn't keep your nose out of police business. You do have a track record, you know."

"Hey! That's not fair. I'm the one who's told Bella we're no Jessica Fletchers a bazillion times."

Lila chuckled. "That doesn't mean you've walked away from your curiosity. I do know you a bit better these days, Haley."

"Don't remind me, okay? Our acquaintance holds some rotten memories, if you think about it."

"Sorry. And sorry again, since what I have to tell you will make a couple more bad ones."

Something twitched in the area near my heart. "Do you really have to tell me, then?"

"I don't have to, but you'll eventually learn the details of KC's toxicology screen. We can't keep much out of the media these days. It came back with a high concentration of Coumadin in her blood. And the autopsy showed no medical need for a blood thinner."

A rush sounded in my ears. My heart pounded in my chest. Air became difficult to take in. I'd known it from the start.

With great difficulty, I cleared my throat. "It's murder, then. Just as I've said from the start."

"Yes, Haley. You're right. Someone made sure KC would bleed to death."

There are times when I'd rather be wrong.

This was one of those times.

9

By the time I got to McDonald's, I knew no hamburger would make it down my throat. Even water was iffy.

Another job. Another murder.

"Are you trying to tell me something, Lord? Did I mess up when I went into interior design? Do you just want me to run Norwalk & Farrell's Auctions?"

Not that I'd done anything to keep that business running since the day KC Richardson died. I'd checked in with Ozzie a couple of times, but the man was so efficient, and he knew his clientele and the world of antiques so well, that it was a breeze for me to just let him run with the ball, so to speak. I was glad I'd talked him into a cell phone though; otherwise, I'd never get ahold of him. He was always on the go.

Still, I had to put in an appearance at the office now and then, if for no other reason than to remember I did own the place and that there was more to my life than dead bodies, bad memories, and high levels of bile in my throat.

The stress was getting to me, and I wasn't dealing with it well. I'd even become a menace at the *dojo*.

I walked into the fast-food place with as much enthusiasm as Michelangelo entering a faux-finish workshop. I spotted Tedd when she got up and flagged me down.

Few would miss the Latin beauty. Although my counselor stands at average height, she catches every eye with her wealth of wavy black hair, her warm olive-toned skin, her enormous brown eyes framed with curly lashes, and the generous smile she enhances with true-red lipstick. The white blouse with tone-on-tone floral embroidery that topped the slim black pencil skirt was eye-catching as well.

She sat back down when I reached her booth. "I'd begun to wonder if you'd decided to stand me up."

"I'd never do that." I plopped down across from her. "I just went to the beach to think, since I had some extra time, but while I was there, I got a call from Lila Tsu."

"The detective?"

"Do I know another Lila Tsu?"

"What did she want?"

"Have you read a newspaper in the last week or so?"

"Sure."

I studied my fingers as I drew a circle on the scarred laminate tabletop. "Then you have to know I was one of the two women who found the dead teen the other day."

"I did notice that." She took a sip from her iced tea, her gaze on me the whole time, even though I refused to look up. "What were you doing there in the first place?"

"Noreen recommended me to Dr. Marshall and his new wife. I went to look at the place, talk with Deedee, and see what she wanted done. You know, the usual interior designer gig."

I looked down, then stole a glance at her from the corner of my eye. She busied herself with her spoonful of yogurt and fruit. After she swallowed, she said, "Why did Lila call you? Are you in trouble with her again?"

I suspect my grin looked more like a grimace than a sign of humor. "I think I've dodged that bullet this time. She called to tell me that tests showed the girl had very high levels of blood thinner in her system. And she'd just given birth. That's why KC bled to death."

"You're telling me someone fed that child something that would increase postpartum bleeding so it would kill her?"

I shrugged and nodded. The burning in my throat kept me from saying a word.

"Haley, that's hideous! Poor child."

I could only manage another jerk of my head. I fought the tears with all I had.

"Who would do such a thing?" She pushed away the rest of her parfait, the wrappers from her burger and fries, and the dewy paper cup of tea. "Who is this KC? Did you know her?"

Yet one more shake of my head, and the first tear spilled out.

"I don't understand any of this," Tedd said. "Why would Lila Tsu call you in particular? I didn't think you'd become so close that she would breach professional conduct."

"We . . . haven't." I felt inordinate pride in those two

words. They were hard to produce. I tried again. "She doesn't want me to blunder into her investigation."

"Wise woman."

That sparked something in me—a very minor, insignificant something. "Hey . . ."

Then Tedd's demeanor changed. "Okay, Haley Farrell. Why'd Tyler make you call me from the studio? And what is going on with you? I just pushed you to where you would normally be all over me, but all you managed was a mousy 'Hey.'"

My last year's progress retreated with supersonic speed. The shakes started up again, the acid burned all the way up to my throat, and the tears poured down my face and onto the table.

"That girl . . . and Marge . . . oh, Tedd, it's been so bad. The dreams just keep coming and coming and coming at me all night long. I wake up crying, screaming. Hour after hour. I can't sleep, I can't eat, I can't work. And then Bella has to go and get herself another demon-possessed cat."

"Let's leave Bella and cats for another time, okay? Tell me about the dreams."

I did, even though I had to struggle to put into words the vividness of the images that haunted me. How can you voice the effect a body in a pool of its just-spilled blood has on you? Especially when you still remember being left for dead in a similar pool yourself.

My broken phrases must have done a good enough job, since I saw my anguish mirrored in Tedd's eyes. She knows where I've been; she's been there too.

When I ran out of steam, she placed a soft, warm hand over mine. "Let me tell you, for whatever it's worth, in your situation I would've had the same kind of dreams. Most people, even without a rape in their past, would be traumatized by what you've seen. Twice now."

"Yeah, but I'm not most people, and I can't shake the dreams. I can't go on like this."

"Give yourself a break, Haley. It's only been a few days since you found KC. It will take some time for you to work your way through this. It's also only been about a year since Marge's murder."

"And here I thought I was doing so well. What a way to fool myself."

"Stop it. You have done well—very well, actually. You're on your way to true healing. But life doesn't always go in a straight line. That's why you have to make sure you lean on the Lord in times like these."

I snorted. "What do you think I've been doing? My Bible gets a whopper workout every day, my knees look like elephant leather from all the time I've spent on them, and my throat hurts from all those cries for help I've sent up to the Father. And look at me. I'm still a mess."

"You're not a mess. You took another hit, and it takes time for a person to regain her balance. Keep on keeping on. The Lord is with you, but you might want to cut down on the screaming. If you talk too loud too much, you won't hear his voice. That's what you need more than anything else right now."

This time I managed a chuckle. "Dad would say I'm kinda deaf when it comes to this kind of thing."

"Nah. You heard the Father's call last year, and that was a horrible, rotten time. Don't tell me you forgot your stay at the Jailhouse Ritz."

I shuddered. "Never. And you're right. That was a horrible time. At least Lila hasn't rattled her snazzy chained bracelets at me this time. She's after Dutch these days."

"Dutch? The builder? How does he come into this?"

"KC was his godchild. Dutch and her father have been feuding for years. Lila's got her mind made up that he had something to do with the death."

Tedd's look made me squirm. Then she asked, "Do you think he could have?"

I'd danced and dodged, not ready to check out my thoughts on this. Trust the canny Latina to force me right to it. But I didn't know what I thought. And I told her that with the hope that she'd let me off easy.

But then she hit me with the single most sordid, repulsive, stomach-turning thought, the one I'd worked hardest to avoid.

"Do you think Dutch might have fathered the child?"

I gagged. Before I totally embarrassed myself, I made a run for the ladies' room. There I slammed shut the metal door to a gray stall and heaved over and over again. I retched. I panted. Cold, heavy sweat drenched my clothes. The sour stench spawned more nausea. I vomited until there was nothing left inside.

Dizziness nearly felled me. I clung to the toilet-paper

holder as if my life depended on its support. It may well have. The hard sharp edge that cut into my palm helped me remember the world beyond the pictures in my head.

Eventually, nothing more came out. Not even tears. Or sweat. I flushed and then just stood there, weak in the knees, bowed over, one arm around my middle, the other still fused to the toilet-paper holder.

"Haley?" Tedd asked. "I called Doc Cowan. I was about to do 9-1-1, but I figured I should check with him first. He says this happens to you on a regular basis, whenever stress or fear get to you. He also said I didn't need an ambulance if you stopped soon enough."

I moaned.

"Should I take that to mean you need an ambulance?"

Tedd sounded so worried, so scared, that I called up what little strength I had left to pull myself upright. "He's right."

"Is there anything I can do to help?"

Obviously, I hadn't eased her mind. I yanked out a mile of toilet paper, wiped my face, neck, and mouth, then dumped the disgusting wad into the toilet and flushed again. A flick of a finger slid the door latch aside. I took a shaky step out of my gray cell. "I'll be okay."

"You don't look okay."

"I know." I splashed handfuls of water on my face again and again and again. After I rinsed my mouth, I drank a sip. When that didn't instigate another upheaval, I swallowed more water, cool and cleansing and soothing.

I wished something would do the same for my head.

When I went to reach for paper towels, Tedd gave me a bunch. "Thanks."

She lowered her gaze. "I don't know what for. I pushed you too far and brought this on you."

"You didn't. It was coming. It was just a matter of time."

"Sure, but I'm the one who sprang it loose. I'm so sorry."

I tossed the towels in the trash before I faced my friend. "Don't apologize. I have to learn to deal with bad stuff. I buckle under that kind of pressure. That's not good."

What I am is a wimp. Crummy stuff always comes down in this fallen world, but when it comes down on me, I crumble.

I squared my shoulders. "I am better, Tedd. At least now I can let myself look at things—especially the worst things—not just avoid the possibility of Dutch's guilt like I have all this time."

Tedd looked unsure, but there wasn't much else I could say. I reached out a hand. She took it and squeezed.

My smile wouldn't have rivaled even the dimmest bulb in a chandelier, but it did put in an appearance. "I really have to head home. I need a shower, toothbrush and tooth-paste, shampoo. You know. Stuff to get normal again."

"You also need food and rest." At my grimace, she shook her head, sent those glossy waves on a graceful flight over her shoulders. "Don't even think it. I'll be checking up on you. You tell your dad to expect a call from me after every meal, and you better sleep too."

"You're such a bully, Tedd Rodriguez!"

"But you love me anyway. And you know I'm right."

I sighed. "Yeah, I do. You're a good friend, and I need every last one I can scrape up."

She looked as though she was about to say something more, but then she smiled. "Get going. You're a mess."

"In more ways than one."

That night I got no sleep. Every time I closed my eyes, images rushed to taunt me. Instead of fighting them off, I decided to read, watch old movies, clean the bathtub, polish faucets, mop the floors.

By the time the sun showed up in the east, I was exhausted but too wired to even consider sleep. Besides, I knew there were a million nightmares I couldn't face just waiting to strike.

I showered and dressed, grabbed a slice of toast and a piece of cheese, then ran to the car. The trip to the warehouse took me only twelve minutes, during which time I managed to nibble about a quarter of an inch of dry toast.

That had to count for something, in case Tedd asked.

With my head as messed up as it was, I knew better than to risk handling dangerous stuff like stripping compounds and nail guns—I wouldn't even be safe with a hot glue gun in my shaky hands. I figured this was as good a time as any to tackle the mounds of paperwork I normally avoid like the plague.

At the desk I stared off into space, not seeing anything, trying to turn my mind into a blank slate. I'd almost succeeded, for all of about a minute, when I heard the electronic door opener hum. Ozzie must have driven the company truck home last night.

I rounded the desk and headed for the belly of the hangarlike building where we store our stock between large sales. Sure enough, my partner sat in the cab of the box truck, his attention on a stack of papers in his hand.

I waved. "Hey there! What're you up to?"

Ozzie opened the truck door, then dropped down to the stained cement floor. "Good morning, Miss Haley. I've just taken a moment to peruse the inventory."

"What inventory?"

He looked puzzled but only shrugged. "I'm sorry. I suppose I didn't make myself clear enough. This is the inventory of the Magruder estate. It took me three days to catalog every last item in that massive three-story mausoleum."

"Who's Magruder?"

This time he blinked his protruding eyes. "Hershel and Sylvia Magruder, of course." He spoke slowly, as though using all his patience. "You handled the telephone call from their grandchildren when they rang us three weeks ago, Miss Haley. Don't you remember?"

I soughed out an impatient sigh. "What? Do you expect me to remember every last little detail of what goes on around here?"

Ozzie took a step back. "Oh dear. Are you quite all right this morning? Do you feel well?"

Not really, but I didn't want to talk about it. "I'm fine. So tell me. Is there . . . ah . . . anything good in the . . . er . . . McCracken's stuff?"

"McCracken? Oh! You mean the Magruders' pieces."

The expression on Ozzie's face was priceless. He knew his greatest fear had come true. His partner was a loon.

I had to try a little harder. "That's right. The Magruders. What'd you come up with? Anything good?"

"Well, miss, you know, of course, that Mrs. Magruder collected antique quilts, and since they lived in central Pennsylvania, her Amish pieces are exceptional. She also had a handful of Civil War quilts that are in excellent condition and should sell very well. Then there are the guns we discussed—quite valuable, I might add—the hand-carved tall clock in pristine condition, a highboy that has the most marvelous patina, boxes and boxes of silver . . ."

As we returned to the office part of the building, I let Ozzie continue enumerating his finds. I didn't remember the quilts, guns, silver, or the phone call about the Magruders. Magruders . . . Magruders . . . Magruders . . .

Nope. Didn't ring any bells.

I cut into his description of a piece of English flow blue transferware that had him in thrall. "How did you fill the truck with all that stuff?"

He gave me another bewildered look. "I didn't, miss. I couldn't possibly have. I drove the truck to SeaTac airport three days ago, left it in long-term parking, flew out to Lancaster, Pennsylvania, did the inventory, packed a number of items to bring with me, made arrangements to ship the rest, flew back, and loaded the truck with what I brought, and now I'm here."

"And I'm supposed to know about this?"

Ozzie began to twist his hands. He blinked over and

over again, his eyes darting from wall to desk to floor. "Oh dear, Miss Haley. Something must be frightfully wrong with you. We spent days making the arrangements for the trip east. I can't believe you've forgotten all that. Are you quite all right?"

"Um . . . I've had a rough couple of nights. Haven't been sleeping well. But it's nothing that a good night's rest won't cure."

I wish.

He looked doubtful. "I hope so, miss. We have a huge sale scheduled for two weeks from today. I certainly hope you haven't forgotten to prepare the catalog or to send out notices to the papers."

I vaguely remembered renting a portion of the convention center for an upcoming sale. "That's fine. I should be able to catch up on my sleep by then."

As long as Dutch, Lila, Deedee, Bella, and the Balis stayed far, far away, that is.

Ozzie gave me another of his nebbish looks, the kind only the most experienced worrywarts can come up with. "Why don't you go home, miss? I can handle things from here on in. It strikes me that you could use a nap."

I went to object but realized I wasn't going to do anyone any good here. "Thanks, Ozzie. I think I'll take you up on your offer. And I'm sorry I gave you reason to worry."

"That's quite all right, miss. You just take care of yourself. The business will be waiting here for you when you are well again."

I hoped I didn't do anything so dumb that I would harm

the legacy Marge Norwalk had left me. She'd worked for years to build up the business. The way I was going, it wouldn't take me more than a couple of hours to tear it all down.

My Honda started right up—at least I could count on that. I drove down the twisty streets of Wilmont, my mind miles and miles away from the steering wheel and the road.

As they had since my episode at McDonald's yesterday, my thoughts returned to Dutch. I'd had reservations about him from the start. His notoriety preceded him, and it had predisposed me to mistrust him.

Now I had no alternative but to question his honesty, his integrity, his character. Was the man who'd saved my life a year ago capable of molesting a teenage girl? Of impregnating her? Of taking out his revenge on an innocent?

Was the man—the only one in five years—who'd caught my eye and sparked a rare and unexpected flash of attraction capable of something as despicable as that?

Could I be attracted for the second time in my life to a man capable of rape?

10

Instead of going home, as I told Ozzie I'd do, I decided to drive by Magnus Mills, one of my absolute favorite places. Old Orville Magnus founded a weaving mill in the 1920s, and it's been in the family since. About ten years ago, when Craig Magnus went into semiretirement, he passed the baton to his daughter, Adrienne, a fabric genius. Adrienne gave the company new life.

With her army of smart buyers, Adrienne has made Magnus Mills a powerhouse in the fabric world. They offer unique material from every continent at bargain prices. She bases her prices on that cost, not on what chichi designers can and will pay. She's no fonder of snooty celebrity decorators than I am.

I'm one of her most devoted clients.

She's the closest thing to a mother I have left.

I've known Adrienne my whole life. She, Marge Norwalk, and my mother were the closest of friends; I called them Auntie Marge and Auntie Adie as a kid. Sometimes a woman needs a dose of mothering, even when the person she hits up for it is a former Hollywood starlet who left the entertainment jungle for love and marriage.

I love Adrienne and her wares.

The lobby of the Magnus Mills office and warehouse complex is an impressive place with floor-to-ceiling gossamer gold silk draperies, black rugs, and creamy chenille-covered sofas. At the reception area, I found a young woman I didn't know manning the phone console.

"May I help you?" she asked.

The black and gold plaque helped me out. "Hi, Emma. I'd like to see Adrienne, please. Would you tell her Haley is here?"

The girl, probably another of Adrienne's kids from Seattle Pacific University, a Christian college she supports in various ways, including jobs for students, gave me an "Are you nuts?" look.

"You're not on her appointment schedule," Emma said. "I can't interrupt her."

"I'm family." That wasn't a real lie; she was my auntie Adie. "Besides, I just spoke to her on the phone." That was all true.

Still skeptical, Emma clicked away at her computer keyboard. Seconds later, the *bing* of incoming email rang out.

"Oh!" she said. "You did talk to her. She says you should go right through to her office."

"Thanks." I pushed the heavy metal doors into the belly of the structure and headed toward the warehouse floor. Unlike many executives, Adrienne prefers to stay close to the heart of things. I rapped on the partly open door to her glass-enclosed cubicle.

"Hey, glamour girl," I called out. "I came to hold you up for some loot. What ya got for me?"

Adrienne slipped out from behind her beat-up old army-surplus desk, arms outstretched. "It's so good to see you, sweetie."

The fashion plate nearly folded herself in two to hug me.

I chuckled. "Hey, jolly green. If you didn't wear those shish-kebab sticks instead of shoes, you wouldn't have to bend down so far to reach the rest of us humans."

She straightened and winked. "Just think. Who will quibble with my prices when I'm bigger than they are?"

I rolled my eyes. "Ooh, I'm shaking in my Birks!"

She buffed her short, square nails on the lapel of her mint-green silk jacket. "I try."

Then she got serious. She looked at me long and hard. "What's wrong?"

I'd come for comfort, not an inquisition. "What's the deal? I barely walk in here and you dig right into my psyche."

Adrienne crossed her arms and tapped the toe of her painfully pointy-toed emerald green Manolo. "Comes with the territory, kid. Don't forget, I've been around you since I had to change your diapers. I know when something's wrong. So tell me, what's up?"

I collapsed into the cloud-soft armchair in front of her desk. She returned to her old leather chair on the other side.

There was no way to avoid Adrienne's concern. I had to come clean. "I'm beginning to think I have a bull's-eye on my back. You know about the dead girl at the plastic surgeon's house last week?"

Adrienne groaned and lowered her forehead to her hands. From behind the silky curtain of prematurely gray hair, she said, "You're in trouble with the cops again."

"Not me. Not this time. But I did find her. And it wasn't pretty."

"That I got from the article in the paper. What happened?"

I told her what I knew and still played a good game of dodge ball when it came to my doubts and fears about Dutch. Even with that little omission—*Little? Yeah, right, Haley*—the story was gruesome enough.

At the end I just sat, drained, miserable, unsure of everything.

Adrienne's chair squeaked when she leaned forward. "Maybe she went to see Stew."

"*You* know the doctor?"

She gave a vague wave. "I've met him at some social events. Brad's firm manages Stew's investments, even though he isn't Brad's personal client. These days my dear hubby runs the company and doesn't do much hands-on investing."

"What do you think of him?"

She looked gorgeous even with her nose all wrinkled up. "He's too slick for my taste. I'd never pay anyone to erase my lines—I've put in years of hard work to earn each one of them."

I laughed. "Uh-huh. The day a wrinkle has the guts to show up on your mug is the day I watch a flock of pigs flit over Mount Rainier's peak."

"I do so have wrinkles. See? Right there, at the corner of my left eye."

Her finger pointed to beautiful skin under minimal makeup.

"Oh, for sure. You need a bucket of Botox right there, right now." I thumbed my chest. "Just look at me. At the rate I'm going, I'll look old enough to be your grandmother by next week."

"Okay, since I refuse to argue with you, why don't you tell me what kind of loot you're after?"

"Wait'll you hear. The doctor's new bride has a thing for pink. You should have seen the look on her face when I brought out my tasteful, chic neutral fabric samples."

"I did hear he'd remarried. And she wants pink? In that fabulous house?" Adrienne shook her head. "What a waste. I'll never forget the Christmas party he held there last year. Gorgeous antiques and excellent fabrics."

"Yup, that's how I see it too. But 'Pink is in,' she says, so pink it is."

"Better you than me." She shuddered and pointed toward the warehouse. "Let's go see what we can come up with."

I followed like a klutzy puppy in its graceful mama's shadow. Her stilettos *click-click*ed against the concrete floor. My Birkenstocks *slap-slap*ped along. Even though my style doesn't sink a thousand ships, Adrienne's kind of shoe is a galaxy or two beyond me. I'd fall flat on my keister if I ever tried them on.

We snaked in and out between ceiling-high stacks of bolts. Adrienne knew what was where and its origin too. Impressive.

"You know, we got a new shipment from India two days ago," she said as we turned yet another corner. "The brocades are wonderful, but most are multicolor, so I'm not sure we could stay in your pink-is-in palette with them. And although I love the cottons myself, I doubt the Marshall house is ready for them. But the sari silk is a wonderful way to go for curtains, and I remember one particularly yummy shade of cerise."

"Sounds like Deedee Marshall, all right."

We took note of a dozen or so different types of goods, some lightweight wool gabardines for upholstery, some black chenille for the ottoman I wanted to use instead of a coffee table—I hate the things; their mission in life is to jump out and bruise legs. Adrienne even found a retro tableclothlike floral in fuchsia, emerald, and white that would be perfect for the new kitchen windows.

At the end I had an armful of awesome samples. "Thanks for your help. I'm not so stressed anymore about the cotton-candy world I'm supposed to make for this woman. You know I don't do precious or cutesy."

"You'll be fine—with the décor, that is. I'm still worried about the effect of KC's death on you."

I hadn't mentioned the name. "You know KC too?"

"Her mother and I have served on the board of the Wilmont Emergency Clinic for about ten years now."

I felt like a total idiot. "Why did you just let me spew for fifteen minutes if you knew all about it?"

"I could tell you needed to talk. A trouble shared is a trouble halved."

She too wanted to dig in places better left alone. Before Adrienne went there with her figurative shovel, I asked, "So what's the mom like?"

"I don't know her well, but as a volunteer, Lori's great. She works like crazy for the clinic, doesn't waste time, doesn't gossip." Adrienne shrugged. "She loved her daughter. She always talked about KC and the things she did."

"Any hint of trouble in the family? Did she know KC was pregnant? When was the last time you talked to her? Do you know the father?"

"No. No. Three weeks ago at the last board meeting. And yes, but only enough to say hi when I bump into him." Her hazel eyes narrowed. "You've been around that homicide detective too long. You sound like a walking, talking question machine. And you know how I hate gossip."

Chalk one up for Lila. "She taught me well. Not well enough to get a decent answer from you though. Please don't play clam on me now. Tell me something about the Richardsons, anything."

"What do you want me to tell you? They're people, Haley, a family like a million others. KC just finished ninth grade, she couldn't wait to take driver's ed, she ran track, scuba dived, and sang in the concert choir. The parents work, volunteer, go to the theater, movies, parties . . ." She shrugged. "I don't know. They're just . . . people."

"What school did KC go to?"

"She transferred to the Carleton-Higgins Academy after sixth grade at public school. She had a learning disability—dyslexia, I think—and the academy's LD teacher is supposed to be great."

"Now, there's a place that brings back fond memories." I grimaced. "Remember when I tracked down Marge's sleazoid husband there last year? He was teaching summer school, and a kid spilled the beans about Steve Norwalk's extracurricular relationships. The headmaster overheard everything and canned the merry widower."

Adrienne nodded. "Ed Hobart was furious with Steve. Ed's the most patient, even-tempered man I know, but everyone at that school board meeting knew how he felt about Steve as soon as he opened his mouth."

"Good grief, Adrienne. You know Mr. Hobart too? Is there anyone you don't know?"

She chuckled. "Lots and lots of people."

"I still can't believe you know the Marshalls and the Richardsons. Now even the principal at that snooty school is your friend."

"Hey, watch it! My kids go to that snooty school."

"So? It still costs a fortune. And what do they get there that they wouldn't get at Wilmont High?"

"I know. But Brad went there, and that's where he wants the kiddos."

"Did your munchkins know KC?"

"Grace did. She's in concert choir."

"Maybe I should talk to Grace. She might know something about KC she hasn't mentioned."

"No problem. Come on over anytime."

"Thanks." I hugged my loot. "I'd better get a move on. I have to come up with a proposal for Deedee that doesn't look like the designer was a cotton-candy machine."

We returned to Adrienne's office, where I gathered my black leather backpack purse and agreed I'd stop by to see fourteen-year-old Grace the next day. At the door I turned for a final good-bye, but I clammed up when I noticed Adrienne's thoughtful expression.

I waited her out.

"You know," she said. "I just remembered something. I wouldn't ordinarily talk about something like this, since it's private—"

"Adrienne! A girl's been murdered here. If you think it might help, then tell me. There's a baby missing, you know."

"No, I don't know. What baby?"

"No one knows where KC's baby is."

"Oh, that's awful."

She closed her eyes, and her lips moved in silent prayer. I took her hand and joined in.

Minutes later when she opened her hazel eyes, I saw the tears. She said, "KC's mom had some work done—a nose job, or maybe a chin tuck. Anyway, Stew did the surgery, and I seem to remember that Lori took KC in to see him when her skin began to break out. Stew treated the acne."

"I thought dermatologists did that."

"So did I, but I guess with all his work on skin, he knows a thing or two about it."

"Fair enough. So KC did know Dr. Marshall. I wonder why she went there when she was in such bad shape."

"Maybe because he's a doctor, one she knew and trusted."

"That would make sense . . . sorta. But why didn't she just go to her family doctor?"

"Maybe she didn't want her parents to know about the baby. I'm pretty sure they had no idea she was pregnant."

"This gets curiouser and curiouser."

"Remember, you're not Alice."

"How can I forget? This villain is way worse than a crazy queen of hearts."

Loaded down with pink, black, and white fabric and mulling over a couple of nuggets of interesting information, I left after another hug. By then I was beat, so I went back to the manse with every intention of crashing once I got there.

Such was not my luck.

Bella lurked in the azaleas outside her place. "Hey there, Haley girl! What you up to?"

I waved the swatches and hurried to the porch. A Bella in the bush is way better than one in hand. Especially with no cats in sight.

But Bella had other plans.

"Can you believe my luck?" she asked, her blue eyes bright. "Detective Tsu actually came to question me. Me!"

That stopped me cold. "Why would she do that? What did she want to know?"

As Bella bustled over, the loose ends of her white belt flapped against the mound of her middle, and her arms waved while she talked.

"She asked me all kinds of questions about the other day when we were at that mansion you're doing."

"And what did you tell her?"

"The truth, just the truth, and nothing but the truth."

"Now you're happy."

"I'll say! I'm like, you know, a real, live part of the investigation."

"No, no, no, no, no, no, no! The *cops* are part of the investigation. Not you, not me, not anyone else."

"I beg to differ with you. Detective Tsu shared valuable information. You know, about the case."

I opened the front door, counted to ten, then a hundred, and was headed for a thousand when it occurred to me that Bella just might know something important.

Resigned to my fate, I asked her in, but not before I checked her out. "You smuggling cats?"

"You're such a dog person, Haley. Get over yourself. Cats are people too."

I wasn't about to touch that one. "Make yourself comfortable, but if a cat pops out from under your clothes, you're outta here. Imagine what Midas would do to the place if he saw one of your beasts in his territory."

"Oh, Midas would just . . ." She waved her pudgy hands in a language all their own, then sat at the table and crumpled a paper napkin. "I don't know, maybe he'd do like the animals in the Bible pictures. You know, the peace and love kingdom."

I poured us both glasses of iced tea. "That's the peaceable kingdom, and I don't think he's anywhere near as noble as a lion on his best behavior." Wild animals act better than Bella's beasts. "Anyway. What were you saying about Lila's information?"

Bella blushed, and her eyes opened wider. "It's murder!"

"You don't have to look so cheerful about it."

She gulped her tea. "Oh, Haley girl. I'm not cheerful about KC being killed. That's pure sin, and sin's serious stuff. It's just that for once I'm in something so . . . so big screen. That movie stuff really does happen, after all."

"Hello!" I had to tiptoe around this one. "Did you miss the part about the killer? The sicko who killed a pregnant girl?"

"Nope. But I know all about Come-on-in. People with Arthur's clauses have to take it."

"Who's Arthur?"

"Not a who, Haley girl. It's that thick arteries disease."

"That's arteriosclerosis."

Her turquoise hair bounced with every nod. "That's what I said. And not everyone can get their hands on that Come-on-in blood thinner. You need a prescription. So we just need to track down who's taking the stuff to know who killed KC."

"Millions of people in America take blood thinners, Bella. There's no way you can figure anything out that way."

She stood in a huff. "Fine. Be that way. But I know something else. I know *someone* else."

I was going to let her go. Really, I was. But my curiosity got the better of me.

"Who do you know, Bella? I mean, I know you know a lot of people—" between Bella and Adrienne, the free world has few strangers "—but who do you know who has something to do with all this?"

"Wanda."

"Wanda who?"

"Wanda Ballard."

"Okay, have your fun. Tell me about Wanda."

"Wanda was a hand model back when I was doing runway jobs. She's lots younger than me, and she's not retired yet. She's a pharmacy clerk at the Wilmont Drugstore these days. I'll bet she knows everybody in town who takes blood thinners."

"But that doesn't mean we can figure out who gave them to KC. The list has to be miles long."

"What does it hurt to ask?"

"I give up. Give me her number. I'll call her after she's finished work and ask her to talk to Lila."

"No way."

"Huh? What was all this about if you don't want me to talk to your friend?"

"Oh, I want you to talk to Wanda, all right."

Busted! By the gleam in her eye.

"No way." I shook my head for emphasis. "No way, no how, nuh-uh, *no*! You are *not* pulling a Jessica Fletcher here."

"You're right. I'm not. Not by myself, that is. You and I are gonna go question our witness. Then we'll follow the clues wherever they lead."

"I'm not going to question Wanda. I'm just going to tell her to talk to Lila Tsu."

Clumps of turquoise fuzz shook from side to side. "Nope. Wanda won't talk to a cop. Never ever."

"Why not?"

"'Cause she's got a record."

Great. "What did she do?"

"She stole some of the rings she modeled way back then."

I groaned.

"It's no big deal. She gave them all back when she was convicted. And she did her time too. She's cool. That's how Wanda became a pharmacy clerk. She worked in the prison hospital."

"And you think she's going to tell you who killed KC Richardson?"

"Sure, she's my friend."

Half of me wanted to send Bella back to her Balis; the other half of me was dying to meet the ring model turned jailbird turned pharmacy clerk, if for no other reason than I'd never met anyone who remotely fit that description. I knew I should've run when I saw Bella in the bushes.

"Oh, all right. What will it hurt? When do you want to go?"

Her smirk told me she'd played me like the expert she is. "We have a date with Wanda tonight at the Seashore

Bowling Lanes. She's in a league, and tonight's their championship. I'll come get you at seven."

When the door closed behind Bella, I fell onto the couch. What had I gotten myself into?

It didn't take long to find out. Bella's friend was an experience, all right. Wanda's team wears lime green bowling shirts with the name Connie's Convicts embroidered across the back. That's right. The members have all done time. And most of them chain-smoke. Around them breathing is optional.

Aside from that, they're a fun bunch. They welcomed us into their midst and asked us to kick back and enjoy the games. Between frames, and between endless bowls of corn chips, potato chips, pretzels, cheese doodles, prefab onion rings, and popcorn in a never-before-seen shade of glowing gold, Wanda told us all she knew about every malady for which she's sold a drug. Every last one. From boils to hemorrhoids to ingrown toenails to irritable bowels.

And I was right, to Bella's extreme dismay. A substantial segment of Wilmont's adult population has crud-filled arteries. No way could we identify a potential suspect from Wanda's vast storehouse of knowledge.

No one even remotely related to the case took Coumadin.

Bella was bummed.

I was thrilled.

Now I could go back home, crawl into bed, and not worry

that my nutty elderly neighbor was about to smash her way onto a killer's radar. Maybe I'd even catch a few z's before the nightmares kicked in.

And maybe in the morning someone would know what had happened to KC's child.

11

"What's that you're working on?" Dad asked the next day.

"Hey there. I didn't realize you were up already. Have some coffee." I moved the Pepto-pink mountain to the side. "I'm about to overdose on all this sweetness and light. It's the design for the Marshalls, but it reminds me of Bella's old hair color."

Dad murmured, "The Marshalls?"

"Yeah. The people where I found the dead girl."

"Oh! I remember. How sad. We brought it up in our prayers at the church board meeting last night."

"It is sad—tragic, really. And no one knows where the baby might be."

"What baby?"

"Dad!" Absentminded he's always been, but this was too much. "The dead girl was pregnant. She'd just given birth. Remember?"

He scratched the back of his head. "Yes . . . I think I do remember something about that. Anyway. You're right. It's tragic."

"Is there something on your mind?"

He crossed to the pantry and withdrew his gross fiber cereal. It is gross—trust me. The cardboard box tastes better.

"Not much." He took a clean bowl from the cabinet. "Besides you, of course. I've been praying for you, honey. You've spent a couple of nights now walking around your room or down here. The nightmares are back, aren't they?"

I hated to worry him. "I'm okay now. It took me a couple of days, but I got some sleep last night." Thanks to nighttime headache medicine that knocked me out when my head felt ready to explode.

He poured the twigs into a bowl, splashed them with his skim milk, then began to crunch. After he swallowed, he said, "Glad to hear that. So what's on your schedule today?"

"I'm taking fabrics to Deedee, letting her choose her pinks."

"That's nice."

Dad worked his way through his daily dose of bark, and with his every crunch I winced. Then the last bite of kindling went down, he took his bowl to the dishwasher. "I'll be at the church until 2:00. I'm seeing a parishioner at that time."

"Okay." I stood. "See ya at dinner."

"God bless you, honey."

"You too, Dad."

Even the large chunk of cheese I gave Midas didn't do a thing for his disposition. His arguments followed me outside, which, of course, is what he wanted to do.

The drive to the Marshalls' mansion was no fun. It'd begun to rain. Yeah, yeah. I know all about the bad rap

Seattle gets for its weather. And it does rain. But it doesn't *always* rain. And when it doesn't, there's nothing as beautiful as the Emerald City and the area surrounding it.

But this wasn't a beautiful day in the neighborhood.

At the Marshalls', Deedee opened the door and stepped aside. "Come on in. I can't wait to see what you have."

Where was Domingo? "You wanted pink."

"Oh, I'm so excited. I've never had a room done by a pro. This is so cool."

Oh boy. "I hope we have fun while we're at it."

She led me to the kitchen, where a silver coffeepot steamed in the center of the table. Two cups and saucers sat opposite each other, and a lemon poppy-seed loaf had been cut into decadent-looking slabs.

"Wow!" My stomach growled—for the first time in a while. "You didn't have to do all this. I had breakfast—" half a slice of toast "—a while ago."

"That's what I figured—a while ago. Sit! Help yourself."

The lemon poppy-seed bread was incredible. And the Starbucks? Need I say more?

Before I could make a glutton of myself, I put down my antique Gorham silver fork, took a last transfusion of caffeine, and unzipped the portfolio.

"I can't wait to see what you think about the cerise silk I found," I told Deedee. "It's going to make wonderful window coverings for the living room."

The sari fabric went over with the kind of success Adrienne had expected. So did the vintage-style floral print, and

even the black-and-white gabardines got passing grades.
So far I'd batted a thousand.

"What about furniture?" the new Mrs. Marshall asked,
her smooth brow furrowed in a frown. "You haven't shown
me any."

"I changed my mind. I brought a catalog with me the
other day, but I think I'd like to take you to a particular
showroom instead. The place I have in mind specializes in
custom work, and I know we'll get what you want there."

Deedee giggled. "We're going shopping! When?"

"They're only open on Tuesdays, Thursdays, and Saturdays. How about Thursday?"

"Thursday? That'll be perfect. Do you want Stew to come
with us?"

"If he wants. But most men are shopping-phobes."

She leaned toward me and glanced over her shoulder.
"He only likes to buy golf clubs and medical equipment.
That's so boring."

I zipped my portfolio back up. "Then that's settled. It'll
be a girls-only deal." Something occurred to me. "Would
you like your mother to come with us?"

Deedee's smile tightened. Interesting. "That's not necessary. She and I don't have the same taste. She likes all this
old stuff around here."

So did I, but why mess with success? "Okay. I'll see you
Thursday at . . . say, ten-ish?"

The beautiful blonde showed me to the door, and I figured
Domingo was history. It was just as well. He'd probably have a
coronary if he saw what Deedee wanted to do to the house.

I covered my head with the portfolio, even though nothing could help my uncivilized hair, and dashed to the Honda. Inside I wiped off the black leather exterior of the portfolio with an old towel and stuck the key in the ignition. But before I gave it a turn, a movement at the right side of the house toward the back caught my attention. A large fern jerked and bobbed with no apparent cause, and then a shrub of some sort did the same.

It wasn't windy.

There was nothing in the landscape that would cast a long, large, male shadow.

This one continued its trip down the Marshalls' landscaping.

Someone was out there.

I knew I should call Lila and her Smurfs, but I didn't want to risk losing the skulker. It could be KC's killer.

The rain continued its steady fall, the sound a comfort to my Pacific Northwestern ears. I especially appreciated its patter today, since it would help mask whatever noise I might make.

Seconds after I stepped out of the car, I was soaked. So much for the portfolio.

I usually wear light cotton skirts in the summer, but the denim one I was wearing was a favorite, and I'd wanted something as far removed from pink as possible. Once saturated, however, denim weighs more than rocks and clings like Saran Wrap. Sneaking became a challenge.

But I persevered. Once I reached the middle of the house, I stepped out from behind the cover of the bushes, intent on

ID'ing my skulker. But I didn't count on Mother Nature's betrayal. I slipped on the mud and mulch, flailed, then grabbed a thick clump of rhododendron.

I might have squeaked. I don't think I went so far as to squeal. Of course, my object was never to wallow in mud, but by now my Birkenstocks felt like cement blocks, and I saw no sign of my feet.

Misery.

Long legs—male legs—blocked my line of vision. "What did I do to deserve you?"

"You!" I glared. "Why can't I turn around without tripping all over you, Dutch Merrill? Why are you mucking in the mud out here?"

"I'm not the mud pie."

A glance revealed my skirt's new random design of brown blobs. "I slipped trying to see who was sneaking around the house. And here it was you the whole time."

"I wasn't sneaking. I've been out here taking measurements for a while now. You're the one hiding behind a shrub."

Then he gave me a wicked smile. "Don't forget what happened the last time I found you snooping."

I shuddered. It had involved rats. And slime. And a trash shed. That's where the Bali H'ai–attracting slime had come from. "You're such a gentleman to remind me."

"You're welcome. Care to share why you felt the need to follow me?"

"I'm not following you. I came to show Deedee a selection of fabrics. I'm doing a redesign here, remember?"

"How can I forget?"

Bitterness underscored Dutch's words. He seemed to sag, and his shoulders bowed as though they bore the weight of the world.

Sympathy came uninvited. "Are you okay?"

"Sure. I just love being accused of the most disgusting things a man could ever do, when all I want is to land a job."

The emotion in his words gave me hope and cleared up the hint of fear I'd felt when I realized who my skulker was. Could a guilty man sound so revolted by KC's fate?

I met his gaze. "I know how accusations feel. Remember? I was there not so long ago."

He studied me for long moments. Rain flowed over him. He looked less powerful, more vulnerable. When he spoke again, it was in a raw, rough voice.

"I'd never hurt a child. *Never*, Haley. You have to believe me."

His anguish struck a familiar chord. "If that's the case, then you'll be fine once Lila finds the killer."

"Don't you get it? I would have thought you of all people would. I don't have all the time in the world here. Lila's on the warpath, and she's sure I'm her man."

Problem was, I did get it. But I couldn't be sure he wasn't playing me for a fool. "Then talk to her—"

"Hah! I've talked and talked until I had no more words in me. What I need is help. Someone who'll help me figure out who killed KC, who got her pregnant in the first place—it *wasn't* me."

"I'm glad you deny it."

Anger returned to his face. "Is that the best you can do?"

He ran long fingers through his drenched hair. "Look, Haley. You did pretty well for yourself last year. Won't you give me a hand here?"

Was he saying what I thought he was saying? "How can I give you a hand?"

"Don't act dumb. It looks terrible on you. Help me find the killer. I have to clear my name. I've already gone through the devastation of a trial, then the delay on the Gerrity job, and now this. I have no money left. Most of what Noreen paid me went to cover my last legal bills."

I was torn. I did know how he felt, that desperation, the feeling that life as you once knew it had come to an end. But Tedd's voice asking that one question echoed in my mind.

The fear felt like a brick wall. Dread gripped my gut. Had Dutch raped and killed KC?

"Look, Haley. I was there for you when you were dying. If I hadn't come along, you'd be dead. Way I see it, you owe me."

"What? Are you nuts? You spent most of that nightmare time trying to put me behind bars. If it hadn't been for Bella going after you, you'd never have come—and at the last minute, I might add."

"But I did come. And you're here now because of me."

"You could've come around sooner, you know, helped me rather than accuse me. Then I wouldn't have had to drink that morphine."

"Who barfed on who?"

"Whom."

"Who cares? I'm not talking grammar here. I'm talking

give and take. I gave you help. You barfed on me. That's two you owe me."

"I did not. It didn't even touch you."

"That's a minor technicality."

"No way. That's the point."

"Forget it. Are you going to help me? Or are you going to let Lila jail me for a murder I didn't commit?"

Last year I'd questioned how so many could think I'd killed Marge, how they could let Lila arrest me. I knew how he felt. And I knew the only way to put my doubts about Dutch to rest was to learn the truth about what had happened to KC.

My contrary alter ego piped up. *You just kinda like him.*

A long moment went by as the thought percolated. Was it true? Did the attraction I felt affect my decision? Did I *want* him to be innocent because I couldn't face the possibility that I'd let another rapist, and this time a murderer, catch my eye?

I met his gaze. There should be a way to see into another person's soul, but all those poets who say the eyes are the windows to that soul? They're wrong. You only see little white balls with circles of varying colors. Facial expressions can be donned and doffed with thespian ease.

Then I remembered an earlier moment of decision. Dutch asked me to trust him last year. And I had. Maybe I made that choice at a safer moment, one where I hadn't worried about criminal intent.

His criminal intent.

He'd seemed genuine then.

And I had to find that missing baby. He could help.

If he was clean.

"I can't promise anything solid," I said. "But I will help you—only if you help me."

"How'm I going to help anyone if I can't even help myself?"

I looked down at the soggy mess I'd made of my favorite sandals. "I can't stop thinking and thinking about it, Dutch. It's tearing me apart. I have to know. I *have* to."

He reached out and touched my arm. His warmth came as a pleasant surprise. I hadn't realized how chilled I was. I took a difficult, earth-laden step toward him.

The clasp grew tighter. "What is it you have to know?"

I met his gaze. "I have to know about the baby. I have to do whatever I can to protect it, to keep it safe. I can't let it die like—"

My words froze in my throat.

For long moments we stood in the rain, not more than ten yards away from where I'd found KC. I felt as though the water should wash our worries away. But it didn't. Only the truth could do that.

He gave a wry chuckle. "This is crazy, you know? Why don't we go somewhere to talk? There's got to be a better place than out in this monsoon."

I chuckled—I tend to laugh when I'm nervous or self-conscious. Right then either emotion could take the blame. "A venti double-shot caramel macchiato should hit the spot. How about you?"

"Coffee sounds good. Starbucks okay?"

"There's another kind?"

He laughed. "I'll meet you at the one at Sands Avenue and Windswept Drive."

"Give me ten minutes. I can't walk in there like this."

He looked down. The laugh was real. "Good enough. But take twenty. You'll need the extra time."

As he walked away, I began to get cold feet—figuratively, of course. Literally speaking, my feet had been freezing for a while now. That mud was cold.

Had I done the right thing? Was helping Dutch a good idea? And what about my motives? Did I simply want to help a fellow man? Or was the attraction I'd only just admitted to at the root of my decision?

That was the most dangerous possibility. The one I had to eliminate. I couldn't afford an attraction. I wasn't ready for one, not yet. Five years wasn't long enough.

And I didn't know if I could trust Dutch Merrill.

I'd have to watch my back.

And guard my emotions.

It took a lot longer than ten minutes to scrape enough gunk from my feet to walk into the laundry room at the manse. There I hiked up a leg, propped it on the edge of the utility sink, and scrubbed globs of clay off my toes. Once done, I repeated the acrobatics with the other foot.

I showered, changed, tied my hair in a knot at the back of my head, and faced Midas.

"Sorry, pal. Those folks at Starbucks don't get the doggy deal. They think you're germy and a troublemaker. I know better than that, so here's a cookie. And if you're good, then I'll take you to the P-A-R-K when I get back."

I'd have two mud balls to clean off, but what's filth compared to doggy bliss?

Midas gave me one of his more human looks, turned, and stomped off. He didn't even wait for the cookie. I was in big, big trouble.

At the coffee shop, Dutch had chosen a booth by the window. I was about to order at the counter, when he waved a venti cup. "Double-shot caramel macchiato, right?"

I hurried. "You're a lifesaver."

"I'm not that round."

"Ugh! I didn't know you suffered from pun-itis."

He lifted one shoulder. "At least I'm trying to laugh."

I took a long swig of caramelly, creamy coffee. The rich flavors woke up all my taste buds, and I began to feel more like myself.

My sympathy showed up again. "It's hard, isn't it?"

"I'm sorry."

"Sorry? What do you mean?"

"I gave you a hard time last year, and now I know what you went through. I made matters worse. I hope you can forgive me."

I gaped.

He reached across the table and, with one long finger, pushed up my jaw. "I'm not that big of a monster, you know."

"I know . . . I mean, you caught me off guard."

"Because I did the decent thing?"

"No. Because it's so hard to ask forgiveness. It's such a God thing to do."

"Whoa. I'm nowhere near there. I just know what's right and what's wrong."

Chalk one up for Dutch. "I'm glad. And, sure, I forgave you."

"Then we should be able to get somewhere, with the crime *and* the remodel and redesign of the Marshall home."

"What a concept! An optimistic man."

"If I let myself think otherwise, I'll go nuts."

I stood. "Been there, done that. Want anything from the counter? I'm going for one of those little wooden stirrers. The caramel's glopped to the bottom."

"Cinnamon would be nice."

"Be right—"

My words died an instant death at the sight of two familiar heads. Together. Lips locked. Not ten feet away.

I stared.

I couldn't move.

"Haley?" Dutch asked. "Are you okay?"

Blinking helped. Shaking my head did too. But when I looked again, nothing had changed.

"Dad's kissing Madeleine Ogleby!"

"Madeleine Ogleby?"

"Yeah, you know. Deedee Marshall's mom."

12

I checked my watch—2:07. "When he said he was seeing a parishioner at two, this wasn't exactly what came to mind."

Dutch gave me a sympathetic look . "Kinda hard to see your dad play the part of boyfriend, huh?"

"And then some!" I didn't know how I felt, but this sure wasn't the time for navel-gazing or anything. "I'll be right back with your cinnamon and my stirrer."

As I approached the counter, the smoochers saw me. "Haley!" my dad called out. "Come on over. I want you to meet someone."

Cinnamon shaker in one hand, stirrer in the other, I approached their table. "I already know Madeleine. I met her at a missionary society meeting."

"Would you believe the coincidence?" he asked. "She's your client's mother."

"Big coincidence." My smile to Madeleine might have been a bit strained. "I took a stack of samples to Deedee this morning. She's excited about the project."

Madeleine nodded. "That's all she'll talk about these days. But tell me. Are you really going to let her fill that fabulous house with pink and black and steel and leather?"

I arched a brow. "Let her? She's the client. I just work with her preferences."

Dad stood and laid a protective arm around my shoulders. "Wait'll you see Haley's work. She's great!"

"I have to second that," Dutch offered.

Weren't we the cozy foursome? "Dad, you remember Dutch Merrill, don't you?"

My father's jaw tightened, but he held out his hand. "How could I forget?"

Dutch shook Dad's hand. "I'm glad to see you again, Reverend. Especially since Haley's much better this time."

When Dad blanched, I knew I had to act. "Let's not go there, okay? Dutch and I have . . . ah . . . er . . . business to discuss. If you'll excuse us—"

"Oh, honey!" Dad's disappointment surprised me. "You can spare a few minutes, can't you? It's such a pleasure to have my two favorite ladies together at one time."

Dutch pulled a chair from the next table and plopped right down.

I glared.

He gave me a deep, meaningful look—which I failed to decipher.

Then he snagged another chair from the adjacent table, and after he parked it right by his side, he patted the vinyl seat.

"Take a load off, Haley. We have all the time in the world for business. Get to know your dad's lady a little better."

He wanted to pump Madeleine for info! I wasn't sure what she could tell us, since she was new to the area and hadn't even been at the Marshalls' when KC died, but I figured it couldn't hurt. Besides, the thought of my father dating a woman other than my late mother needed time to sink in. Might as well start with that right away.

We talked about Seattle, Wilmont, and Portland, the merits and demerits of each. Deedee's predilection for a color made infamous by indigestion medication came up after that. Eventually, to my dismay and to Dutch's obvious relief, he was able to lead the conversation to the two-hundred-pound gorilla at the table.

"Have the police told you or Deedee anything new about KC?" he asked.

Madeleine shook her head. "Nothing. But I am worried. I think Deanna's obsession with the house is a result of the stress she's under. I can't imagine what it must be like to have that detective show up at all hours of the day."

Dutch and I swapped looks.

"Did Deedee know KC?" I asked. "I understand Dr. Marshall treated her for a skin condition."

"I wouldn't know," Madeleine said. "But Deedee's only been in Wilmont since the wedding four months ago. She and Stewart met in Portland. He used to come down to see her rather than the other way around. I'm not sure she knows many of his acquaintances yet."

"Have you talked to your son-in-law? About the murder, that is."

She flinched at the word. "Just that first day. He came

home, and the detective was still there. She took him into the library and questioned him there—just as she did with Deanna and me."

"When he came out, did he say anything?"

Madeleine paused, thought. "He was upset that the girl died, and on his property, of course. But I think what bothered him most was the effect it would have on his brand-new marriage. Deanna was a wreck by the time the detective left."

"Haley," Dad said, worry in his voice and on his face. "This is weighing heavily on Madeleine. She hates to see her daughter under so much strain, and I can understand her feelings. I hate to ask, but since you had such success last year, would you be willing to dig around a little to see what you can find out? For a worried mother's sake, of course."

"Oh, she needn't bother, Hale," Madeleine said. "I'm sure the police can handle everything just fine."

"Ah . . . you know how Lila Tsu feels about me stepping on her toes, Dad. I'm not sure it's such a good—Ow!"

Dutch's under-the-table kick did permanent damage. "Excuse my yelp. Dutch has no idea how big his feet are, or how heavily he treads."

It was Dutch's turn to glare. "Sorry. Didn't mean to hurt you. Just needed to stretch my legs."

Dad's eyes narrowed, no doubt in memory of Dutch's past transgressions against me. "One should always tread lightly, not run roughshod over anyone in one's path."

My sideways glance caught Dutch's blush. "You're right, sir," he said. "I'll be more careful in the future."

I swallowed a laugh. So much for my shy, humble father. "Oh, why not?" It was what I wanted to do anyway. "Sure, Dad. I'll do a little snooping, as Bella would say."

Madeleine's eyes widened in alarm. "Don't tell me you plan to take the madwoman with the wildcats along!"

"Bella's not a madwoman—"

"Bella's okay—"

"She's not as bad as she looks—"

Dad, Dutch, and I stopped our simultaneous defense.

I chuckled. "Bella's harmless. But the jury's still out on the cats."

Dutch laughed. "Haley's had a run-in or two with Bali H'ai. It's a personal thing."

"Bella's a lonely widow," Dad said. "Bali H'ai's all she has, and she spoils the cat too much. I think you can understand that, my dear."

Madeleine smiled for his benefit. "I understand the loneliness, but I would never take in a pair of feral beasts." She shuddered. "Domingo found his slippers torn to shreds after Bella and her cats left. He was furious, and he's not especially charming at his best."

That brought up an interesting point. "I didn't see him this morning. Is Domingo on vacation?"

"You might say that."

"A *permanent* vacation?"

"Not exactly," Madeleine said, her cheeks a bit pink.

"Let's just say that Stewart felt Deanna and the butler's relationship needed time to cool down."

I'll bet. And I wouldn't count on Domingo's return either. "I see."

Dad stood. "Well. It's been great to talk with you two, but we really must leave if we want to get decent seats for today's lecture."

"I didn't know you were going out," I said.

Madeleine slipped her arm through his. "The University of Washington is hosting a series of talks by an art historian who's guest-teaching there this semester. The first two have been fascinating and very well attended. I talked Hale into coming with me today."

Dad? At an artsy lecture? "Okay. Have fun."

I waited until the glass door closed behind them, then turned to Dutch. "Nothing she told us was worth my crushed ankle."

"Oh, I don't know. You can pump her for information when she thinks you're helping her. Besides, the bride-groom's awfully cool about a patient's death, and I find the vacationing butler interesting."

"I don't. Didn't you hear Deedee and Domingo? I thought for sure they'd go for each other's throats. And if Dr. Marshall treated KC a while ago and only briefly, then I don't know if he should be all broken up about it."

As soon as I said those words, I knew I'd messed up. Dutch went ballistic.

"Anyone with half a heart would be torn up about a little

girl's murder. I can't believe you're not taking this more seriously. I know you're a flake, but this is murder—"

"Hey! That's not true. I'm not a flake, and I *do* take it seriously. More seriously than you'll ever know." I shot up a quick prayer. "Theoretically, yes. Everyone should care deeply. Practically, not necessarily. Remember your own response to Marge's murder."

He took in a sharp breath. "Okay. Point well taken. So where do we stand?"

"Right back at the beginning. And you know Lila's going to go ballistic if she finds out what I'm up to."

"So what do you want to do? You promised you'd help."

"I figure I'll do what I did last year. I'll talk to everyone who knew KC. I'll start with the kids at school. Maybe you should call her family, offer condolences."

"Oh, that's a good one, Haley. Give Ron another reason to call the cops on me."

"Maybe if you called while he was at work, talked to her mom."

"That might be an even worse idea." His blush kicked up a few more notches. "Um . . . I used to date Lori."

"You what?"

"We were high school sweethearts, even though she was a senior and I a freshman when we started going together." He ran a hand through his hair, his discomfort obvious. " She met Ron when I went to college, and Ron was my RA—residence advisor. Lori came to visit me, and, as they say, the rest is history—history that doesn't make for great covert telephone conversation, if you get my drift."

Yikes! "Fine. I guess I'm on my own again."

"That's not fair. I just don't want to make things worse."

"And we know how good a job you can do at that."

He winced. "Okay. I'll try the call, but don't expect a whole lot."

"At least you'll have tried."

He stood. "I should go back to the Marshalls' and finish the measurements."

"And I'm going to talk to a girl who was in concert choir with KC."

Arms crossed, he gave me a hard look. "You planned to snoop all along, didn't you? But you still made me beg. What was that? Payback?"

"No, of course not. I didn't make you beg, and I told you I wanted to find that baby. I still do."

"Seems to me," he said, "the sooner you find out who fathered it, the sooner we'll find KC's killer."

I slung my backpack purse on one shoulder and headed for the door. "That's exactly what I'm going to do."

"Look at me."

I did.

"It wasn't me."

At that moment I believed him. "I'll let you know what I find out."

But would I still believe him after I raked up a little more muck?

Adrienne's daughter Grace hadn't known KC very well,
so she couldn't tell me much about the dead girl. She knew
KC had loved scuba diving and that she'd dated Jackson
Maurer through all of ninth grade. Jackson's address was
right in the school directory.

In a perfect world, I'd meet Jackson and he'd look con-
trite and admit to more than movie dates with KC. Only
this isn't a perfect world. And Lila had said the boyfriend
hadn't known about the pregnancy. Had he told the truth?
When I spoke with him, would I be able to tell?

Jackson's neighborhood was nothing like the Marshalls'.
Neat Craftsman bungalows, very typical of the Pacific
Northwest, lined both sides. The house number, 6109, was
painted in muted shades of tan and brown on a mellow
olive green background. I climbed the stairs to the deep
porch and rang the doorbell.

A blond woman opened up. "May I help you?"

I hadn't thought ahead, so I went with the truth. "I'm a
friend of the Marshalls, and I have a few questions for Jackson. About KC. She died on the Marshall's back patio—"

"I know." Her lips turned white at the edges. "The police
were already here. I don't know what you would have to
do with any of this."

"I've spoken with Detective Tsu—" a true statement "—
and with Mrs. Marshall—" also true "—and we wonder if
Jackson could help us understand a few things."

Heavy footsteps approached from the rear of the house.
"It's okay, Mom. I'll talk to the lady. I don't have anything
to hide. It's not as if I had anything to do with . . ."

He closed his eyes, and pity swamped me. His grief for the girl was deep and sincere. Jackson had clearly cared for his girlfriend.

"Would you like to join me here on the porch, or would you be more comfortable inside your home?"

A long, warm look passed between mother and son. He sighed and walked outside. The mother, a familiar look of concern mixed with love on her face, closed the door.

Jackson sat on the top porch step. "What do you want to know?"

"How long did you and KC date?"

"I've known her since grade school, but we only got together for real when she started ninth grade—almost a year ago."

No wonder he was having such a tough time. "I know this is hard for you, but I'm sure you want to find out what happened to her."

"Yeah. I guess."

I met his gray gaze, and something there told me he'd grown too old in a few short days. I looked away to give him space.

"But nothing's going to bring her back," he added.

"I hear you." I studied my hands, then came to a decision. "Last year a woman who was like my second mother was murdered. It was tough for a while there."

Silence.

I took a deep breath. "You know I have to ask this, but do you have any idea what happened?"

"Give me a break, lady. KC bled to death after she had a kid. I'm not dumb, you know."

"I didn't think you were." So much for common ground. "So tell me something else. What about the baby?"

He erupted to his full six-foot height. "I know nothing about the baby. I didn't know she was pregnant. She didn't look pregnant, and I don't know how she hid the belly. I had no reason to ask, 'cause I just didn't know."

One long lunge took him down to the concrete walk. Then he got in my face. "It sure wasn't mine. We never— you hear me?—*never* had sex. I made the True Love Waits promise the same day KC did."

The raw emotion in his face and in his words left little doubt as to his honesty. I nodded slowly. "Then let me ask you this. Do you know who else KC hung around with? When she wasn't with you, I mean."

His long fingers curled into tight fists; the knuckles turned white. "She got into diving a couple of years ago, but not like this last year. At first, she did a bunch of snorkeling, then she started the junior diver program—they dive shallow stuff, maybe . . . oh, I don't know, I think she said about twenty feet deep. But then she began to spend all her time down at that place on the pier, especially the last couple of months, and she decided, now that she was fourteen, to go for her open-water certification. We had a fight about it, about all the time she spent at the dive shop. I lost. If I wanted to keep on seeing her, it was going to have to be during leftover time. Scuba came first."

"I take it you're not into scuba, then."

He snorted. "I can't afford all that stuff. My part-time job barely covers car insurance, gas, and a couple of dates a week."

"So you're thinking—"

"You want to know who KC's kid's dad is?" When I nodded he went on. "Then you'd better check out those diver guys at the shop. After KC got so serious about diving, I was lucky to see her once a week, sometimes even only every two weeks. She didn't have much time for me. Now we know why."

He spun and strode down the street, his smooth gait that of an athlete, an angry athlete.

I was torn. My heart ached for the betrayed teenager. His pain was almost palpable.

As was his anger.

Jackson Maurer probably would've slain dragons and walked on sizzling embers for KC Richardson. He'd loved her enough to respect her.

But that anger . . .

Did it get the better of him when he learned the extent of her betrayal?

Jackson might have killed *for* KC. Had he killed her?

13

"So have you gone to the scuba shop?" Tedd asked. She leaned back in her desk chair and watched me wriggle in my chair.

I'd caved. I'd called her after I found myself staring at the bottle of nighttime headache medicine hours after my talk with Jackson Maurer. I knew better than to fall into the trap of the easy out offered by a drug, even an over-the-counter one.

"That's my plan for tomorrow. I haven't had enough sleep to do any good as it is."

"Want to tell me about it? What's keeping you awake now?"

"The same thing. The baby."

As I poured out my fears, Tedd took a couple of notes, but for the most part, she listened. That's one of the best things about her. Whatever you tell her, you know she hears it. And she remembers.

I have to watch what I say around her.

But I don't do so well with that. When I mentioned my agreement with Madeleine, she gave me a long look. "Was that a good idea?"

"It seemed pretty good at the time."

"And now?"

"I don't know."

So I told her about my agreement to help Dutch.

She asked the same questions.

This time I gave her a different answer. "I feel pretty rotten about it, Tedd, but I don't know if I trust him."

"Why should you feel rotten? You don't know who killed KC."

"Yeah, but he's so torn up about it—she was his godchild, you know."

"You told me. But he hadn't seen her in years."

"That's because of her father. From what I can figure out, KC's dad is no great prize. He and Dutch fought about . . . a scheme he couldn't stomach is how Dutch put it."

"And you're sure that Dutch was on the right side of that disagreement?"

"I'm sure I want him to be."

"Why?"

I stood and paced. "Because he saved my life."

"Is that all?"

"No, and you know it."

"Want to tell me about that?"

"No." I chuckled. "And you know that too."

"You know, Haley, it's wise to use caution in this case, but you can't go through life suspecting every man you meet."

"I don't. It's just that . . . well, Dutch has all those connec-
tions. He was Lori Richardson's boyfriend. She dumped him
for Ron. Then he was Ron Richardson's partner. They fought.
Dutch lost a bundle there too. He was KC's godfather, but
he lost her too after the fight."

I dropped back into the chair and laced my fingers tight.
When I looked up, Tedd's gaze seemed to reach right into
all my pain. Tears welled up.

"I'm scared," I said, my voice little more than a whisper.

"What are you scared of?"

Lots, but that wasn't what Tedd meant. "I'm scared I'm
going to learn that Dutch . . . that he . . . he's the baby's father, and then killed KC. And then . . . that he might have
done something to the baby."

By the time I got out the last word, my cheeks were wet
and a knot had a choke hold on my throat. I shook as though
I'd been out in the cold for a long, long time.

"Why does that scare you? Has he done—or said—anything to make you think he's the baby's father? That he
might have hurt the baby? Or KC? Has he threatened
you?"

"No, of course not. It's just . . . well, you know. Rape is
. . . rape."

Lame, but it was all I could come up with. The word said
enough. "I just don't want him to be like that . . ."

Almost like water that bursts through a dam, my feelings rushed up, and I sobbed. Big, painful bursts of sound
ripped up from the deepest part of me, and tears poured
in streams from my eyes.

"She's dead," I managed to choke out. "But the baby, Tedd. I have to protect the baby . . ."

My voice broke, and fresh sobs made it impossible for me to say more.

Tedd let me cry. Then, when I thought I couldn't squeeze another drop from under my eyelids, she called my name.

I looked up. I felt the urge to run. "No, please. Don't . . ."

"Why don't you tell me about the baby. Why are you so obsessed with KC's newborn?"

"Because I couldn't save mine! I have to save hers."

I'd never talked about the miscarriage I suffered three months after I was raped. Not to Marge before she died and not even to my father, who drove me to the hospital, my legs drenched with blood.

But I told Tedd.

"It was horrible, especially for Dad." I could still remember his stricken face. "For the second time, he feared he was about to lose me. But the one we lost was his grandchild."

"Had you told him you were pregnant?"

"I could barely accept it myself. How was I to tell him or Mom?"

"So you dealt with it on your own." It wasn't a question.

I shrugged. "I didn't know what to feel when I learned I was pregnant—by my rapist. I hated him. I didn't want a child to remind me of what he'd done."

The anger surged, and the memories burned inside me. In seconds I relived those days of helpless desperation, of wanting to be anyone but me. All my efforts were futile, of course, and the futility brought its own burden of despair.

"You didn't want the child?" Tedd asked after a while.

I wrapped my arms around my middle, trying to hold myself together. "I didn't really know how I felt about it. I spent those months in the hell that comes from not knowing anything anymore. Some days I just wanted to turn back the clock."

I scoffed. "Stupid, right? Other days all I could do was scream my rage out at God. How could he let it all happen to me? How could he let a baby happen?"

The memory of those days reached up and pulled on me, dragged me back toward the pit where I'd lived those agonizing days. But something deep inside me resisted. I couldn't go there. Not again. I'd fought too hard to drag myself out.

A sob broke in my throat. "Then there were the days when I thought about the child itself. I didn't want a child, certainly not *his* child, but in the end I couldn't hate the baby . . . my baby."

This time Tedd waited me out. When my thoughts slowed their dizzying whirl, I said, "When I began to bleed . . . well, that's when I knew I wanted my child. But by then it was too late."

Tears filled my eyes again, sad tears, not hot and angry like the earlier ones. "He stole so much from me . . . I lost so much. First my trust, my faith, my innocence. Then my child. For a while there, I wanted to die."

Another wave of stifling darkness hovered just a finger's

length away, but it didn't consume me like it had back then. I had survived.

"I guess God had a different plan," I told Tedd. "And maybe this is why I'm still around. So that I can make sure this baby doesn't wind up like its mom."

"Do you think God wants you to risk drawing the killer's attention for the sake of that child?"

"He wouldn't want me to ignore the danger the baby's in."

"How do you know it's in danger?"

I burst from the chair and leaned over her desk. "Where is it, Tedd? Who has it?" I stared until she met my gaze. "Who's feeding it? Clothing it? Loving it?"

"Talk to Lila, Haley. It's her job to find out."

"Sure. I'll talk to her. Then she and her Smurfs can go and arrest Dutch. That's what they're ready to do, just like they did to me. And no matter how scared I am, I'm not sure he's guilty of anything—other than being a hardhead who argued and lost to someone who wanted to do business the dirty way."

Tedd gave me a mild smile. "I like you better when you're mad. Not like you were the other day, so scared you turned yourself inside out. Your anger tells me you're closer each day to that healing we've talked about."

I slapped my hands on the top of her desk. "I'll tell you what's going to really help me heal. When I can hand that baby to someone who'll care for it, that's when I'll be able to breathe again."

"You know you can't go back."

"I know. But I can go forward."

"I don't think this is the best thing for you to do."

"It may not be the smartest, but it's the only thing I can do."

"There is another thing you can do."

Her tone of voice rubbed me wrong. "I'm not going to like this, am I?"

Another smile. "Probably not. But I'm right. And you'll agree—someday."

I took a long, deep breath of fresh air. "Hit me with your best shot, Doc."

"You've got to come to grips with your lack of trust."

When I went to object, she held out a hand. "Hear me out, will you? I know trust is a precious gift, and no one should fling it around like fairy dust. But you also can't go forward if you continue to hold yourself apart. You're part of the human race, one of God's children, and you have to find the good in those you meet."

"You want me to see Christ in everyone."

She nodded.

"Well, guess what? That's just not possible. After Paul raped me, there was no shred of Christ to be found in him. And nothing you say can change how I feel about that."

"That's true. I can't change how you feel, but the Lord can. And the only way he will is if you start to flex your trust muscle."

I rolled my eyes. "I'm allergic to exercise—other than Tyler-style workouts, that is."

"It all comes together in a neat package—if you let it. It took a great deal of trust to let Tyler, a big, powerful man, flip you and kick at you, especially back when you were still so raw."

"I never thought of it that way."

"Then maybe you better start. And you better get ready to trust some more."

Uh-oh. "What's in that squirrelly brain of yours?"

"You're the one who gave me the idea in the first place. You plan to go to the scuba shop tomorrow, right?"

I nodded and gave brief thought to flight.

"Well, there you go. You'll just have to sign up for classes while you're there."

"What? Are you nuts?"

"I'm perfectly sane. I don't know any other activity where you have to trust flat out. You have to put your life in your teacher's hands. Your teacher will control your air, how long you're underwater, how well you learn to handle yourself in another world"

What I should do is trust my instincts a whole lot more. What I also should've done is gotten out while the getting was good, not stayed to listen to a therapist in need of therapy herself. "And you seriously want me to do that? To let some stranger decide whether I breathe or not?"

"Why would that stranger not want you to breathe?"

"Why did someone want KC dead?"

"Someone had a reason for that. Feeding a postpartum woman blood thinner took some planning. Someone had something against her. A scuba teacher would want you to stay safe and alive. It's not good for business if you kill your students, you know."

"Okay. All right. You have a point." I gave it a thought, but I couldn't see my way clear. "I'll pass."

"You can't let fear run the rest of your life, you know."

"It's not running my life now."

"Sure it is. That's why you won't agree with me."

"I won't agree with you because I'm not crazy."

"So prove me wrong. Take a scuba class."

I stood to leave. "Nope."

"I dare you, Haley."

Even with my eyes scrunched shut, I could see Tedd taunting me. I knew perfectly well what she was doing. She really did know me well. There was that little character flaw I never let anyone see, not even Tedd. She just knew what made me tick. I've never been able to walk away from a dare.

But this one? This one I could turn down. "I'm outta here—"

"I dare you."

"No way."

"Dare."

I crossed to the threshold, wrapped my hand around the doorknob. "I'll keep you up on my snooping."

"I dare you, Haley Farrell. I dare you to prove me wrong."

I whirled. "Why are you doing this to me? I thought you were my friend."

"I am your friend. And your therapist."

"You're a lousy therapist. You're fired."

"You can't fire a friend."

"I can walk out on one."

"No, you can't."

I groaned. She had me there. I couldn't. I returned to the chair. My body melted, all my oomph burned in the heat of our argument. Still, the thought of going deep into the ocean, my ability to breathe dependent on a tank of air filled by a stranger, was so foreign I couldn't get my head around it.

But Tedd had dared me. And something inside me urged me to do it, to show her I could do the scuba deal and still know I had to watch my back. I could trust Tedd most of the time, Bella some of the time, and Dad and Midas all of the time. But the rest of the world?

In a pig's eye!

But I could trust God. "Okay, you want me to play Jacques Cousteau? Fine. I'll do it. But that won't prove a thing. Other than whatever doesn't kill me—"

"Will only make you stronger. My point precisely."

I'd walked right into that one. "You win this hand. I'll do what you want me to do. But don't blame me if I drown or something."

"You won't."

"Good, because I'm going to come up with something so awful, so scary, for you to do that you'll know exactly what you put me through."

Tedd was silent for a moment. Then she said, "Remember who you're talking to. I've already walked every mile in your shoes."

And she had. She also had been raped. She knew how hard it was to come back. There was nothing more I could say.

"I'll let you know how it goes."

"God bless you, Haley."

"Thanks." I opened her office door and took a deep breath. "I'm going to need it."

Sometimes I love Tedd. Others times I want to shake her.

Today I wanted to shake her.

I stood outside the waterfront strip of shops, staring at the one with air tanks, wet suits, rubber fins, and hoses and gauges of all shapes, colors, and types displayed in the huge front window. Asking questions took a certain amount of nerve, but that wasn't my problem.

I'd given Tedd my word, but I'd rather eat ground glass than enroll in a scuba diving class.

There was no way I wanted to take a class—that was sure. Could I even do it? Was I capable of giving control to someone I didn't know?

Out of nowhere, the words of a song I'd recently heard on Christian radio came to mind. "God is in control," the woman had sung. If I didn't believe that, then I was sunk—figuratively as well as literally.

I didn't have to trust a teacher at the diving school. I had to trust God.

"You got it," I said, my eyes on the partly cloudy sky above. "You're the boss, and I really hope you see that air goes through that air thingy once I go down. I'm counting on you."

As usual, God didn't answer, but I took the slight clearing over me as a positive sign.

I reached for the handle on the glass door, but it swung out toward me. An oldy-moldy Beach Boys' tune blared out with enough decibels to knock me on my backside—but I held fast. Two guys in sleek wet suits, both in their late teens or maybe early twenties, came out, their faces animated.

"Man," the blond one said. "I knew there was good stuff down there."

The redhead laughed. "No joke. And it's old, dude."

"Yeah, I hear they're at least a hundred years old."

"That's awesome. And they're in awesome shape."

"Bet they'll sell for a fortune."

"For sure. That'll buy a lot of dive time, you know."

"Can you believe Tom's luck? Man! I wish I'd gone down with him. Then maybe I could cash in on a bit of his loot, you know, talk him into sharing the wealth, dude."

Hmm . . . loot . . . that would sell for a fortune . . . and about a hundred years old . . .

They could only be talking about one thing. It'd been splashed all over the *Seattle Post-Intelligencer*. A local diver had made a major find when he explored the coast of nearby Edmonds. The antique glass bottles of various shapes, colors, and sizes were considered an absolute treasure, and the antiques community in the Pacific Northwest was all abuzz.

I had no idea the dive shop in my backyard, so to speak, had sponsored the dive that made the find.

My grin spanned from ear to ear. Wild Tasmanian devils couldn't keep me from that shop now. "Look out scuba people, Auctioneer Haley is on her way."

14

The scuba shop couldn't have felt more foreign had it been parked out on Mars. The Beach Boys and their little Deuce Coupe threatened my hearing, and the stench of rubbery, vinyly, plasticky stuff made me long for a pair of nose plugs—which they didn't seem to sell. Nothing was familiar.

Well, I did recognize air tanks and wet suits from TV shows and movies. And there aren't many people in the civilized world who don't know what swim fins and masks look like. But everything else in the shop overwhelmed me. Hoses, gauges, wicked-looking knives, weird guns, and other gizmos littered the front window and the glass shelves at the checkout counter.

Then I saw them.

The bottles.

"Ah . . ." No wonder the papers had been full of raves.

"Hey there!" The guy with a shaved head, somewhere in his early twenties, gave me a smile. "Like our latest find?"

I approached the table in the right corner of the crowded shop, my eyes on the brown, clear, green, and blue bottles, most of which, unless I was horribly off the mark, were worth in the vicinity of fifteen hundred dollars apiece.

"Love it," I said, a finger on a fabulous cobalt one. "Did you find them?"

"Dude, I was on the dive, but it was Tom Pitney who found them."

"Do you know what he wants to do with them?"

"He wants to sell them, but he hasn't made up his mind how."

Oh yeah! "Maybe I could help him with that. You see, I own Norwalk & Farrell's Auctions, and we could get him top dollar for the collection."

The guy crossed his massively muscled arms over the bikini-clad woman on his purple tank top. "You and a thousand others, lady."

Bummer. "I guess he must have been contacted by every major antiques dealer in the west by now. I'm surprised he hasn't done anything about them yet."

"Well, Tom's been . . . um . . . well, a friend of his died recently, and he's, like, been dealing with that. Dude'll get back to diving and his bottles when he's ready."

"I'm sorry to hear about his loss." Could it be KC? "I'd like to leave you my business card anyway. I can wait until he's ready. Losing a loved one's a rough deal."

"I don't know about a loved one," he said, discomfort on his face. "He was her dive buddy. You know, 'cause she's kinda young and had to dive with someone older. They'd become good friends."

My heartbeat sped up. "I lost a very close friend last year. It was hard, and it's taken me a long time to deal with the pain."

"Yeah, well, people don't come here to talk about dead people. Can I help you with something?"

He had no idea how much he'd already helped. "I recently—" no need to tell him how recently "—became interested in scuba and am thinking of taking lessons. I was told you guys were pretty good."

"The best. Hey, I'm Max Higgins, and I, like, run the shop for Stingray two or three times a week."

"Stingray, huh?"

"The owner's name is Raymond Jones. Not exactly a stellar name, you know?" He winked. "So the dude likes Stingray better. I would too."

"Stingray it is. Tell me about scuba, Max. Why should I spend the time and money?"

"Aw, dude, it's everything. There's nothing else like it on good ol' planet Earth. See, it's, like, a different world *in* the world. There's no noise, it's not crowded, you can just sit and watch the sun and clouds move across the sky from under the water, or you can go find fish . . ."

I let him ramble, only half in tune with his State of the Scuba Union address. The bottles on the table had a grip on my attention, and my hands just itched to go and really check them out. I'm not as good as Ozzie at actual appraisals, but I can tell when something's worth my time.

With about forty of them covering the tabletop, I figured these would fetch somewhere in the vicinity of sixty thousand dollars—definitely worth my time. And then there was the connection to KC. That was something I had to pursue.

"Listen, Max. You sold me." He didn't need to know on just what. "Where do I sign on the dotted line, and when does the next beginner's class start?"

My interruption startled him. "Uh . . . yeah, dude. Here. This is our latest schedule. Check it out."

A quick scan of the bright red flyer revealed a full roster of lessons. One could scuba dive anytime between sunrise and sunset, weather permitting. I noticed instructors' names listed by the lessons, and Max's appeared beside the skilled level classes.

"I'm impressed," I said. "Since it seems you're an expert, I wonder if you ever teach know-nothings like me."

"Sometimes, but Stingray's had Tom teaching newbies for a couple of months. He'll probably be your instructor."

"I thought you said he was so broken up he wasn't diving these days."

"Well, not since KC died, he hasn't, but, like, he'll come back to teach his lessons for sure. He needs the bucks to pay for school."

Bingo! "KC? Is that the poor girl who died at the doctor's house?"

Max's eyes narrowed. "Yeah . . . she was a friend."

"Did you know her too?"

"We all did. She was a regular here since she did her

bubbler gig a couple of years ago. She snorkeled a whole bunch for a while too. She got her junior certification after that, and when she turned fourteen, she decided to go for her open-water certification. Stingray was working with her on that. She was real excited when she did great on the academic stuff you have to do before each dive."

"So was Tom her boyfriend?" Sometimes it pays to act dumb.

"Naw. She was, like, dating some kid from her school. But Tom's not that old either, nineteen, and he had it bad for her. But she just didn't even notice anyone, and she was younger than Tom. Besides, all she ever wanted was to dive."

"That is sad." I had probably pumped Max to his max, so I pulled out my checkbook. "How much to enroll? Do I pay for the lessons up front? And what kind of equipment do I need? Can I rent?"

Max took me through the enrollment process in no time, and then his eyes gleamed again. He gestured toward the gadgets and gizmos. "You'll learn all about the gear on your first lesson. That's when the fun starts. And all you'll need to bring is a swimsuit. Your first lessons will be in the pool out back."

"A pool? Not the ocean?"

"Not right up front."

I couldn't hide my relief. "That's great! I can handle that."

Max's expression told me he'd heard more than I'd want him to. "Dude. You sure you want to do this? Diving's not like collecting stamps. Either you're serious or you're out. We can't have idiots on a dive. Everyone's life depends on everyone else who's down there."

My stomach flipped. "You're right. It's serious business, and yes, I do want to do this. It's just that it's new for me, and I'm not ready for the ocean."

He gave me an exasperated head shake. "No joke. That's why we only let you into the pool at first. Then you go off the end of the pier. You're not going into the Sound for real until you know what you're doing."

"Thanks. That makes me feel a lot better."

He gave me another weird look—well, his look wasn't weird. It just was the kind of look that told me he thought I was weird.

If he only knew.

"Why don't you, like, take a look at some of the books over there," he said. "Some of the more basic ones will help you get an idea what you'll be doing."

"Great. I'll take a few minutes to do that. Thanks."

Since it's always better to know something about any new endeavor you're about to undertake, I scoped out the titles in the pair of side-by-side seven-foot-tall shelves. I really wanted something like *Scuba for Dummies*, but they didn't seem to stock it. The books with glossy photos appealed to the artist in me, but I knew those weren't the ones I needed most. Then, on the third shelf down, I found one with the word *basic* in the title. That was the one.

I opened to the table of contents and then heard a door open and close in the back of the shop.

"Hey, Max!" a young man called out.

"Tom, dude! What's up, man?"

The conversation continued more quietly than their greeting, but I turned just enough to catch a surreptitious look at the newcomer from behind the cover of my canyon of books. How many Toms would walk into the shop with that much familiarity?

At about five foot ten, Tom stood a couple of inches shorter than Max. He also lacked the overblown muscle mass that Max displayed in his tank top. Blond and tanned, Tom looked like a poster boy for Southern California living. I snagged another diving book and stepped toward the checkout counter without letting my Birkenstocks slap.

Sure, I eavesdropped—shamelessly.

". . . You sure you're ready to come back? Stingray said you could take off as long as you wanted."

Tom shrugged, his expression grim. "It's not like it's going to do me any good. I'm not making any money, and sitting around all miserable isn't going to bring KC back."

"I'll tell Stingray to put you on the schedule for next week, then."

"That works."

Max scribbled something on a tablet hung by the back door. "Monday okay?"

"Yeah, sure."

Tom turned to leave the way he'd come in, and Max walked the other way, right past the bottle-topped table. "Hey, man. Before I forget. Some woman just left who wanted to talk to you about your bottles. She gave me her card for you, says she, like, owns some auction place or something."

"I must've heard from every one of them in the country since the *Intelligencer* got ahold of the story."

"Well, have you given it all some thought?"

"Are you crazy? A couple of bottles aren't no big deal to me right now. Sure, I'm gonna want to sell them. They'll pay a good chunk of tuition, but, man, give me a break. I can barely think or sleep or eat for thinking of KC."

"I hear you." Max reached into his shorts pocket. "Here. This is her card. I'll tell you, this one's . . . different. She wasn't so big on the bottles as some of the others."

"Really?" Tom said, his gaze on my card. "You mean she didn't start hitting you with dollar amounts up front?"

"No, not really. She just, like, got this great big grin when she saw the bottles, touched one of them like it was . . . oh, I don't know, dude. A treasure, a *real* treasure."

"That's a change."

"Yeah, man. I'm not gonna forget real quick the guy who wanted to rip you off and tried to sneak away with two of the blue ones."

"That ripped me." He shook his head. "But I can't get all worked up about a chunk of old glass right now. Know what I mean?"

"Yeah, but you gotta think about it, dude. School starts up again before you know it. Those bills are big."

Tom flicked the card against his thumb. "Maybe I will give her a call."

Here I stood, dying to talk to Tom but embarrassed to be

outed as a snoop. What to do? Did I somehow try to sneak
out the front and then barge back in? Or did I just guts my
way out and go shake the guy's hand?

Since I couldn't very well walk out without being heard—
they had that dopey chime hooked up to the electronic motion sensor on the door—that wasn't much of an option. I
really didn't have any choice but to go meet Tom.

"Max!" I called out, the dumb act once again my ally.
"Max, I'd like to buy these two books. They're great. I just
started flipping through them, and I couldn't stop reading—oh! I'm sorry. I see you're busy."

The look Max gave me spoke a thousand words, none of
which I liked. He'd seen right through my dumb act. Tom,
on the other hand, barely spared me a glance.

"Sure thing, Haley," Max said. "And since you were
so busy reading, I'd better introduce you to Tom Pitney,
right? I'm sure you, like, have lots to talk to him about his
bottles."

Tom's frown didn't give much encouragement. "This
your card?"

I held out my hand. "I'm Haley Farrell. I own Norwalk
& Farrell's Auctions, as you can see on the card. And yes.
I'm interested in handling the sale of your bottles."

He looked me up and down with a clear, direct stare.
"Why should I agree to have you sell them instead of all
the other people who've called?"

I hadn't expected a job interview. "Ah . . . well, because
I'm local, for one thing. Norwalk & Farrell's Auctions is
located right here in Wilmont."

Ginny Aiken   183

"What difference does that make? A New York check's not going to be any different from a Wilmont check."

He was no dummy. "No, but it's always a good idea to patronize local commerce." Lame, lame, lame.

He knew it too. "I'm only in this area because I'm at U-dub. Once I graduate I'll turn my back on the grand old University of Washington and leave this soggy place."

"Hey! We get good weather too."

My outburst made him chuckle. "Okay," he said. "That's better. At least you got some human in there with all the business babble."

"So you're interested in testing me."

"Well, it's a whole bunch of expensive bottles we're talking about."

"Do you know just how expensive they are?"

"Not really. I only found them three weeks ago, and then KC . . ."

The wounded look I'd first seen on his face returned. Here was another young man devastated by KC's death. I had to be careful. It wouldn't be difficult. I knew how he felt.

"I'm sorry, Tom. I understand you knew KC Richardson. By a weird coincidence, I'm one of the people who found her."

He closed his eyes and averted his face.

I reached out and placed a hand on his shoulder. "This isn't the time to get into details about the bottles, and I know it." I took a deep breath. "My business—Norwalk & Farrell's Auctions? I inherited it from a woman who was like a mother to me. She was murdered last year."

He tensed up under my hand, but he did face me. "I guess you do know."

"Yeah. And I also found her. I can't tell you how hard it was to see her like that, and then to walk out onto that patio a year later and find KC there."

He drew in a ragged breath.

My squeeze to his shoulder was an inadequate gesture of understanding, but it was all I felt I could do under the circumstances. "You have my card. I'll be there at those phone numbers whenever you're ready. I hope you do decide to go with us for the sale."

I gave him a final, awkward pat, then walked to the register, where Max stood, his attention glued to us. I rummaged through my backpack purse. "Here's my credit card."

"Dude. You're okay, you know?"

I smiled. "Thanks. But I didn't do much."

"You didn't hit him up hard for the bottles, and you were nice about KC too."

"I told you I know what it's like to lose a loved one."

"Guess you do."

"Haley," Tom said. "I don't need to think about it. I'd like you to sell the bottles for me, but I'm not ready to do a whole lot of thinking right now. Give me some time, and then we can talk about money and stuff."

Instead of feeling triumphant, I felt humbled. To my surprise, my eyes prickled with tears. "Thank you for your trust, Tom. It means a great deal. And I do understand. Like I said, you can reach me at those phone numbers any time you're ready."

The register pinged the total for the books, then clacked out the receipt. I signed, stuck the yellow copy in my wallet, and grabbed the bagged books.

"I'll see you next week," I said on my way to the door. "Oh, Tom. Before I forget. We have a secured warehouse and can keep the bottles safe there for you if you'd like."

"That's a good idea. I'll call you on Monday to make arrangements."

"Hey, dude," Max said. "You're going to be teaching her on Monday. You guys can talk all about old bottles then."

I grinned. "That works."

Tom nodded. "Good deal."

Satisfied with all I'd accomplished in my brief visit, I reached for the door handle, only to have it fly outward. I nearly fell flat on my face.

"Easy there," a tall, middle-aged man said, his hands on my shoulders. "I'm sorry. I didn't see you the other side."

"Oh, it's not your fault," I answered, flustered. "I wasn't paying any attention. I was too busy talking. I'm starting lessons on Monday, and the guys were telling me about them. Oh, and the bottles too. Those are great . . ."

I let the babble dry up at the amused look on his face.

"I'm always glad to see a newcomer show so much enthusiasm." He held out his hand. "I'm Stewart Marshall. I spend much of my free time here. I'm sure we'll get to know each other very soon."

This was Deedee's husband? Another scuba diver?

Oh man. KC's murder had more strings than an Oriental rug's fringe. "Funny you should say that, Dr. Marshall."

His eyebrows shot up.

I shook his hand. "I'm Haley Farrell, your interior designer. Unfortunately, I'm the one who was with Deedee the other day. We found KC."

His fingers spasmed around mine, and he released my hand. His expression took on a troubled cast. "I'm sure it's a pleasure to meet you, Haley, but I do wish the circumstances were different. It's a tragedy when a girl that young dies in such a terrible way."

I studied his reaction. He looked sad—not too much, but appropriately so. "I'd much rather meet you once the job is done," I replied. "When everyone can celebrate the new look of your home."

He shrugged and gave a dry little chuckle. "I have no problem with the way the house is right now, but Deedee is such a cheerful woman. I can see why she wants a different look to the place." His voice turned tender. "She has brought such joy to my life that I'm willing to put up with all the upheaval."

"I see you know what it means to redesign a house."

"My ex-wife tore the place apart back when we first bought it. It took us a year and half to finish the work. I hope it won't take that long this time."

"Can't make any promises yet. Deedee and I are going shopping tomorrow, and I have to check in with the contractor. Oh, and Deedee said something about a pool. Have to look into that too."

With a huge, dramatic gesture, the doctor reached into his back pocket and waved his wallet in the air high over his head. "No! You can't have my last dollar. Have mercy on an old man."

I laughed. "I'll do my best. I can see this is going to be an interesting job."

"I hope you and Deedee have fun. Goodness knows, a murder victim on your patio is hardly the best way to start a marriage. She's been distraught since that day—understandably so."

"No doubt. It's weighed on me too."

His look was full of kindness and concern. "I hope you're getting more sleep and eating better than Deedee is."

I grimaced. "Okay. You busted me. I'm not doing too well, but I'm sure that as time goes by I'll be fine."

He reached out and placed a comforting hand on my shoulder. "I'm sorry that was your welcome to my home. Please take care of yourself, and I promise to improve our hospitality on your next visit."

"Thanks." I fell silent, and the moment grew longer, awkward. "Well! I'd better get going. I have a house to redesign, after all."

"It was nice to meet you," Dr. Marshall said. "And I hope you enjoy your scuba lessons."

As I walked to my Honda, I tallied up the afternoon. It had been productive . . . sort of. I enrolled for classes; I met Tom and got him to agree to let me sell his bottle collection; I learned he too had loved KC Richardson, and I witnessed his genuine grief over her death; I met Dr. Marshall and found him to be a nice, gentle, funny man; and I bought two books on scuba diving.

But none of that had brought me any closer to knowing what had happened to KC. I knew no more about the missing baby than I'd known before.

I still stood at square one.

15

"I love that!" Bella squealed later that evening. "You are so talented, Haley girl."

"Even though I'm a feline Philippine, huh?"

Bella narrowed her blue eyes. "That, dear girl, is Philistine. Get it right, will you?"

I chuckled. "So you like what I've come up with so far for the Marshalls' kitchen."

"It's absolutely fantabulous! I can just picture myself with my morning tea in the breakfast nook looking out over the pool." She turned thoughtful. "I wonder if Deedee will swim before or after breakfast."

"Maybe both."

"It'll be a heated pool, right?"

"In the Pacific Northwest? Of course! Otherwise, they might get to use it all of two days out of a year."

Bella shook a stubby finger at me. "Don't you turn eggs Benedict on me. I've always thought you were a good egg; now you're bad-mouthing our weather."

I raised my arms in the universal "Don't blame me" gesture. "Hey, I'm a native. I'm allowed to bad-mouth our weather. It's foreigners who can't."

"That's an interesting way to put it," Dad said from the doorway. "How'd your day go, honey?"

I waggled a hand in the air. "So-so. Busy though. Oh, and I think you'll get a kick out of this. Guess what I signed up for today?"

"You didn't say anything about signing up for anything," Bella said, accusation in her voice. "Why didn't you tell me you were up to something cool again?"

I could've just kicked myself. That slip of my tongue was sure to bring an avalanche of consequences.

"Um . . . I forgot, Bella. Sorry."

Was there any way I could get out of this?

As I scrambled for a conversational diversion, Dad walked over to the cupboard and took out a tall glass. At the refrigerator he helped himself to ice and fresh-brewed tea. He sliced a lemon, plunked the yellow circle in his drink, then faced us again.

I stared as if I'd never seen Dad serve himself tea before.

"Well, Haley," he said, "are you going to tell us what you signed up for?"

Oh well. "I'm starting scuba diving lessons on Monday."

You know that expression "You could hear a pin drop"? Well, you could've if you'd dropped a pin in our kitchen just then—even a feather would've busted eardrums. Bella's eyes looked ready to pop from their sockets, and Dad just stood there and gaped.

With impeccable timing, Midas parked himself by the cabinet where the doggy cookies live and *woo-woo-woo*ed for another treat. Thank goodness this golden wasn't silent.

My father took more care than needed to set his glass down on the counter. "I never knew you had an interest in the activity."

"I didn't. At least, not until the other day when Tedd . . . um . . . *suggested* I try it."

Dad's gaze zeroed in on me, concern all over his face. But instead of speaking, he picked up his tea and took a long drink.

Bella, on the other hand, popped up from her seat, indignation all over her pretty face. "You've been keeping secrets, Haley girl. How come you didn't tell me you had a boyfriend? How'm I gonna know if he's good enough for you if you don't let me check him out?"

The gymnastics of Bella's mind never cease to amaze me. "I don't have a boyfriend. How did scuba lessons translate into a boyfriend?"

"What? Do I look stupid or something?" She parked her fists on her hips. "This Ted's gotten close enough to you that he's sending you underwater. Who is he? How long have you been seeing him? How does he feel about Midas? And how soon is the wedding?"

"Good grief, Bella Cahill! You really need to be writing books, or at the very least screenplays. How'd you get to a wedding from just hearing me mention Tedd?"

Her chin jutted farther, and she continued to glare.

With a sigh, I stood, placed my hands on her shoulders,

and gave her a gentle squeeze. "Bella, my dear, Tedd's a friend, a *girl*friend. Her full name is Teodora Rodriguez, and I've known her for about a year now."

Bella sagged. "Oh."

"Sorry. It's not that exciting, is it?"

"Not really." Then she perked up again—to my regret. "But the scuba stuff is. When'd you decide to become the wrinkly French guy who used to do the shows they reran on TV when you were a kid?"

I fought a chuckle. "That's Jacques Cousteau, Bella."

Dad turned on the tap to rinse out his glass. "What Cousteau didn't know about the ocean and diving isn't worth learning."

"Well, I'm not going to try to beat his knowledge, that's for sure. Tedd just figured I could do with some . . . trust building, and from where I stand, I don't know anything else that calls for anywhere near as much blind faith as scuba. I'm not sure it'll work. I'm not even sure she's right, but she wouldn't let up. You know how persuasive she can be."

Dad met my gaze and held it for a moment. I couldn't tell for sure, but I suspected he also sent a brief prayer heavenward.

"I can't think of a better activity for you," he finally said.

When Bella's smile put in an appearance, I knew I was in for a rocky ride.

"You know?" she said. "This sounds like it's right up my alley. And I can't let our Haley girl go off and do something so risky without someone looking out for her." She bustled to the door. "Wonder what kind of cute clothes you get to wear for scuba diving."

The door slammed as she trotted off.

"No—"

"Don't even try," Dad said, a mischievous sparkle in his eyes. "You know better than to get in the way of Hurricane Bella. I just want to be around to see the divers' faces when she takes them on."

I dropped into a chair. "Lucky me. It looks like I get a front-row seat."

Whether I wanted one or not.

The next day I got an early call from Dutch. He'd set up an appointment at the Marshall home with the pool installer. In spite of the tragedy at the outset of the job, I couldn't shut down my excitement over the designs we were working on, especially the nonpink elements.

At 2:30 I drove up to the mansion, parked, and rang the doorbell. Deedee answered.

"Hi, Haley." She gave me a hug—surprised the daylights out of me. "It's so good to see you. I loved the furniture showroom, but this is going to be so much more fun. I can't wait for my tropical-paradise pool to go in."

Furniture shopping with Deedee was . . . interesting. The more shiny chrome and steel any piece had, the more she liked it. Sparkly stuff, pink on pink, and geometric lines all over the place didn't really excite me, but the design challenge those restrictions presented did.

"I'm glad. Is the pool guy here yet? How about Dutch?"

"They both got here about two minutes ago. I took them out back. Let's go see what we can come up with."

I experienced a weird sensation as we took the same path as on the day we found KC. At the kitchen door, I shuddered. But mercifully, when we stepped outside we only saw Dutch and a chunky, red-ponytailed guy. Each man had a hand pointed at a different end of the yard.

"Uh-oh." I shook my head. "Not a moment too soon, Deedee. It looks like a testosterone match is on out here. Let's go bring some sanity to your pool project."

Deedee giggled as we walked up to the posturing males.

"Hey there, Dutch."

He nodded his greeting.

Then I held out my hand to the redhead at his side. "I'm Haley Farrell, the designer on the project. Pleased to meet you."

"Good to meet you." The chunky guy's paw tightened like a vise around my fingers. "I'm Doug Carter. I specialize in tropical styles. Perfect Pools assigned me to your project."

My hand would never be the same. I shook it out as discreetly as I could. "Let me tell you what we're doing with the house. That way you'll have a better idea what we can and can't do with the pool."

Although the pool guy frowned, I knew I couldn't let him just plunk his hole in the ground wherever he wanted. I showed him my preliminary sketch for the rear elevation of the house and made sure both he and Dutch realized the kitchen's glass wall had to take center stage.

After a bit of verbal wrangling and some horse-trader-type compromise, we came to an agreement. The pool would sit thirty-five feet away from the new Pennsylvania bluestone patio, just in front of the first evergreens in the northernmost corner of the yard. Doug would stack under the trees themselves the boulders we needed for the waterfall into the lagoon-style pool. I could already envision their gray tones in perfect contrast with the deep emerald foliage.

Once the men were done and on their way back through the house, I turned to Deedee. "I still need a couple more measurements in the kitchen. Do you mind if I stay behind while you show the guys out?"

She gave an airy wave. "Of course not. Go ahead and do what you need, Haley. I just, like, want everything to be perfect. Of course you need to do your measurements over and over to be sure it all turns out the way I want it . . ."

Her fluffy, feathery voice carried back as she followed the men. I grinned. Who'd have thought I'd one day redesign a home for the up-to-date cross between Marilyn Monroe and Barbie?

I pulled out my hundred-foot tape measure and made for the pantry. The day I returned to take photos and measurements, I'd had the time only to take a quick peek into this area. Now I needed precision to design new storage configurations once we tore down the pantry walls.

My design would nestle the new breakfast nook in a half-hexagon bay window area we planned to build based on the space we'd gain once we removed the pantry itself. I measured the wall between the pantry and the kitchen, then opened the door to measure the exact depth of the small room.

Floor-to-ceiling shelves sagged under canned goods, boxes of various cereals, pastas, and every type of tea known to mankind, dozens of pans and baking dishes, serving pieces, and all sorts of other kitchen paraphernalia.

To reach the back wall, I would have to move stuff out of my way. I began with the shelf right under my nose. The stacked skillets—eight of them in different sizes!—went down on the floor behind me.

Once those were out of my way, I went to work on the multiple commercial-sized containers of ibuprofen, cold and sinus tablets, antacids, laxatives, vitamins, and prescription-type bottles of medication.

I moved bottles of Celebrex, Lipitor, Vicodin, and a couple other serious painkillers. Then I froze.

My hand hovered over a particular pill bottle on that shelf. My heart pounded hard in my chest. My breath grew shallow. Nausea struck. I began to pray.

The good doctor and his wife had a large bottle of RU-486, the notorious morning-after abortifacient, in their kitchen among a veritable cocktail of drugs, many of them controlled substances.

Why?

Like a lightbulb, the idea flashed to life. I scrabbled among the remaining bottles, intent on one thing: did a bottle of Coumadin lurk among the Marshalls' kitchen stash? I was so focused that I never heard a thing.

A heavy hand landed on my shoulder.

"What do you think you're doing, snooping in our kitchen cupboards?" Deedee's shrillest tones pierced my eardrums. "And I trusted you. How dare you dig around in our things? We're not paying you to mess with our private business. You're just here to decorate the house, not to sniff out every last little thing about us. I should call the police on you. You just wait till I tell Stew—"

"Chill, Deedee," I said, anything but chilled-out myself. "I told you I needed to measure the pantry. I couldn't reach the back wall with all that stuff in the way, so I had to move it around. I put the pans on the floor—be careful you don't step on them and trip. And I had to make a path for my tape measure between your meds. Everything is stacked so high and tight in here that I couldn't see the wall, much less take any measurements."

"Oh." She narrowed her eyes. "I guess you could be right. The pantry is full. I had the grocery store restock everything, since it was getting kinda bare now that Domingo's been gone for a while."

Her frown didn't ease, but she'd at least considered my explanation—which was the truth, of course. I couldn't have measured if I hadn't moved things. I didn't think it prudent to discuss the arsenal of drugs.

To prove my point, I stretched out my tape measure. "The room's exactly nine feet and seven and an eighth inches wide and thirteen feet and five and a third inches deep."

I made a big deal of the notation in the notepad I took from my portfolio, which I'd propped against the door frame. Then I faced my client again. "All done!"

That seemed to relieve her. "Good. I'm all stressed out now. I need a nap."

Okay. "I'm jealous. I have a ton of things to do, so I'll leave you to your z's. I'll put together the ideas we've talked about and then give you a call early next week so we can go over some initial drawings for the kitchen and sunroom."

"I'll be waiting for your call."

I hurried outside, jumped in my car, and didn't allow myself a deep breath until I reached the brick columns at the end of the drive. There'd been no Coumadin on the shelf—at least, none that I'd found. But I'd only cleared a small area on the one shelf. Who knew what skulked behind the canned shrimp and truffles and lemon-curd jars?

What really troubled me, though, was that one awful bottle. Why would a plastic surgeon have a container of morning-after pills at his home?

Did the nice man I'd met at the dive shop have a darker, more dangerous alter ego? Even though I hadn't found Coumadin, did Stewart Marshall have some stashed away somewhere? Had he given it to KC? And why had Deedee freaked out like that if she didn't have anything to hide?

Was she afraid of her much-older husband?

All good questions. But I had no answers.

Not yet.

Once I drove out past the wrought-iron gate, I pulled over onto the shoulder of the road and called Tedd. "I hope you're free right now."

"Take a look at your watch. My last client left about ten minutes ago, and we just locked our doors."

"Don't go anywhere. I'll be there in less than fifteen minutes. Please."

"Are you okay?"

"I'll tell you when I get there."

My hands shook so much I don't know how I made it to Tedd's office in one piece. I was a safety hazard on the road, but I had to get away from the Marshall mansion. I had to talk to Tedd.

She was looking out for me in her waiting room, just inside the glass door. I walked in, she locked up again, and we headed back to her private office. Once we both sat, I met her gaze.

"The Marshalls have RU-486 in their pantry. They also have a ton of heavy-duty prescription narcotics there."

Tedd frowned. "They have the morning-after pill in their kitchen?"

"In their kitchen. And major painkillers too."

She gave me an ironic smile. "That sounds slightly illegal."

"Yeah, right. Slightly. Try totally."

"So what does it mean?"

"I'm not sure. And I didn't find any Coumadin. But I didn't have a chance to look through everything there, much less other parts of the house. I can't be sure it's not hidden somewhere else. Besides, you should've seen Deedee. She totally freaked when she saw me moving pill bottles around."

"There's only one use for the morning-after pill."

"Yep."

"You wouldn't think a husband and wife would use something that radical for birth control."

"Nope."

Tedd fell silent, and I sat there and shook. My mind filled with ugly images, from my past and from the scene of KC's death.

The longer the silence drew, the more troubled Tedd looked. Finally she said, "I'm not sure how to go about this."

"What do you mean?"

"I just thought of something a client told me. It occurs to me that it might help you connect some dots. But I have a problem with confidentiality."

I wanted to scream at her, to remind her that murder had happened here. But I had to hold my tongue. She did have an ethical issue to deal with.

I tried to wait her out, but my patience was nothing to write home about. Prayer helped—only for so long.

"Come on, Tedd. Give me a break here." I stood and paced; patience wasn't getting us anywhere. "We're talking about a dead kid. Tell me what you're thinking—whatever you know. Please."

Tedd waved me back into my chair. "I know what's at stake, Haley. But I can't ignore what's at the core of what I do."

I'd never seen her so troubled. She continued, her voice serious, her gaze intent. "According to a client, and I have no reason to doubt her, we have a local doc who performs illegal late-term abortions. True, the RU-486 has nothing to do with late-term abortions, but how many doctors do we have in town? In little old Wilmont? Then, out of those, how many would even have that med in the first place?"

Tedd stood, turned her back to me. "Please go out to the waiting room while I make a phone call."

When I rose, my knees threatened to give way. I've never been able to get my head around the concept of abortion, much less the so-called late-term ones. To me, it's murder, plain and simple.

"I'll be waiting," I said.

In the waiting room, I sat and prayed; I prayed for myself, for Tedd, for her client, for KC, for my dad, for Deedee and Stewart Marshall, for Dutch.

Most of all, I prayed for the little babies who wouldn't live long enough to breathe, to be held, to be loved, to learn to pray for themselves. Silent tears flowed unchecked.

I didn't need anyone to tell me who the local abortionist

was. I didn't need anyone to tell me what had happened to KC's child.

I knew. And I wished I didn't.

Stewart Marshall had killed KC's child.

What I needed to learn was whether he'd also killed KC.

And why.

16

I went straight home after I left Tedd's office. Dad wasn't there; more than likely, he and Madeleine had gone somewhere. They'd become inseparable.

It didn't matter. What mattered most was that the house would be empty. I didn't know when the events of the afternoon would hit me, but I expected the hit to be hard when they did. I didn't want Dad there to see me fall apart again, to wind up worried about me yet another time.

My Bible offered comfort. I read a little, but my attention strayed too often to continue, so I turned to prayer. I poured out my heart to the Lord. I confessed my fear, my lack of courage. I asked for strength, for guidance, for the wisdom to recognize his leading.

Then I just sat, my Bible held close to my heart. My foot pushed my mother's rocker into an easy, steady rhythm. By the time the doorbell rang, I'd come to realize that although the afternoon had been traumatic in every possible way, I hadn't fallen apart. Yes, I felt wrung out, my emotions all on the edge, but I hadn't plunged into one of the deep, dark pits of despair I'd so often visited in the past.

Midas and I opened the door for Dutch.

"Oh," I said. "Did I forget a meeting or something?"

"I wish. I just had another run-in with Lila Tsu, and I wondered if you'd come up with anything in the last few days. Can I come in?"

"I'm sorry. Of course you can." I stepped aside, dragged Midas away from the open door and doggy freedom, then gestured toward the sofa. "Take a seat. I hope you don't mind making a new best friend. Midas is not known for shyness."

"I've met him before, remember?"

Groan. "And every time I was at a disadvantage."

"Seems you've left that habit in the past."

"What makes you say that?"

"This time I'm the one in trouble, aren't I?"

I thought about the scuba lessons but decided not to mention them. Instead, I said, "What's the deal with Lila? Does she have new evidence? Anything to tie you closer to the crime?"

I hoped not; I'd come to accept my attraction to Dutch.

He ran a hand through his dark hair. "No, not really. I get the sense she's under pressure to solve the case but isn't getting anywhere. Since she's back to square one, she figured it was time to torture me some more."

"Sounds like Lila. That's her modus operandi, you know. At least, that's how she handled her suspicion of me last year."

"I wish she'd quit with me and start to look for the killer somewhere else. It sure wasn't me, and I want to hurry up and prove it."

Should I share what I'd learned? If he was really as innocent as I'd begun to believe, then it wouldn't matter. If, on the other hand, he was as guilty as he'd initially appeared, as guilty as Lila believed him to be, then telling him important information would help him cover his tracks even better.

Another quick prayer went heavenward, and I decided to buy myself some time to chill a bit, get a good handle on my feelings.

"Can I get you something to drink?" I'd never thought of myself as a Martha Stewart hostess, but this even I could handle. "I have coffee, tea, and lemonade, and I suspect there may be a can or two of soda somewhere in the kitchen."

"If you can track down the soda, I'd like that."

"Give me a minute, and I'll be right back."

In the kitchen I prayed again. The sodas were way back in the lower cupboard next to the sink, but it took a bit of digging around to reach them. I filled a glass with ice, then, can in hand, returned to the living room.

I'd come full circle on my fears and suspicions and had realized all I could do was to leave the outcome to God. He wouldn't let me down.

"Here you go." I gave Dutch the cold glass and popped-open can. "I'd like to buy the world a Coke . . ."

"I was just thirsty, Haley. I didn't really need a song-and-dance commercial to go with it."

He took a drink.

"I learned a couple of things, Dutch. For one, KC's boy-friend did love her, and he swears he's not the father. He's

really broken up about her death but angry and bitter about
her obsession with scuba diving. She spent every possible
minute down at the shop, and he barely saw her once she
got serious with diving. If you ask me, he loved her enough
to respect her. Which tells me he didn't touch her. He isn't
the baby's father. And I'm not sure his anger made him
snap and . . ."

Dutch took his time but then lifted a shoulder and
nodded.

I continued. "There's a guy down at the scuba shop who's
also crazy about her. He's just as messed up right now, but I
don't think she encouraged his feelings. Max, the one who
was running the shop when I went there, says KC was pretty
serious about the real boyfriend. I met Tom, the diver, but I
didn't get a chance to ask him that kind of question."

Dutch gave me an "Are you nuts?" look. "Do you really
think it works that way? To just go up to a guy and accuse
him of fathering a dead teen's baby?"

My temper decided to join us. "No, Dutch. I'm not that
dumb. I signed up for lessons with Tom on Monday. I'll
get more details as my lessons go along. I know I can get
info out of him sooner or later. But I have no intention of
hounding him for answers."

"I get it." His eyes warned of incoming sarcasm. "You're
going to put on your flippers and snorkel, go under, and
then do a '*Glu glub. Bub blub glup*' bit. Hope you hire a
translator."

"Good thing you didn't go into clowning. It doesn't come
naturally, you know."

"Neither does detecting come so naturally to you, but when has that stopped you?"

"Hey! You asked me to help."

"How will your scuba lessons help me?"

"They might if you'd let me tell you the rest. I had a close encounter of the intriguing kind down at the shop. Guess who else is a devoted diver?"

He shrugged and swigged more soda.

"Fine. I'll tell you. Dr. Marshall walked in just as I was leaving the shop."

That caught Dutch's attention. He clunked his drink down on the coffee table, leaned forward, and met my gaze. "It is interesting that he'd be down there, right where KC supposedly spent most of her time. I'm getting an inkling where you're going with this."

"Well, *bing, bing, bing*! The man just won the giant stuffed panda. You're lucky I'm on your side, buddy. I'm going to give you more than an inkling here. After you and the pool guy left the mansion, I had to measure the pantry. That's why I stayed behind when Deedee walked you guys to the door. And that's where I hit the mother lode."

He peered at me, surprised me with the hint of mischief on his face. "You don't look like you're in danger of starvation, so I can't imagine why you'd think of groceries as the mother lode."

If looks could kill, Dutch would need an undertaker. "You have a lot of nerve! I'll have you know I'm not fat."

He had the gall to laugh. "I never said you were. In fact, I think you're pretty close to perfect—in the weight category, that is. In the realm of sanity, though, the jury's still out."

"*Do* you want to know what else I found out?"

He nodded.

"Then just zip your lips and let me tell you. I went into the pantry, and those shelves were packed. I couldn't see the walls because of all the food and kitchen equipment they've stashed in there. I had to shuffle stuff around to get to the wall with my tape measure, and that's when I hit pay dirt."

"Are you going to make me beg for the info?"

"Maybe I should, after all the grief you've put me through."

"I didn't make you beg when you were poisoned—"

"Fine, fine. You win. I won't make you beg. The Marshalls could open a pharmacy with all the drugs they keep in that kitchen. They specialize in narcotics. Legal ones—if prescribed by a physician, that is. And . . ."

For drama I mouthed a fake drumroll.

Dutch shot daggers at me.

I thought better of more teasing. In any case, it wasn't a laughing matter, no matter how much humor helped me get through the tough stuff.

"They have a pretty big container of RU-486. That's the morning-after pill."

I doubt he would've looked any worse if I'd thwacked him between the brows with a two-by-four. I let a minute or two go by before I continued.

"Now, according to the autopsy, KC delivered a child.

I suspect that means the ME found her uterus distended enough to have carried an infant fairly far along."

"Where are you going with that?"

"Only to say the morning-after pill played no part in KC's death." He went to speak, but I held up a hand to stop him. "Hear me out. The morning-after pill wasn't part of KC's murder, but I have to wonder why a plastic surgeon would have that particular drug in his home."

"Why would you think it's his?"

"He's a doctor. He can get his hands on all kinds of drugs."

"Yeah, but an abortion pill? A plastic surgeon?" He shook his head. "*You* stick with *me* here, okay?"

I nodded.

"Wouldn't it make more sense for Deedee to be the owner of the medicine? I heard back when the FDA was going over all the tests and trials to decide whether to approve it or not that women in Europe get the stuff ahead of time. They want to have it on hand for possible 'accidents' rather than lose time after the fact with the need for a doctor's prescription."

"But why would Deedee want to kill KC?"

"Why would Stewart Marshall want to kill her—and the baby?"

"Okay. But even if one of them fed her the morning-after pill, it didn't work, did it? The baby grew. So what I'm trying to say is that the scenario doesn't make sense—"

"*You* think it doesn't make sense? How do you think I

feel? I'm the one Lila's trying to pin the whole thing on. The pregnancy, the murder, and who knows what else she'll try to get me for. Maybe global warming or the hole in the ozone layer."

"Don't get sarcastic on me—"

The ring of the phone cut me off. I grabbed the receiver and answered.

"Is this Haley Farrell?" a woman asked.

The voice wasn't familiar. "Yes . . . who is this?"

"My name . . . I'm Alicia Daniels. I'm Tedd's client. She called a while ago and said I should speak with you. She insisted it was very, very important."

My heart ached at the tremor in her voice. I had a good idea how hard this was.

I responded in a gentle voice. "I'm so glad you decided to call. I believe there've been at least two deaths, and an innocent man might wind up in jail instead of the one who did commit the crimes."

"That's pretty much what Tedd said, and believe me, if she hadn't insisted it's a matter of life and death, I would never have called you."

Thank you, Lord. "I'm glad you did. And please understand—I do appreciate how difficult this is for you. I'll keep whatever you say in confidence—"

"I know you'll try to be discreet, but if this leads where I think it's going, then I have to be the one to call the cops."

I sighed in relief. "What can you tell me?"

Alicia's voice gained strength as she spoke. "A couple of

years ago, I had a stupid relationship with a married man, a Seattle politician, and I wound up pregnant. I was dumb enough to think he'd divorce his rich wife and then marry me for true love."

The bitterness in her voice stung. I didn't comment.

She went on. "Instead of a divorce lawyer, he called a friend who'd do us a favor, 'take care' of our little problem. Then he gave me a check for twenty-five thousand dollars, as if my feelings would disappear in the face of money. Of course, the procedure was on the house."

"And . . . ?"

"And I had the abortion. I wasn't more than three months into the pregnancy, but I learned this so-called doctor specializes in late-term abortions. Makes a ton of money that way too."

I felt sick; my stomach churned and my head pounded. "They say crime pays . . ."

"It sure does for him. My procedure was a cheapy. If he'd charged for it, it would have only been a couple hundred dollars. And had I suspected conception immediately after the critical time . . . well, *right* after the fact, then he would've been happy to provide me with enough morning-after pills to get rid of the 'problem.'"

I fell back onto the rocker. Dutch came to my side, took hold of my icy free hand. Worry colored his gaze a couple of shades darker than normal.

To my surprise, that warm clasp gave me a whole lot of comfort. It also helped me get my next words out.

"But you say he specializes in late-term abortions."

"Yes. The rich society families in Seattle take their way-ward daughters to him when they need to take care of the consequences of their indiscretions. And even though it doesn't matter here, I want you to know that I've regretted my decision every single day. I did kill my child."

I couldn't take any more. "Alicia, I think you'd better call homicide detective Lila Tsu at the Wilmont PD. This is what I thought I'd hear, and she needs to know."

Tedd's client took a long, shaky breath. "I never thought counseling for postabortion trauma syndrome would re-quire a call to the cops." She scoffed. "What am I saying? I didn't even think of consequences when I started that affair. But I've learned my lesson. What was that old law in school? For every action there is an equal but opposite reaction."

"Amazing how true all that schoolwork turns out to be sooner or later."

She asked if I wanted the doctor's name.

"From what you've said, I have a pretty good idea who the doctor is, but go ahead. I have to be sure."

She told me.

I was right.

After a few more words, we exchanged good-byes. I hung up and set the phone down on the coffee table. I turned to Dutch. "Your patience is awesome. I would've been jumping all over you, trying to yank the phone away."

He winked. "That's the difference between us, Haley. I'm

mature, and you're . . ." He gave a helpless wave. "You're not."

"If that's the way you want to be about it, then I'll just go on upstairs and take a nap. You can wait until your friend Lila and her giant Smurfs come and fit you for your shiny new bracelets—"

"Forget it. The look on your face as you talked with whoever that was on the phone is the first thing that's given me hope since the day KC died."

I reached out and touched his forearm. "All kidding aside, Dutch. You have good reason to hope. I'm sure you've figured out that I just spoke with a woman who went to Stewart Marshall for an abortion. Hers was a first-trimester one, but it seems he has a corner on the local late-term market."

Instead of the relief I expected to see on his handsome face, Dutch's rugged good looks took on a ruddy undertone. His eyes narrowed.

He stood, clenched fists at his sides. "I wonder if Ron and Lori know their good friend killed not just their unwanted grandchild but their darling daughter too?"

I stood and met his gaze. "Good question. One we need answered. Have you had your talk with the Richardsons?"

He turned away. "No. I . . . well, I just put it off and put it off because I really don't want to come face-to-face with Ron again."

"But you know you have to. Especially now."

"Especially now." He looked over his shoulder. His dark eyes pleaded. "Will you come with me? Please?"

"I thought you'd never ask."

Dad and Madeleine Ogleby walked in the door as we were on our way out. Both were beaming.

"Haley, dear." Dad's voice was jolly. "Come and give us a hug. We're celebrating today."

I gave him a wary look. "What's so special about today?"

He opened his arms, and I took my time to walk into his hug.

"Today," he said, "this wonderful, beautiful woman has agreed to become my wife."

I backed up. "Huh?"

Oh yeah. I tend toward high eloquence when stunned.

Madeleine reached out and took my hand. "Your father, Haley, the nicest man I've met in years, has asked me to marry him. Of course, I agreed."

I shot wild looks at everyone in the room. Dad and Madeleine looked like matching nodder dolls. And Dutch? Well, when I snagged Dutch's gaze, I saw him fight the urge to laugh. Then the big jerk began to sing. Seems he's figured out I'm a fan of old movies.

"Sisters," he warbled. "Sisters. There were never such devoted sisters."

Evil.

Wicked.

Foul and fiendish.

That's what Dutch Merrill really is. To think he'd take such grisly glee in the face of my distress.

Sure, I was distressed. I was also stunned, stupefied, stressed—take your pick. Because if Dad went ahead and married Madeleine, then yes, Deedee would become my stepsister.

How much worse could things get?

17

I suspect Dutch shot question after question at me on the drive to the Richardsons to try to take my mind off Dad's impending nuptials. Mind you, I have nothing against my father finding happiness again. It's just that he hasn't known Madeleine all that long. And there's that minor matter of her pink-obsessed daughter.

"Earth to Haley!"

"Hey! Give me a break here, will ya?" I blew a tangle of wild curls off my forehead. "After all, it's my dad who's gone bonkers on me."

"I don't think an engagement is a sign of going bonkers."

I didn't like the hint of laughter in his voice.

He went on. "It's Deedee that's bugging you, isn't it?"

"Yeah, okay. You're right. The thought of Barbie as a stepsister does give me the willies. I'd almost rather get Bali and Faux Bali, and you know how I feel about them."

Dutch chuckled. "Aw . . . she's not that bad, is she? You're always down on Bali H'ai. Poor kitty. And she's *so* sweet too."

I rolled my eyes. "And you're Bert and Ernie, Cookie Monster, Elmo, the Count, and Kermit in one."

He laughed louder.

"No, really. Give me a break here. It bugs me that Dad's asked Deedee's mother to marry him. Wouldn't it bother you too? I found KC at Deedee's home. Then her kitchen's stocked with more drugs than General Hospital. Plus, don't forget her husband's a baby killer. Would you get all giddy about future family members like them?"

Dutch sighed. "I hoped if I teased you enough you wouldn't make the connection right away."

"Yeah, right. How could I not?"

"Well, I tried. Anyway, even if the woman you spoke with does call Lila, and even if she does come through and testify against Stewart Marshall, without hard evidence to prove her allegations, it'll be a case of he said, she said all the way."

"You're leagues ahead of me." I'd been too busy bemoaning my family situation to think of the more horrific matters before us. "Sorry. I just zoned out. You have to admit, it was a shock."

"Sure was." He gave me a gentle look. "But what do you think? Where are we going to find evidence of those late-term abortions? I know you know that's what happened to KC."

"Of course I do. But don't forget the Coumadin. Without that her death would be maybe second-degree murder. The blood thinner makes it a whole other ball game. And even if we find a container of the stuff in his house somewhere, we still need a motive. You don't think he killed the girl just because he did her late-term abortion, do you?"

"No. If that were the case, then he'd have a trail of dead women behind him. There's got to be more than that here. Why would he want KC dead?"

I had no answer, so I kept silent. We were in his truck, a shaky, rackety exemplar of decrepit Detroit art, and while the vehicle was horrible, Dutch's driving was sure and safe. I chalked that up on Dutch's plus column.

"You know," I ventured. "I can think of one possible motive."

"What's that?"

"What if, like Alicia Daniels, KC expected more from the father?"

"Do you mean marriage?"

I shrugged. "More, Dutch, more than he was ready to give. And if he's the son of a prominent family . . . You know. Maybe he has a brilliant future as a rocket scientist or Einstein the second, or maybe he'll be the one to make Michael Jordan look like a dud on the court."

"I suppose a powerful parent can demand anything if he's willing to shell out enough dough. And Marshall likes money—or at least, what money can buy him. But how do you make the leap from abortion to murder?"

"I don't know—yet. But I do know the Coumadin's important. You can't forget the Coumadin."

After a while he slanted me a look. "I haven't forgotten the Coumadin, Haley. Yes, the autopsy found it, but we still need hard evidence to connect it to Stewart Marshall. We need evidence to prove he's in the abortion business and not just the nip-and-tuck market."

"We could contact more of his patients—victims, really."

"No way. The fact that Alicia is willing to come forward is almost a miracle. Women go to butchers like Marshall because they don't want anyone to know about their pregnancies. Remember, abortion's legal—"

"Only to a certain point in gestation."

"Which goes to prove my point. For whatever reason, they can't—or won't—go to a regular abortion clinic. You'll never get his average patient—victim—to talk."

The thought I fought so hard to keep in the back of my mind pushed its way forward. A bead of sweat formed on my forehead, my hands went ice cold, and bile filled my throat.

Lord Jesus, please don't make me go there.

The silence in the truck's cab lengthened. I shivered, my emotions again in an uproar. Dutch gave me time, time I didn't want. When he stopped for a red light, I had to smother the urge to jump out and run.

Where would I go? I didn't know. I just wanted to get away from all of this. I wanted to forget, to get beyond all that had happened to me, to get away from KC's murder and its implications.

But I couldn't escape.

This was reality.

"Where's the evidence?" Dutch asked again, his voice gentle.

"We . . . we need to find out where he . . . where he disposes . . ." *Oh, Lord, help me!* "We need to find out what he
does with the babies he . . . he kills."

Dutch's hand, warm, gentle, strong, landed on my knotted fingers. I looked at him with gratitude.

"I'm sorry," he said. "It's really ugly, isn't it? And it's my
fault you're in it this deep."

"Don't forget, I'm the one who walked out on that patio
and found KC."

He squeezed my hands. Almost without conscious thought,
I opened one and laced my fingers through his. "I'm in this
with you all the way."

"Thanks." His voice sounded husky.

I thought for the next couple of miles. "Since there's two
of us, we can concentrate on different things. Why don't I
check out the house and the dive shop while you take Dr.
Marshall's office?"

The *click-click* of the turn signal alerted me to our location.
We'd reached the Richardsons' very ritzy Seattle neighborhood. Dutch put on the brakes. We stopped outside a
sculptural, cedar-and-glass contemporary masterpiece.

"We're here." He took his key from the ignition, then
turned in his seat. "Will you promise me one thing?"

My "He's gonna make a sucker of you" alert went off.
"What's that?"

He leaned closer. "Promise you'll be careful. That you
won't try to take on Stewart Marshall on your own."

"What do you mean, promise to be careful? I'm always
careful—"

"I don't want to argue. I just want you to know how hard it hit me when I walked in last year and found you passed out on the floor, your body full of morphine. I don't want you hurt again."

His expression, the sincerity in his voice, touched me. I ditched the bravado. "Thanks, Dutch. I really mean it. For caring, and for what you did last year. And yes, I promise I'll be careful. I'll keep an eye out for Dr. Marshall, and I won't do anything stupid like try to catch him, not by myself. I'll call Lila the minute I even think something might come down."

My words did nothing to ease his troubled look.

"I know you mean that," he said, "but I just can't help it. I'm afraid something's going to go wrong, that you're going to wind up on the wrong end of whatever that might be."

"Then we'll have to trust God, won't we?"

"You think God'll come through? That he's going to keep an eye out for the two of us? Don't you think he might be a little busy these days? There are wars and floods and famines and earthquakes, you know."

"He sent you after me last year."

"And here I thought all along it was Bella who sent me to find you."

"He used Bella and you to keep me alive. I have to believe he had a reason not to take me home then, and I have to believe he'll see me through this time. You too."

He sat for a moment, silent. Then he smiled. "Let's get back to this God talk later on. We have to get the show on the road."

"Before you chicken out, right?"

"Something like that."

"Hey, I'm here to hold your hand . . . or something like that."

We got out of the truck. I walked around to the sidewalk and took hold of his outstretched hand.

"Partners?" he asked.

"Partners."

We walked to the glass front door, hands tightly clasped.

The brunette who opened the door burst into tears. "Oh, Dutch . . ."

Her face was blotchy, her eyes bloodshot, her nose red. She held a crumpled tissue in one hand and reached out for Dutch with the other.

Lori Richardson was gorgeous, even now, ravaged by grief. Dutch untangled himself from the embrace, said hello, then reached back for my hand. I avoided his touch but stepped up to stand at his side.

"Lori," he said, "this is—"

"What are *you* doing here?" The six-foot-plus, burly man looked as torn up as Lori. I assumed he was Dutch's former partner, Ron. "Come to gloat?"

The compassion on Dutch's face stole my breath.

He reached out a hand. "Not at all, Ron."

Ron looked at it as if it were a snake.

Dutch didn't back down. "I came because I know you're devastated. Didn't need to see you guys to know it. And . . . and I really want to put the past behind us. When something like this happens, it makes everything else look stupid."

Ron still wasn't buying. Contempt twisted his features. "I don't need your pity."

"Ron!" Lori cried. "He came in peace—"

"Sure he did. He's just trying to save his—"

Lori's warning look cut off her husband's words.

He shrugged. "He's trying to save his sorry hide, all right? Don't you read the papers, Lori? Didn't you hear that Detective Tsu woman on TV? She said she had a suspect, and the newscast was all about him after that. This . . . this scum is the one who killed KC. Revenge is his game."

Dutch took a step toward the enraged man. "I'm sorry you feel that way. I haven't seen KC since you and I argued some time after her baptism. And I never tried to get revenge. Yeah, I was angry, have been for years. But that doesn't mean I'd do anything to hurt you. Or her."

The red in Ron's face darkened. "Get out—"

"Listen to me," Dutch said. "Please. Give me a minute of your time. That's all I ask. When I'm done, you can kick me out. But please. Give me a chance to talk."

Ron's struggle showed. Finally he seemed to surrender. His shoulders sagged, and he looked about thirty years older. "Go ahead. But make it quick. The ME's going to release KC's . . ." His voice broke. "He's done his thing, and we have an appointment with an undertaker."

Tears filled the man's eyes.

Lori sobbed.

I slanted a glance at Dutch. He looked haggard; grief etched deep lines on his face.

"Look, Ron," he said. "When did I ever go behind your back for anything? You know I never made a secret of how I felt. That's how I've always operated—still do. I lay my cards on the table, and everyone knows where I stand."

Ron didn't respond.

Dutch pressed on. "I wouldn't hurt anyone, not intentionally. And much, much less your daughter. No matter how mad I was at you—and I don't deny my rage—it never crossed my mind to lash out at you. Not at you, not at Lori, and never, *never* at little KC. One of my greatest regrets over the years is that I didn't get to know her."

The rough quality of his voice brought me to tears. I looked over and saw the dampness in his eyes. There was something so real, so open about his revelation.

I was glad I'd agreed to help. Dutch is a good man.

"I believe you," Lori said. "I never thought the detective's suspicions were right. Or Ron's."

Her husband shot her a glare. "Yeah, seems you're still stuck on him, even after all these years."

"That's not true, Ron." I admired Lori's composure in the face of the accusation. "I love you. I married you because I loved you then, and I still love you now. But that doesn't mean I don't sometimes want to grab you by the ears and shake you. This is one of those times, pal."

Dutch chuckled without humor. "Give me a break, Ron. Every step of the way, you came out on top. Did I ever come at you because Lori chose you over me?"

Ron didn't reply.

"I didn't. I even agreed to stand up for you at the wedding."

"You did?" I asked before I could stop myself. "Wow! You're nigh unto angelic for that one."

Lori smiled through her tears. "Let's not get carried away here. These two are too obstinate for anything like that."

I could come to like this woman. "Oh, I've bumped my head against that wall a couple of times."

"Dutch never got to the introductions," Lori added. "But let me tell you. I never thought I'd see the day I'd meet the woman willing to take on this ornery beast. How long have you two been married?"

"Oh no!" A blush sizzled all the way to my hairline. "We're not . . . we're . . ."

What were we? I turned to him for help but found him frozen in place, his gaze glued to me, his jaw gaping wide.

I was on my own for this one. Better to start at the beginning. I held out a hand. "Haley Farrell. I'm an interior designer, and I've worked with Dutch before. Deedee and Stewart Marshall hired the two of us for the remodel and redesign of their home. I was the one who . . . who found your daughter that day."

Lori's tears resumed, as did her soft sobs, but she also took my hand in both of hers. She didn't speak; she couldn't, but she patted my fingers in a sad, distracted way.

"Haley's agreed to help me clear my name," Dutch finally said. "She's been where I am. She's Marge Norwalk's heir."

Husband and wife traded glances; then Lori cleared her throat. "I remember the story in the papers last year. You're the one who cracked that case, aren't you?"

I nodded. "And Dutch pulled a white-knight rescue. I was on the floor, dying from an overdose of morphine—not self-inflicted, you understand. If he hadn't charged in when he did, a killer would've gotten off scot-free. And I'd be dead. I owe him, and I especially want to help since I know he didn't kill your daughter."

At my words, Lori underwent a transformation. She stood tall, took a deep breath, and stepped to the side.

"This is ridiculous," she said. "Come on in to the living room. We need to talk. And, Ron." She glared at her husband. "It's way past time you and Dutch buried the hatchet. You've come a long way from the man you were fourteen years ago. Besides, neither one of you is blameless in the falling-out, so give it up."

With a shrug, Ron led the way to the soaring living space. A full wall of stone housed a huge fireplace. Floor-to-ceiling sheets of glass made up the far length of the room and offered a fabulous view of Lake Washington. Hardwood floors gleamed underfoot. Crossbeams held up the matching ceiling. We sat on leather furniture that felt softer than whipped cream. I wished I'd been the one to design the gorgeous space.

Then we got down to business.

I shared what I'd learned. I had no qualms about talking. Now that I'd met them, I had no doubt KC's parents had played no part in her death. Not that I'd seriously entertained the possibility. It was clear they hadn't known about the pregnancy, and they said so over and over again.

At first they seemed reluctant to give my suspicions much credit. But as Dutch and I filled in the blanks with all we'd learned, anger and determination replaced their consuming grief.

By the time we stood to leave, Dutch and Ron had made great strides.

At the door Ron gave a loud "Ahem."

Dutch met his former partner's gaze.

"I . . . ah . . ." Ron took a deep breath, then seemed to gain the strength to go on. "Over the years I've refused to admit what I knew even back then. In my hunt for success, I made many terrible choices and associated with people I knew I shouldn't. Then later I heard rumors about Stew, but I chose to ignore them. I even sent my wife and daughter to him when they needed minor medical care, and now I have to live with the consequences of my hunger for money, position, power."

Dutch remained rigid, his eyes riveted to Ron.

In an abrupt gesture, Ron shoved his hand toward Dutch. "I'm sorry, man. You were right and I was wrong. I took the shady road, cursed you, hit you with everything the legal system allowed, but I lost in the end. All this—" he gestured at the house "—isn't worth a thing in the end. You were right."

Dutch took the extended hand. "We all lost. Especially KC."

The big man sobbed. "And that's what I'll live with for the rest of my life."

Dutch pulled on Ron's hand and gave him a brusque hug. Ron's sobs echoed through the house.

I wept for the dead girl, for the family torn to shreds, for the grief that sin had brought down on them. In the midst of the grief, as if a small voice had spoken, I realized that some good would come out of the evil we'd seen. Shared grief had thrown a blanket over years of hate. Two men would no longer live with an old rage that ate at them.

"We'll get him," I said, my voice soft but certain.

"Let me know what I can do," Lori said.

The men pulled apart, their hands still locked together.

"I'll call every day," Dutch said, his voice raw with emotion. "I'll let you know anything that happens as soon as it comes down."

Ron nodded. "I can't just sit still here, you know. I'm going to look into everything he's done for the last . . . I don't know, twenty years at least. We are going to get him."

Dutch opened the door, turned, and looked at Ron. "Thanks."

Tears again welled in KC's father's eyes. "No. I'm the one who owes you the thanks. I hope you can someday forgive me. I harmed you, not the other way around."

"I forgive you, Ron. I'm just glad we can put the past behind us. Let's look to the future, to getting Marshall. After that we'll have all the time in the world to talk."

We walked to the truck in silence. Once inside the cabin, I reached out and touched Dutch's cheek. "You're all right."

"What took you so long to figure it out?"

I blushed. "I've been known to be single-minded to the point of—"

"Does blindness come to mind?"

"Watch it! You're about to blow your spiffy new good-guy image."

His laugh came out in a big burst, as if a dam had broken and the water rushed out to find its level. I supposed that was how he felt. Years of pain and anger had been set aside by a shared tragedy.

Too bad it had taken a girl's death to reach that point.

After a bit he said, "Nah. You know me better than that. You know who I really am. C'mon. We've got work to do. There's at least one last thing KC's godfather can do for her. Let's go make sure Stewart Marshall doesn't get away with murder."

18

The weekend had to be the weirdest ever. My first scuba lesson was scheduled for Monday morning, and I still wasn't all that psyched to go play underwater with Tom as my only protection against a watery end. True, I can swim, but that business of playing under the sea in an octopus's garden made my stomach wriggle. One would think I'd swallowed an honest-to-goodness yellow submarine.

To distract myself I worked on the design board for the Marshall job.

Now, there was an exercise in futility. On the one hand, I did my best to come up with a stunning look—in spite of the pink—for that gorgeous old home. I always aim for my best. On the other hand, I was just as determined to come up with enough evidence to put my client behind bars.

The *Twilight Zone* theme song followed me wherever I went.

But always, in the back of my mind, sadness lurked. Three deaths. Three children gone: my own miscarried child . . . KC Richardson . . . her baby as well.

Then on Sunday, at the end of the worship service, Dad asked the congregation to give him the luxury of a few minutes to share his good fortune.

He beamed from the pulpit. "I'd like all of you to know that a new member of our church, Madeleine Ogleby, has done me a great honor and has agreed to become my wife."

The scoffs, snorts, and gasps of the faithful could have propelled the church building to Mars and back again. Dad didn't seem to notice. Instead, he gestured for Madeleine, my future stepmother, to join him at the pulpit.

"Since neither one of us is especially young, we aren't planning on a long engagement. Please join us on the third Saturday in July for our wedding."

Boy, was the gossip gonna buzz! I didn't even make it to the church door; members of the missionary society ambushed me right at the end of my pew. Ina Appleton looked curious. Penny Harham disapproved. The others landed somewhere in between. Needless to say, Bella took the lead.

"How come you kept such a major secret from me, Haley girl? I thought we were friends."

Oh brother. "We are. I've just been very, very busy."

"Bogus! It doesn't take but a minute to give me a call."

The ladies chimed in with support for Bella.

My hands went up in surrender. "All right. Okay. You guys win. I blew it."

Bella donned a satisfied smirk.

I continued. "Except that I did nothing wrong. The news wasn't exactly mine to share, was it? I think it's up to Dad to tell people about his engagement, don't you think? Isn't that what you would want if you were in his and Madeleine's place?"

No one argued further, not even Bella.

She blushed, then slunk away.

I grinned and headed home, where the nightmare in pink glowed at me from my design board. As much as the challenge exerted a powerful lure, my disgust for and my anger toward Stewart Marshall repelled just as much.

Dutch's phone call distracted me for a while. I took the opportunity to ask a question that had teased my thoughts for a while.

"Exactly how old are you?"

"Does my age matter?"

"I'm just curious. I understand you went to school with Ron and Lori, and they're old enough to have had a teenage daughter. Were you some kind of prodigy?"

He laughed. "I guess I look young for my age. Remember, Lori was an 'older woman.' Ron was older too, and they married before they finished college, right after they met my freshman year. KC came along nine months later. Oh, and for the record, I just turned thirty-one."

"Whoa! Six years older than I am." He sure didn't look it. "You're nothing but an old geezer, then. Gotta watch out for you."

"I seem to remember remarking on the matter of maturity a time or two . . ."

Before he had the chance to remind me of my various awkward moments, I switched the subject. I asked again if he'd thought of anything, remembered anything that might help, but he hadn't. Since he had nothing new to report, we soon said good-bye.

The day dragged on until I finally caved in to Midas's demands. We went to the park with his Frisbee in the late afternoon.

Dinner was a quick meal of zapped leftovers with a tossed salad on the side. Then I went to bed.

I dreamt of Captain Ahab and Moby Dick.

I dreamt of Jonah and his whale.

I dreamt of Jaws.

Even Flipper the dolphin and Jules Verne's Captain Nemo cavorted in my dreams. Things went downhill from there.

By the time the sun crawled up the eastern horizon, I'd revisited every movie, TV show, or book that dealt with an underwater creature. It didn't bode well for my scuba diving gig.

Regardless, I showed up at the shop. Tom caught me off guard when he met me with a snorkel in hand.

I pointed. "What's that for? Are you confused or something? I signed up for scuba lessons, not snorkeling."

"I thought you'd bought some how-to books. Didn't you take a look at them?"

"Ah . . . umm . . . I've been kinda busy these days. What did I miss?"

"Everyone starts out snorkeling. I'll teach you how to clear your mask and how to swim on the surface and breathe through the snorkel. Then I'll have you hold your breath and dive deeper in the pool."

"Oh. You mean I don't have to mess with the hoses and stuff?"

"Not for a while."

"Phew!"

He laughed. "Aw, you'll do fine. Trust me. You're going to love diving. Everybody does."

I responded with a wry grin. "Even those who were dared into signing up for lessons—"

"Yoo-hoo!" a familiar voice called out.

I shut my eyes tight.

I shook my head.

I wailed, "No . . ."

But nothing changed. I opened my eyes to see Bella march up to us, excitement smeared all over her round, pretty face, her rotund body sausaged into an orange one-piece swimsuit that didn't go well with her Southwestern Turquoise hair.

"Can you believe my luck, Haley girl? I got a chance to sign up for lessons with you. You and I are gonna have so much fun."

Fun wasn't exactly what I would have called it right then.

But I would have been wrong. To my surprise, I enjoyed every minute of the class. And the next one. And the one after that. And I couldn't wait for the day when I got to go on my first real dive.

When I wasn't paddling around in the dive shop's pool or handling the details of Norwalk & Farrell's Auctions' large sale of Pennsylvania antiques, I paid the Marshall home multiple visits. I tried every conceivable trick to try to sneak into the various nooks, crannies, and corners all over the place. But no dice. Deedee wasn't about to let me go snoop. Not after the pantry fiasco.

On the other hand, there was nothing she could do to keep me from nosing around the yard, which I did to my heart's content.

But I came up with nothing—nada, zip, zilch. I found no fresh digs, no unexplainable mounds, no unusual trash containers. In other words, I came up with no evidence at the Marshall estate to show how the doctor disposed of his tiny victims' corpses.

Dutch had the same kind of luck.

We touched base on the phone almost every day and met at Starbucks to commiserate more than once. The only thing that gave us hope was that Lila hadn't come back to hound him.

Yet.

Deedee and Stewart approved my designs. They signed off on the funds Dutch needed to start demolition. They signed checks for furniture, fabrics, rugs, paints, artwork, and tchotchkes. I was going to have to go through with my pink, pink, pink design after all.

Then, early the day before I was scheduled to go for my first saltwater dive off the end of the Wilmont pier, I got a call from Lori Richardson. She wanted to meet me for lunch at a downtown Seattle café. The invite nearly shocked my socks off.

She said she'd done little but think about our visit and

had remembered something she'd heard a while back. When I pressed her for details, she insisted we needed to meet, that what she had to tell me was odd, that she wasn't sure how important it might be, but should really be shared in person.

"Dutch must've told you about me," I muttered.

"I haven't talked to him since the day you two came over. He's called Ron a couple of times, but that's it. Why would you think he'd talked to me about you?"

Great. I'd set myself up for it. "Because he thinks I'm too curious, and this would fit his idea of torture for me."

Lori chuckled. "Torture, huh?"

"Chinese water torture wouldn't work as well."

"See you in an hour, then."

At the café we ordered soups and salads, iced tea, and decadent stuffed cannoli. We swapped light chatter, but when the waiter brought our food, I decided I'd been patient enough.

"What is it, Lori? What did you want to tell me?"

She sighed and put down the fork she'd picked up. "I don't know if it matters or not . . . You know that Ron urged me to go to Stew for some minor work I wanted done."

"Yes."

"And you know I took KC to see him for her skin." When I nodded, she continued. "Well, one time when we went to his office for follow-ups, we saw Deedee there—she's kind of hard to miss. This was before they were married, of course."

"Hmm . . . I thought he met her in Portland, that he went there to visit her. But you're saying that she came here? Was she a patient?"

"She was that day. He . . . um . . . did her breasts."

Chalk up another one for Bella. She'd called it right on Deedee's silicone assets.

"So Deedee wasn't really from Portland? Dr. Marshall didn't go visit her during their dating days?"

"I don't know a thing about Portland. She might have met him there and then come up here for surgery. Anything's possible."

"Okay. That could be."

"Anyway, she was there with another woman, a friend. They were talking—pretty loud too—and I couldn't avoid overhearing them. Deedee told her friend that she was going to marry him. I didn't know who the him was at that time. She also said she knew exactly how to make sure this one didn't get away."

Barbie doll Deedee? "Hmm . . ."

"Hmm indeed." Lori stirred her soup. "She also said she was sick and tried of living her dull old life. She was tired of wanting things and never having enough money to buy them. She was ready to trade in her life for a new one. She was ready to trade places with the kind of woman who always got what she wanted."

So much for admiring her inner strength. "Calculating, don't you think?"

"Devious. Then, just as KC and I were called to go to the examination room, I heard Deedee say she'd learned enough about him that she knew how to make him pop the question, and she'd soon be headed down a very swanky aisle."

I leaned forward and stared. "Do you mean . . . black-mail?"

"In hindsight that's what it sounds like to me."

"Oh boy." I flopped back into my chair. To think I'd come to like the woman. "She must have learned about his sideline."

"That's what Ron and I figure."

"Do you think she's been helping him?"

"I don't know. She doesn't strike me as the kind who's about to do a day's work. Not even for all the money in Stew's bank accounts. I'd say she's more likely to make sure he keeps his nose to the grindstone."

I nodded slowly. Boy, had I missed the mark on this one or what? "That might explain why she reacted like she did when I found the meds in the pantry."

"I'm sure she doesn't want his sideline exposed. I suspect it brings in even more than his outrageous prices for legit care."

My stomach grumbled, and I dug into my lunch. All the while my head churned the bits and pieces of information I'd gathered since the day KC died. Nothing seemed to want to gel into a solid picture. I knew I didn't have all the facts yet.

After my last scrumptious mouthful of crisp wafer and creamy filling, I pushed back from the table and stood. "I hate to use the old cliché, but I really do have to eat and run. I want to catch up with Dutch, tell him about Deedee, see if he's learned anything in the last couple of days."

"Let me know as soon as you have something solid."

"Of course. You and Ron will be the first to know."

To my surprise, Lori got up and hugged me.

"Thanks," she said, her voice husky.

"Don't thank me until I do something or come up with something helpful."

"I can thank you for caring. And for trying."

We said good-bye, and I ran to my car. I phoned Dutch. We agreed to meet for coffee later that evening. I went down to the auction house warehouse and pretended to work. But in reality I counted down the hours, minutes, and seconds, then drove to Starbucks, still unable to link together the information I'd gleaned.

When I told Dutch about my lunch with Lori, he smiled. "She's a great lady. I'm glad you like her."

"What's not to like?" Then I turned to the topic at hand. I told him about Deedee's surgery, about her conversation with her friend, about Lori's and my suspicion that Deedee had blackmailed Stewart Marshall into marriage.

He let out a long, low whistle. "So much for the ditzy naïve blonde. Are those two a pair or what?"

"But that still doesn't get us from point A to point B."

"No, but maybe we can find Deedee's friend. She might know what Deedee had on Stewart—obviously, the abortion mill. That would give us another witness who knows about it. And she wouldn't have anything to fear from testifying against him."

"Road trip!"

"Wanna go to Portland, do you?"

"Don't you?"

"Not particularly, but I've a feeling it won't matter what I want."

"You're right. And there's just one more thing to decide."

"What's that?"

"Your car or mine?"

"Since I don't own a car in the first place, then I think we'd better choose yours rather than my junky truck."

"You're on, Merrill."

"You're nuts, Farrell."

"Takes one to know one." I was itching to go. "So we're agreed. We go to Portland tomorrow after my first real dive."

"I hope you have some idea what you want to do down there. Don't forget. Portland's a pretty big place. I don't know how you figure you can drive in and pick Deedee's friend out of the thousands of women who live there."

"Got it covered." I puffed on the fingernails of my right hand, then buffed them on my T-shirt. "I'm going to hit up my soon to be stepmom for info on my future stepsister's old pals. I'll say something about a surprise house-warming party for Deedee, and that I'd need her friends to help me plan it."

The look he gave me came full of admiration. "A little devious, but I think it could work."

And it did. By 9:00 that night, I had the names and addresses of four of Deedee's closest friends. I even wrangled from Madeleine which one Deedee trusted most. Tomorrow Dutch and I would be on the hunt for one Jackie Jordan, my future stepsister's best friend.

Before we could shuffle off to Portland, I had the minor matter of my first saltwater dive to survive. Well, it wasn't all mine. Bella was coming too.

She'd surprised me by how quickly she'd picked up on diving and how much she was enjoying herself. I've always loved the loony woman, but my admiration for her enthusiasm grew by leaps and bounds with each class we took. I hoped I was a little like her when I got to be her age. Minus the monster cats, of course.

But I didn't dare tell her. I'd live to regret it, and soon.

At the dive shop, six or seven divers were preparing their gear. Some tested valves; others checked the seal on their masks; one strapped a mega-sized knife on his leg; two guys packed their collection bags. Into the bags went pry bars, other unfamiliar tools, and the lift bags they'd fill, balloonlike, from their regulators to get whatever loot they found up to the surface. I'd often wondered if all the stuff they took with them weighed them down, but it must not have, since they all hauled the mesh laundry bag look-alikes along every time they went on a dive.

I found Tom at the back of the store where the bottles had once reigned supreme. These days they lived under safer conditions in my warehouse.

"Are you ready?" he asked when he saw me.

"Aside from the butterflies in my stomach, I think so."

"You can't dive if you're not psyched about it." He waved toward the divers hanging around outside. "Just ask them."

The ring of the bell on the door kept me from responding.

"I'm sorry I'm late." Bella huffed and puffed toward us. "I . . . ah . . . had a minor problem with . . . um . . . my housemates."

"Housemates?" I howled. "Hah! Those maniac cats aren't housemates. They're a nightmare. What'd they do this time?"

Bella averted her blue eyes. "Oh, it's not important. Let's go diving."

Sooner or later I'd get out of her what Bali and Faux Bali's latest mischief had been. Right now I had to agree with her. "Let's go diving."

Although Bella and I would only go off the pier, the experienced divers planned to start at the same spot. Then they'd wind their way along a natural ridge. It started a few yards from the end of the dock and followed the coast to the south. I noticed Stewart Marshall among the others. Just the sight of him made my stomach hinky.

I turned my back to him. "Let's get this show on the road." *Before my stomach has a chance to embarrass me.*

The dive went great. I had to give Tedd credit for pushing me. I'd fallen in love with the sport, and I had her to thank. There was something so peaceful about going underwater. No sound penetrated the depths but that of your own breathing and the buzz of the occasional powerboat going by. The sun glowed down in sparkly silver ribbons that wove throughout the greater swirl of blue, and I wished I could mimic that iridescence in a paint technique.

I moved my arms and legs in a slow rhythm, so different from the rush I normally experienced up top, and noticed that the dance of the seaweed had a grace all its own. I couldn't wait until Tom determined I was ready for the real thing, until he gave me the go-ahead for a dive where I could see more of the ocean, where schools of fish would swim around me, where I could explore this new world I'd never known before.

During the time we were down, every now and then I noticed the movements of the other divers off at a distance. Just when Tom gestured for us to head for the surface, I saw a flash of green and black.

Bands of those colors had swirled across the legs of Dr. Marshall's wet suit.

I tried to see where he went, what he was doing, but the translucent water and the distance between us worked against me. All I could see was that he no longer swam with the others. He'd separated from the group, and unless I was mistaken, he was taking an underwater detour. Curiosity made me move toward him.

Tom was having none of that.

He grabbed my arm and yanked me back toward the pier. He made a rough upward gesture with his thumb, and his anger came through loud and clear in spite of the mask he wore. It wouldn't be pretty for me once we were topside again.

As soon as I surfaced, the chewing out began.

"What were you thinking?" he yelled. "You barely know how to breathe underwater, and you decide to go off on your own? Are you crazy? Or do you just have a death wish?"

Bella watched, her face white as bleached muslin.

"I'm sorry. I didn't mean to worry you guys. I just got so into the whole world underneath that I forgot to . . ."

What more could I say? Not that I wanted to follow a killer, that's for sure. So I chose to leave things as they were.

But Tom didn't want to do that. And I guess he was right.

"If you ever even think of doing anything that stupid again," he said, his teeth gritted, his face red, "you'll be banned from the school. You get it? I'll make sure you can't come back. What if I had to go chase after you, Haley? What about Bella? You think it would've been right for me to leave her there to make sure you didn't kill yourself? Just think of the risk I'd have to take with her safety."

I shuddered. "I'm sorry. I really am. And this is one major wake-up call. I'm not about to lose track of what I'm doing again. I'd never want anything to happen to Bella."

"Oh, Haley girl," she said. "I would've been fine. I was right by the dock. But you? Nuh-uh. You have to be more careful. Especially after I made sure Dutch saved you last year."

Tom narrowed his eyes. "Are you telling me she's in the habit of doing wacko things all the time?"

"I don't do wacko things—"

"Well . . ." Bella cut me off. "They're not really wacko, the things she does. But wacko things do happen to her all the time. More than to everyone else, as far as I know."

I raised my hands in surrender. "Okay, guys. I've done my mea culpa, and I'm not going to sit here and let you beat up on me any more. I've got someone waiting. So trust me. I'm really sorry I messed up. It won't happen again. But now I'm outta here."

Portland, Jackie Jordan, and the rest of Deedee's pals, ready or not, here I come.

19

By the time we made it into Portland, both Dutch and I were exhausted and talked out, and worse yet, he'd become a grouch. He even accused me of rampant grumpiness, but of course, he was wrong.

It was late, just the right time to catch a nurse on her way home after her shift. We parked ourselves outside Jackie Jordan's cute little Craftsman bungalow to wait for her to show up.

We waited. And waited.

It felt as though we sat there for days, weeks, decades. But it couldn't have been longer than thirty-five minutes at most. Then a snazzy little red car, some Asian import I didn't recognize, pulled into the driveway. A tall, willowy redhead in a mint green nurse's top and crisp white pants got out of the car, locked it, and headed for the bungalow's side door, key in hand.

"Jackie?" I called.

She spun, stuck a hand in her purse, withdrew a shiny canister, and took aim.

"Don't shoot!" The last thing I needed was a blast of mace. "We just have some questions for you. About a friend of yours."

"Get off my property before I call the cops."

Her other hand dove into her purse, and out came a cell phone. This woman was prepared; she meant business.

"No, really," I said. "Madeleine Ogleby gave us your name. She said you're Deedee's best friend."

"Madeleine who?"

Dutch and I exchanged looks. I pressed on. "You know. Deedee Marshall's mother. Deedee, the blonde who married the plastic surgeon in Wilmont, Washington."

Recognition dawned. "You mean Madeleine remarried—again?"

"Remarried *again*?" I didn't like where this was going. "I thought she was a recent widow. How many times has she been married?"

Jackie shrugged. "I don't know. I lost count back when we were in junior high. Maybe seven, eight times."

No wonder Madeleine had moved in on Dad so fast—she was a pro at that game. "So Ogleby's not Deedee's maiden name."

"That's not the name I know."

"So what is that name?"

Misgiving crossed her face. "How do I know you're okay? That you're not here to try to use me to hurt the Smiths? Deedee's my best friend, and her mom's been through a lot lately. I don't want to be part of any setback. How do I know you even really know them?"

Deedee and Madeleine Smith. It has that certain ring of slithery anonymity, doesn't it?

With a deep breath for courage, and Dutch's warm hand at my back, I went for broke. "I know you've been Deedee's friend for years. I know the two of you would switch off and spend every second night at each other's homes during the summer. I know you were her maid of honor four and a half months ago. And I know you went with her when she had her—"

I glanced at Dutch, then shrugged. Delicacy didn't matter. "You went with her to Seattle when she had breast surgery."

The can of mace went down. "You know a lot about Deedee and me. How about you tell me about you?"

I stuck to the truth, just not all of it. I told her Madeleine was about to marry Dad, that Deedee had hired me to re-design her new home, and that I'd talked to Madeleine about the possibility of throwing a surprise housewarming for Deedee.

"Of course, that's not something I would go ahead and do without your input—you *are* her best friend, aren't you? That's why I'm here."

Lingering doubt showed on Jackie's face. "You had to come all the way from Wilmont to Portland to plan a party? And then you had to wait for me in the dark? What are you, crazy?"

Dutch snickered.

I stomped on a gargantuan foot.

He yelped.

I grinned.

"No." I scrambled for some plausible explanation. "Ah . . . not really. . . ."

What good was my two-hundred-pound sidekick if he wasn't going to give me a hand? I turned to the ape and gave him a forced smile. "I . . . ah . . . *we* came to Portland—"

"On business," he finally said. Then he held out a hand. "Hi, Jackie. I'm Dutch Merrill. I'm the contractor on Deedee's remodel. Haley and I had to come to Portland for something for the Marshall job, and she couldn't wait to start on the party. I'm just a tag-along now."

Hmm . . . what a slick way to avoid a lie and still sound almost believable.

I turned to Jackie and rolled my eyes. "Yeah, he's like one of those evil cartoon shadows. You know. The ones that never do what the person does, but instead loom over the character and scare the pants off the little kids who watch the dumb show."

That at least got a smile. "Okay. So let's say you really do want to plan a party. Why didn't you just call me?"

"Ah . . . we were in the neighborhood." What can I say? It was late, we were—literally—in her neighborhood, and it was the best I could do besides cook up a lie. Lame. Really, really lame.

"Look, I had a long night. One of my patients developed unexpected complications. It was rough, and I'm dead on my feet. Why don't you just call me tomorrow, and we'll talk then?"

I traded looks with my accomplice. "Okay. We'll still be in town."

"How about we treat you to brunch?" He slathered on his up-to-now absent charm. "To make up for scaring you. We are sorry about that. And that'll give you and Haley plenty of time to talk."

We agreed on details of when and where, then drove off. We'd made reservations at a nearby motel before we left home, and I couldn't wait to hit first the shower and then a bed. We checked in. I waved good-night.

"See ya in the morning." I shuffled off to my room.

Dutch called out something in response, but by then I was too far gone. I found my room, dropped my bag, hurried to the shower, used their complimentary bath and shower jams and jellies, dried off, and collapsed onto the lumpy mattress and skinny pillows. I didn't care. The built-up exhaustion of weeks of stress finally hit me like the demolition of a brick fireplace wall.

Next thing I knew, sunlight arrowed between the panels of the blue and green striped curtains, and someone was determined to break down my door.

"Open up already!" Dutch yelled.

"Hang on! Why do you have to take out your aggressions on my door at the crack of dawn? We're not supposed to meet Jackie until 10:30, and it's only . . ." I glanced at the clock. "It's only 6:39."

I muttered a truckload of threats to his life and limbs while I scrabbled through my overnight bag for the clean clothes I'd packed. I hurried to the bathroom, gave my poor bladder much-needed relief, brushed my teeth, and yanked open the door.

"Morning." Sure, I growled. I'm not a morning person.

"Chirpy, aren't you, sunshine?" He waved a handful of papers and kicked the door shut. "Wait'll you get a load of these."

I yawned, certain he wouldn't go away until he'd punched every last detail on those papers into my foggy brain. "They look like plain old eight and a half by elevens. What's the big deal?"

"The big deal's that I took some time to surf the Net when I couldn't sleep last night. I Googled Deedee's name—her real name—and I hit the jackpot in a couple of old Oregon newspapers' archives. Take a look."

Thank goodness I'm a quick reader. There was page after page after page of newspaper stories about my future stepsister and stepmother, none of them particularly flattering either.

"They're con artists!" I cried. "They've been arrested more times than Mike Tyson. We've got to do something. That woman can't marry my dad."

His smirk reeked of smug. "See why I woke you up? Doesn't it feel good to know you and Lori were on the right path? Deedee's career of choice is fleecing unsuspecting males."

"But she never got one of her victims to marry her—unlike her mom, who's married just about everyone in pants."

"Ah-ah-ah," Dutch said, "what you mean is that she never found that good a sucker until now."

"Until she had the goods to really turn the screw." Then I remembered Dr. Marshall's concern for his new wife when we met at the dive shop. "There's always the outside chance that he married her for love—prodded on by the blackmail. As they say, there's a sucker born every minute. She could've mesmerized him into love, then closed the deal with the other."

"Too bad it's not the same on her part."

"Oh, I don't know, Dutch. I don't think she can separate the guy from the dough, so she might be in love too." Then I grimaced. "Oh, forget that. Neither one of them deserves pity. They deserve each other, and that's what they've got—for better or worse."

"Still wanna go to breakfast with Jackie?"

"Are you kidding? I want you back in Wilmont to do your he-man pounding thing on Lila's door. This may not be the proof we need, but it sure is enough to put her on the right path."

"Call Jackie and tell her something came up. Give her some excuse, and let's get out of here. We got what we came for."

In less than fifteen minutes, after a strange conversation with the sleepy and befuddled Jackie, we got in my Honda and headed for Wilmont, our hope renewed. That's when it hit me.

"Oh no." I dropped my face onto my hands. "No, no, no, no, no, no, *no!*"

Dutch slanted me a look. "What's wrong?"

"Oh, Dutch, this is really nasty. What on earth am I going to tell Dad?"

He winced. "'Hey, Dad. Your fiancée is as crooked as a shepherd's hook and nowhere near as nice,' won't exactly go over well, will it?"

"And he's so happy."

"I don't know what you can tell him," Dutch said. "But I'll be there with you, okay?"

I shook my head. "This is one of those times I'm going to have to suck it up and do the right thing by myself. But thanks anyway."

Sometimes being a grown-up really stinks.

Dad's steady gray gaze never strayed from mine. "I'm so disappointed in you, Haley. I never would have expected you to be so resentful. Madeleine isn't interested in replacing you. She and I just feel blessed to have found each other at this time of our lives. I wish you'd share our joy."

Tears of rage and frustration filled my eyes. "Dad! I'm not resentful. I'm not even jealous. I want nothing more than your happiness. But this woman's got some weird agenda. Just look at the stuff Dutch downloaded from the Portland papers. *Please.*"

"I admit I don't know much about that www stuff." Dad stood, anger in his jutted jaw, his narrowed eyes, and his flared nostrils. "But I do know enough to realize that you can concoct any kind of hoax if you piece together anything that's out there. I have faith in the woman I love."

That hurt. "And you have no faith in the daughter you've raised."

"That's not fair, Haley. I do have faith in you. I've believed in you, supported you, and prayed for you, even when you were your least lovable. I'd hoped you'd at least support my happiness in return."

"I do want your happiness." I stood. "And that's why I'm warning you. I don't want you to wind up like the last seven guys Madeleine lured to the altar. She divorced four and took them to the cleaners, and the other three are now six feet under in a couple of Portland cemeteries."

"That's enough." He reached for his reading glasses but didn't find them in his pocket. He patted his pants, looked over the counters, picked up the basket where I keep paper napkins, even lifted his plate—nothing.

I reached up and slipped them off his balding head. "Here you go. And just like you needed me to help you see where you had your glasses, you need me to help you see Madeleine's deception. I don't know why she'd want to marry you—other than that you're a wonderful man. After all, you're her first normal guy. The others all had major bucks in the bank."

"Have you thought she might have had a change of heart?"

"It's possible. But since her daughter's just launched her career into rich-guy fleecing, I doubt it. Who knows what those two women are up to."

"I've heard enough, Haley. And I hope you never bring it up again. I won't listen to you speak ill of the woman who'll soon become your stepmother." He turned and went to the back door. "I'll be in my office the rest of the day."

The knot in my throat didn't let me do more than nod. At least I'd tried. I hadn't gotten anywhere, but I'd tried. The best I could do now was trust God and follow through with what I knew I still had to do.

I flipped open my cell phone and called Dutch.

"Hey," I said. "It's me. It went down even worse than I expected, but I did my best."

"You ready, then?"

"Let's go get Lila."

"Be there in five."

Ten minutes later we walked into the Wilmont PD.

Homicide detective Lila Tsu wasn't alone in her office. To my dismay, my sixth-grade nemesis, Chris Thomas, sat sprawled in the wooden chair across from her desk.

Lila's look came full of curiosity "This is a surprise. Interesting company you're keeping these days, Haley."

"You take what you can get," I said. "And we don't have time to trade swipes with you right now." I glared at Chris. "And you'd better forget your stupid jokes. We have information about Deedee Marshall and her mother—"

"Among other things," Dutch said, clearly impatient. "I don't know where your investigation is right now, but we think you need to know what we've learned."

Chris had the decency to stand and give me the chair. Then he stepped outside and dragged in a couple of metal folding chairs for Dutch and him. Once everyone was seated, I began.

I told Lila and Chris everything I'd done and learned. When I mentioned the scuba lessons, Chris nearly swallowed his tongue—he was stunned, didn't think I had it in me. I gloated.

But not for long.

"So that's why I haven't seen you at the *dojo* lately," Karate Chop Cop commented.

"I only have so many hours in my day, and I felt I had to do this. But my sports interests aren't important here. What matters is that Stewart Marshall is also an avid diver just like KC was."

Dutch jumped in, clearly unhappy with the way I told the story. He spit out details, dates, times, places. He told about our visit to Ron and Lori Richardson's home. He even took it upon himself to tell the detective about the lunch conversation Lori and I had shared—the nerve of the man! That was my conversation, not his, to retell.

So I cut him off. "That's when I decided we needed to find out something, anything, about Deedee and Madeleine. Since Madeleine's now engaged to my dad, I asked her a couple of questions, and she didn't suspect a thing. We went down to Portland and met Deedee's best friend—she's nice. Aside from knowing that Madeleine's been married more times than Liz Taylor, I don't think she knows about Deedee and Madeleine's darker side."

Lila did a "Get on with it" kind of wave, and I did.

As I went on, Dutch handed over his printouts. Lila

scanned the pages, then raised her head and gave me her laser stare. "You've been busy, haven't you? Just as busy as we have. We know all this, so you didn't need to blunder into our investigation."

I met her gaze full on. "Since I know how forceful you can be, and since I also know how close you came to nailing me for a murder I didn't commit, I knew I had to help Dutch. He's not guilty, and I think by now you can see that Stewart Marshall's your man."

She gave a noncommittal shrug. "It doesn't look good for him. But I think you forgot a few details. Yes, he may have performed a late-term abortion on KC, but who paid for it? He's not likely to have done it out of the goodness of his heart, not from what you've told me or from what we know."

"Does that matter—"

"*And*," she added as if I hadn't said a word, "even if he did do it pro bono, you have to remember that KC didn't simply hemorrhage spontaneously. Where's the smoking gun, Haley? Where's the Coumadin?"

"He's a doctor, isn't he? I'm sure he can come up with the stuff from . . . oh, I don't know. Maybe one of his doctor pals slipped him some." I glared. "What? Do you want me to do all your work for you now?"

She stared back, her delicate features expressionless. "I'd rather you didn't do any of my work. But since I can't seem to stop you, short of jailing you, here's a final question. Why? Why would Stewart Marshall give KC a blood thinner? Why would he want to hurt her? What did he gain by killing her? Why do you think he's the killer?"

I fell back into my chair. I heard Dutch bring up the usual litany: Marshall had the opportunity, he could certainly get hold of the means, and one really doesn't have to prove motive for an arrest or an indictment, much less a conviction. Besides, maybe it was as simple as KC threatening to reveal his little business.

But in the back of my mind, the matter of the Coumadin remained. I thought back to Bella's and my time at the bowling alley. Wanda had given us a glimpse into her photographic memory. She'd recited a list of prescriptions for Deedee and Stewart Marshall, all three Richardsons, and Jackson Maurer and his parents and sisters.

Oh yeah. Wanda'd been busy all right. After Bella alerted her to our forthcoming grilling, Wanda had her model fingers tap out a dance of discovery on the keys of the pharmacy's computer. She hadn't come up with a hit.

"You know, Detective Tsu," I said. "You probably have enough to get a search warrant—a couple of them. One for the Marshall home and another for Dr. Marshall's office. I'm sure you can even get one for the dive shop, even though I haven't found a thing there. I would think that would have occurred to you without my help."

"Give her a break, will ya, Haley?" Chris said. "She knows what she's doing, and we do need probable cause. Yeah, we can get him on the abortion deal, but that's not what we really want. If he's guilty—" He held up a hand to stop my objection. "If he's guilty of murder, then that's the rap we want. We can't jump the gun. You're just going to have to trust us, be patient, and let us good ol' boy cop grunts dawdle along on our lazy, lousy investigation, y'hear?"

I blushed. "I'm sorry. I didn't mean to call you incompetent—"

"Really, now?" The detective's words dripped sarcasm. "Why would you think we haven't already thought this through? We've been looking into Marshall's sideline for a while now. But we can't prove a thing. Yes, the woman you referred to me will testify, but that's just her word against that of a respected member of our medical community. We need more. We need evidence."

Dutch cleared his throat. I looked at him.

I sighed. "Yes, we do. We need evidence—hard evidence. We need to find where he disposes of . . ."

"Yes, Haley," Lila said in a gentler tone. "We need to find those tiny corpses. And we haven't been able to do that. We have no idea what he's done with his tiniest victims."

The usual roiling started up in my gut, so I sat back and just thought. The dead babies . . . the Coumadin . . . no evidence at the home, at the office, or the dive shop . . .

God, I know I'm on the right track. But something's missing, or maybe I'm just not seeing things the way I should. Open up my eyes. Help me see what I've missed so far.

The other's voices swirled around me, but I didn't bother to listen. I focused on what was milling around in my head and tried to grab the kaleidoscopic images that danced and dodged each other just beyond my reach. And through it all the Coumadin wove in and out like a ribbon of darkness, a trail of blood.

Then, out of that gray muddle, a couple of phrases I hadn't thought about for a while leaped in vivid Technicolor to the front of my thoughts. "You want to know who KC's kid's dad is?" Jackson Maurer had said. "Then you'd better check out those crazy diver guys at the shop."

Images dazzled across my mental screen. Water. Tanks. The shop. The pier. Divers and books and masks and sun.

"That's it," I whispered.

I bolted to my feet.

Lila, Chris, and Dutch looked at me as if I'd suddenly taken flight. And in a way I had. At least my thoughts had. And I was sure they'd landed on the X—the right X, the one that marked the spot. In my heart of hearts, I knew what had happened. I knew who'd killed KC, why, and how.

Now all I had to do was prove it.

20

Lila, Chris, and Dutch were now sure I was certifiable. When a woman leaps up from a chair, babbles incoherently, then runs out, there's good reason to question her sanity. More often than not, little guys in white coats follow, fit her with the latest in straightjacket couture, then haul her back to the nearest hospital's psychiatric ward.

I raced to Tyler's *dojo*, which was only two blocks away from the PD. By the time I got there, my back was nearly black and blue from the beating it took under the pounding of my backpack purse.

I ignored the sore ache. I had more important things to think about, much worse injuries to worry about.

My *sensei* took one look at me and pointed straight to Asian World. I made a beeline to his office and then just waited for him to join me.

"I'm okay," I said by way of greeting. "Really, I am. I just need a moment to pull myself together. Then there's a bunch of things I have to do."

Tyler's dark brown eyes narrowed. "Do I need to call Tedd?"

"You can, but it's not about me right now. It's about the dead teen and her baby. I know what happened. And I have to figure out what I'm going to do next."

His muscles bulged when he crossed his arms. "You're going to call Lila Tsu right now, is what you're going to do next. You're not going to pull another kamikaze stunt like you did last year, sister. Not while I'm here to stop you."

"Of course I'm not." I waved dismissively. "I'm not going to do anything crazy. I just need some time to think, to clear my head. I'm not even sure how I know or how to make sense of it all."

"And you had to come to my office to think? What's wrong with home, Haley?"

I averted my gaze. "That's part of the problem, Ty. Dad's got himself engaged to a woman with a rotten past. She's even got a rap sheet, for goodness' sake. And her daughter's part of the problem. I need some peace and quiet. Don't worry. I won't do anything stupid."

He barked out a dry laugh. "Depends on what you call stupid."

"Look. I promise I won't do anything dangerous. I'll go home in a little while, make and eat dinner, take Midas for a walk, go to bed, take my scuba lesson tomorrow. I won't do anything out of the ordinary. And I promise I'll call to run any changes in my regular plans by you. Deal?"

He didn't look too sure. "Deal. Just don't leave until I'm done with my next class. I want to talk to you, see where your head is, before I send you home."

"Go. Your adoring fans await you. And you wouldn't be sending me home, *sensei*. I can come and go on my own."

"That's what's got me worried sick."

After he left I wrestled down my niggle of guilt. I hadn't

lied. I made no change in my plans. I just orchestrated a few side events that would support what I'd figured out.

First off I called Bella. "You wanted to help me investigate, didn't you?"

She was silent—in rapturous joy, I'm sure. Then, "Does Seattle stink of coffee?"

"Okay, Bella. Here's what you have to do. And it's really, really important. I have to know I can count on you."

Emotion filled her assurances. Although it took some doing, I got her to agree to back out of tomorrow's dive. It was easier for her to agree to latch on to Dad. All I had to do was tell her his safety, his very life, depended on her surveillance and protection.

True, I laid it on a bit thick, but if either of the shady Smith women got a whiff of what I was up to, Dad would be in danger. They'd use him to get to me. It was best to keep him at church, focused on whatever problem Bella brought him.

I can always count on Bella for trouble.

Then I called Tom to tell him Bella wouldn't join us, and I hit my first hitch. He was in bed with a stomach virus and wasn't able to do tomorrow's dive. I didn't have to fake dismay.

"Don't worry." His voice wobbled. "Ken Harris agreed to take my place. He's good. You'll like him."

It occurred to me as I hung up that a substitute instructor might be even better for my plans. All I had to do was sweet-talk him into letting me do my thing.

When I called Dutch, he was worried. "Are you sure you're okay?"

I dumped a landslide of assurances on him, none of which seemed to take. "I'm okay," I said for the thousandth time. "I'm at the *dojo* and am on my way home in about . . ." I checked my watch. "In about twelve minutes. Ty asked me to wait until he finished his class."

"You're going straight home then?" When I assured him that was the case, he added, "I'll pick you up. I don't want you out alone in the dark. Remember, I drove you to Lila's office. You're on foot if I don't come."

I would rather have walked, for the privacy, if not for the exercise, but he wasn't having any of that.

"Wait for me. I'll be there." His voice had that steely note.

In the end I was fine. I answered both Ty's and Dutch's questions truthfully. They weren't convinced, but that was their problem, as I told each of them. And finally I got home.

Dad had left a note. He and Madeleine would be out late. They'd gone to dinner and another art lecture. I ate a frozen dinner; fed, watered, and walked Midas; then holed up in my room. I made a couple more phone calls, confirmed some of my suspicions, turned to my Bible, prayed, and eventually slept.

To my surprise, I awoke rested and alert the next morning. I'd managed more sleep than I otherwise would have in a week. *Thank you, Jesus.*

Since I didn't want to give Dad a chance to lecture or question me, I grabbed two slices of bread, smeared them with peanut butter, and called it breakfast on my way to the dive shop.

There I found Max at the counter and a middle-aged man in a wet suit arguing the merits of various brands of valves.

"Hey, Haley," Max said. "This is Ken Harris. He's taking over Tom's lessons until he gets over his stomach bug."

"Hi, Ken. It's good to meet you."

Ken nodded, slapped the top of the counter, then said, "Let's go check our gear. I'm ready to roll." When he reached the door, he turned. "Oh, by the way. The other woman, Bella something—"

"Cahill."

"Yeah, that's it. Bella Cahill couldn't make it today, so it'll just be the two of us."

"That's too bad. She's always psyched to go down." I stepped out into the partly cloudy day. "So what do you have planned for today's dive?"

"Tom says you're ready to go out as far as the ridge."

My eyes nearly popped. It couldn't be that easy, could it? "You're serious?"

"As a judge. I still remember how it feels."

He might remember how it feels to finally head off to a true dive, but that wasn't the cause for my excitement. I was on a mission. My goal was the area along the ridge where Stewart Marshall and his little collection bag had disappeared the other day.

Ken and I did the usual check of our tanks, valves, regulators, and masks. Every diver is adamant about this one thing: safety is everything.

Finally we took off for the pier. Just as we reached the end, the sun broke through the splotchy cloud cover. I looked up and smiled. *Thank you, Father.*

As I went over the edge and into the water, I spotted a familiar figure. Great. Why was Dutch out here?

Well, it didn't matter anymore. I was underwater, and he couldn't just jump in and stop me. I put him out of my thoughts and turned my attention to my dive.

I followed Ken out from the end of the dock, so thankful that the sun had come out, even if only for a short while. The eerily beautiful landscape beneath the water beckoned; it lured me farther and farther into the depths.

The ridge itself was awesome. It looked just like something you'd see in a book about the bottom of the sea. Craggy rocks jutted in irregular angles. Lacy seaweed swayed in rhythmic waves. I flipped out when a silvery fish darted out from behind a bulky stone.

This was so cool. I owed Tedd big time for turning me on to diving. I could see why it had become a consuming passion for KC.

The thought of the dead teen stole a chunk of my enjoyment. I wasn't down here for nothing more than a walk in the park. This wasn't just a pleasure dive. I had a job to do.

As I followed my instructor, I realized why I'd known I had to check out what Stewart Marshall had been up to. The ridge itself was pocked with dark areas that might be nooks and crannies. If that's what they were, they'd make perfect hiding spots for whatever a guilty person might want to hide.

I signaled to Ken, indicated that I wanted to get closer to the rocks. He gestured for me to follow, and we approached the area. What I saw kicked my excitement up a notch.

Not only was the ridge dotted with dark little nooks, but it also sported a dark opening, one that really looked like a small cave with an entrance about four feet in diameter. I pointed at the spot, and Ken shook his head and pointed it the opposite direction.

I put my hands together and pleaded.

His head shakes grew more determined. He reached for my arm with one hand, while with the other he pointed away again.

But before he could stop me, I darted inside. He followed right at my heels, still shaking his head. Forceful jabs toward the opening of the narrow but deep cave made too clear his intention, but now that I'd reached my goal, I wasn't about to let him drag me back out until I was good and ready.

I had snooping to do.

As I swam farther into the darkness, I began to take deeper and deeper breaths. I tried to calm myself, knowing that my oxygen would go faster if I let my breathing continue at a more excited rate. I turned on my underwater light and nearly gasped out my regulator mouthpiece.

Lined up along the right side of the cave's wall, I counted dozens of lift bags held down with the lead weights divers use to help them stay at the bottom of the sea. My heart began to pound. I remembered Stewart Marshall swimming away from his fellow divers, collection bag at his side. I knew he'd had one of these lift bags among his more innocuous gear. I know I should open one to make sure it contained what I feared, but I also knew myself. I couldn't, just couldn't, handle that hideous sight.

I felt sick. I grew lightheaded. I struggled to breathe.

Another deep drag brought no relief to my lungs.

That's when I began to panic. I turned to look for Ken and saw him tugging at and checking his gear. I did the same. I pulled my air pressure gauge out from where I'd tucked it in my dive vest, and I saw it read full. I saw nothing strange—everything was hooked up as it should be and was working correctly.

But I still had to fight for the smallest breath. And unless I was very wrong, my instructor was having the same problem. Just then he stopped checking his gear and jerked a thumb toward the front of the cave.

This time he didn't have to ask me one more time.

We headed out, but I saw him struggle, slow his pace, and weaken his kicks. His expression through the mask was frantic. It seemed that as a larger person, his oxygen was running out even faster than mine. I reached out and checked his gauge, and then it hit me.

Both gauges read full. Completely full.

Neither registered the air we'd used so far.

Something was very, very wrong.

I grabbed Ken's arm. He fought me off, shook his head, pushed me out.

I grabbed again and began to pull. We would either both make it out of here, or neither of us would. I was not about to leave a living human in that cave. I wasn't about to give Stewart Marshall any more kills. Not if I could help it.

There was no coincidence here. Someone had tampered with our tanks. The only person who would want to harm me—and I knew I was the target rather than Ken—was the doctor whose filthy, murderous secret I'd uncovered.

As I'd been taught to do in case of emergency, I held my breath to conserve air. I tugged at Ken and dragged him out of the cave. When I could no longer stand it, I took another small breath. Then Ken went limp in my grasp.

No! He couldn't die. I wouldn't let him.

I kicked harder, aimed for the surface, fought against what was now a near dead weight. But I made no headway. I wasn't strong enough.

I had a decision to make.

If Ken was to have any chance at all, we would have to have help. And that wouldn't happen if I didn't make it up. I simply couldn't surface and drag him with me. And my air was dangerously low.

Praying for forgiveness, for the Lord's protection, for mercy for Ken, I let go and watched him sink the foot and a half to the bottom. I took the deepest breath I could, filled my lungs like balloons, and kicked up with all I had. Those few seconds were the longest of my life.

Hurry, hurry!

I urged my legs to kick harder and harder, felt the air in my lungs buoy me up . . . and then I finally broke through. I spit out my mouthpiece and sucked in clean, fresh, life-giving air.

Then I screamed with all I had.

"Help!"

"Hang on!" Dutch called back. "I'm almost there."

I saw him chug toward me in the dive shop's dinghy, its motor loud and rough. As I watched, Stingray and Max slipped over the little boat's side and under the water.

"Stay there," Dutch said. "They need you to mark where you and Ken were so they can find him."

"How . . . how'd you know . . ." I shivered so hard that I had to stop talking.

"Give me a minute, will ya?" He cut off the engine and paddled with the oar. I felt a tug at my flipper, looked down, and saw Max give me the thumbs up. All I saw of Stingray was the back of his heels as he swam down for Ken.

I started to cry.

"Here," Dutch said. "Grab on tight and let me pull you in."

A second later he hauled me up the side of the boat and into his arms. I collapsed against him and sobbed. "Thanks . . ."

"Hush. Don't try to talk."

I cried some more. "How did you . . . how did you know to come?"

"Give me some credit, okay? I knew you were up to something last night. So I followed you here this morning. I wasn't going to do anything unless I thought you were in trouble."

"But *how* did you know . . .?"

"I didn't. Stingray came in right after you and Ken took off. He began to check his gear, and saw that something wasn't right with the tank he planned to use. He said it felt light, even though the pressure gauge showed three thousand pounds of pressure."

"Ours read full too, but we ran out of air."

Dutch's big hand trembled when he cradled my head closer to his chest. "Well, when Stingray checked it out, the gauge was stuck. Not only that one but also all the other gauges on the dive shop's tanks."

Anger stirred in my gut. "I was right. No coincidence." I shuddered. "And it's no coincidence that I found a cave lined on one side with bags. I had to do the dive to make sure I wouldn't send the Smurfs on a wild goose chase, even though Ken did everything he could to stop me. We have to call Lila. I was right. She has to send someone to check out the bags."

"She should be here any second now. I called as soon as I knew what had happened with the tanks."

"Dude!" Max yelled. "Give us a hand here. Ken's still alive."

In a blur of activity, Dutch helped Max and Stingray get Ken into the dinghy. Dutch took over for Stingray, who'd shared his oxygen with Ken and was now giving him mouth-to-mouth while he and Max swam the unconscious man toward the boat.

"Start the engine," Max told me. "You just get this thing to the pier. We'll swim. And hurry!"

I'd never operated any kind of boat, but either divine inspiration or sheer, raw fear guided me. I got the dinghy back to the dock, where EMTs, Lila, and three of her giant Smurfs were waiting.

The EMTs took over Ken, while the detective and the Smurfs surrounded me. The questions began to fly.

I lost it. "Come on! We don't have time for this. You have to hurry. Don't waste time on me."

"What are you talking about?" Lila asked.

I yanked off my flippers and made for my Honda. "Dr. Marshall. You can't let him get away. The medics will take care of Ken, but go! Go find Stewart Marshall. He messed with our tanks, and I found his burial ground in a cave in the ridge. Hurry!"

Lila's heels tapped on the wooden dock right behind me. "You'd better know what you're talking about."

Over my right shoulder, I shot her a glare. "I do."

She called out to the Smurfs and gave them instructions. The three men took off, sirens fading in seconds. I stepped off the pier and onto the rocky beach terrain. My pace slowed considerably even though I felt as determined as ever. I had to get to my car. There were things I had to do; I had to make sure everything went down as it should.

Lila followed me, and even though she wobbled on the rocks when she reached my side, she held out a hand and we steadied each other as we limped over the rocks. I glanced back and saw the EMTs in action. Ken lay on the dock, an oxygen mask over his face. Dutch stood about five feet to the side, concern on his face.

"Is he . . . will he live?" I called out, tears in my eyes.

A woman with short brown hair looked up. "We're doing our best."

I nodded.

Lila put a hand on my shoulder. "Are you really okay?"

"Not yet, but I will be in a while."

"How does it feel to be right—again? Since the doctor's office is so close, my guys are probably there by now, and he'll soon be wearing handcuffs."

On my way to the car, I detoured toward the dive shop, where I'd left my belongings in a locker, but then I noticed Dutch's pickup in the parking lot. Rather than waste time going inside, digging through the locker, dressing, and all that other fluff, I yelled for Dutch.

"Hurry! I need your help."

He loped toward us, questions in his eyes.

I turned to Lila. "You and your Smurfs better have some extra pairs of those spiffy bracelets of yours."

She looked puzzled. "More handcuffs? What are you up to now, Haley?"

I saw that Dutch had slowed down to a walk. "Hey! Get a move on. We have more work to do yet."

Lila stepped into my path. "You're not going anywhere but home. This is in the hands of the police."

"Wanna spar for it?"

Her eyes narrowed. She remembered our infamous

match at Ty's *dojo* last year. She followed me to the parking lot.

I continued. "Because we're really not finished yet. Yeah, Stewart Marshall performed KC's abortion, a late-term one, since from what I can tell, she hid her pregnancy almost to the end, but he didn't kill her."

Dutch loped up. "What do you mean, he didn't kill her? Who killed KC?"

I stepped toward his truck. Lila again moved into my path.

Dutch grabbed my arm. "What's going on—"

"Haley Farrell, I'm going to put you under arrest if you—"

My shrill whistle cut them both off. I took my fingers out of my mouth. "Will you listen to me already? Yes, Stewart Marshall is a baby butcher, but he didn't kill KC. We have to hurry, or Deedee and Madeleine will get away."

"What?" Lila asked.

Dutch scratched his head. "How do you figure?"

"Remember Jackie? Remember she said Madeleine had been through a lot lately? That she didn't want any part in a setback? I called Jackie again last night to sort of talk about the party but really for info. Turns out Madeleine's a stroke survivor. And Bella's friend Wanda does have magic fingers. I called her too. Go check Madeleine's medicine chest. She's the one with the Coumadin. She hadn't transferred her prescription from Portland when Wanda first checked."

Understanding dawned on the detective's face. "I'm on my way."

Now we knew all the whos.

The only thing we still didn't know was why.

21

Dutch and I followed Lila, who wisely gave up any further attempt to discourage us. But to my dismay, we got caught behind a red traffic light.

"It's nice to know you're such a law-abiding citizen," I commented, tongue in cheek.

"Didn't I tell you I was innocent from the start?"

"I meant the traffic light, you goof. But with the other deal, didn't I help you? Didn't I risk my life for you?"

The light turned green. "Oh, right. Not only did you help me just like I helped you last year, remember? But now you feel you have to one-up me with the death-defying factor? Women!"

"Hey! That's a low blow. This has nothing to do with gender. Where's the thanks, pal? How 'bout some groveling?" I waggled my fingers in a gimme gesture. "Come on. I'm waiting."

He shot me an impish grin. "You know I'm grateful, and you're just being a pain. Thank you ever so much, Haley Farrell. Now that you've saved my sorry hide, it's all yours.

Don't forget that old saying, the one about being responsible for the life you save."

I rolled my eyes. "That's all I need. One ornery contractor. All my own. Thanks, but no thanks. You can have your sorry self back."

"Don't be so quick to turn down that generous offer. There are those who consider me quite a catch."

"Sure. Like catfish and carp are big catches too."

"Oh, you wound me so . . ."

I tipped up my chin. "I'm going to ignore you. I'm going to think of the future. I'm going to think of seeing the princess of pink in a fashionable orange jumpsuit."

He turned the corner to the Marshalls' street, and the twin brick columns appeared up ahead and to our right. He angled the nose of the truck to enter the Marshall estate.

Dutch treated me to a wicked smile. "The orange won't go with her complexion, you know—"

"Hey! Look at that."

A pink convertible approached the columns from behind a thicket of shrubs to the left of the gates. "Hurry!" I yelled. "Don't let her get away."

The pink car sped up; the landscaping bit the dust. Deedee leaned forward, a look of pure hate on her twisted features.

My gut clenched. "Dutch! She's not going to stop."

"Wanna make a bet?" He spun the steering wheel hard left, and the truck skidded sideways between the columns, blocking the opening. "Hang on tight, Haley. You were right. She's not going to stop."

He lunged over me. Deedee barreled her fancy foreign car into the side of the truck bed. The impact jarred me, even my back molars, but a second later I was able to open the door and jump out. Deedee had the same idea, but I was in far better condition than she was.

I tackled her.

She fell.

Dutch cheered.

From my vantage point on top of Deedee, I turned to see him give a victory *V*. "Face it, Farrell," he said. "We make one wicked good team."

And then it hit me. We really did.

What's worse, I liked him. And I was glad we'd succeeded.

I nodded slowly, not sure what it all meant. Especially for the future. "Oh yeah, Merrill, we're pure peanut butter and jelly on wheels."

As if on cue, Lila and her Smurfs came down from the house and clapped bracelets on the enraged Deedee. Lila told us that when she'd called the Smurfs on her way to the mansion, the blue crew had found the now-shackled Stewart Marshall at his office. And he'd conveniently packed a suitcase for his visit to the Jailhouse Ritz.

That first wave of Smurfs had asked Lila for backup after she told them to nab the Barbie-doll bride, and now that the criminal bride and groom were neatly tied up, the whole blue army was combing the vast property for every last shred of evidence they might find. It would probably take them the better part of the day . . . maybe even night.

Lila and Chris bundled Deedee into the detective's unmarked car and drove away.

Then it was just the two of us. Oh, and Dutch's totaled
truck.

I pointed to the demolished side. "What are you going
to do now?"

He shrugged. "It wasn't my smartest move, was it?"

"Especially now that you're unemployed."

"What can I say? Truth must prevail." I watched the slow
smile dawn. "Well, well, well . . ."

I was in trouble—even if I didn't know how.

When I didn't comment, his smile broadened. "Seems
this is my lucky day after all. Remember what I said about
saving my life and you owning it and all that? Well, whether
you like it or not, I'm all yours."

"I already told you to forget it, Merrill."

He laid a chummy arm over my shoulders. "And it just
so happens that you're loaded, Farrell. Since I saved your
hide too, and since in our joint pursuit of a crook, I did
my splendid vehicle sore harm, you can demonstrate your
largesse and replace old Barney here—"

"Not!"

"Hey, don't forget I helped you avoid that fate worse
than death that you so feared."

I frowned. "What fate was that?"

"Sisters . . . sisters . . . there were never such devoted
sisters—"

Sisters . . . mothers . . .

"Get in the truck! We have to go. Madeleine's out

there, and Dad's only protection is Bella and maybe her Balis."

I didn't have to repeat myself. Dutch leaped back into the driver's seat, tossed me his cell phone, and cranked up the engine. "Call Lila. See if anyone has Madeleine yet."

My call lasted less than ten seconds. No one had found Deedee's mommy dearest yet.

I turned to Dutch. "Hurry."

He slanted me a look that gave me no comfort. "Pray," he said.

I did.

I'd never been so thankful for Wilmont's tiny size. We reached the manse in less than seven and a half minutes. From the street nothing looked any different than when I'd left that morning. But I knew looks could be deceiving. Who would ever think women as lovely as Deedee and her Grace Kelly, princess of Monaco, look-alike mother were so vile? That Stewart Marshall's gentlemanly exterior hid a baby killer?

Dutch barely had a chance to put on the brakes before I yanked open the passenger's-side door and bailed. I ran up the front steps and into the house.

"Dad? Bella? Are you guys here—"

"Hello, Haley dear." Madeleine held a small black gun in her elegant hand. She waved the pistol at me, and the light caught intricate mother-of-pearl inlay on its sides. "Please join your father and Bella on the couch. We were just having ourselves a pleasant little chat."

I held my breath and stepped forward. I listened but heard no steps behind me. I hoped Dutch didn't just barge in like I had. He was our only hope.

As is often the case, I chose to go for the dumb effect. "That's a beautiful antique. Are you a collector?"

Madeleine's laugh rang out soft and musical. "I suppose I am, in a way. But I don't collect firearms. This was just a gift. From one of my former husbands."

"Oh, I get it," I said. "You collect spouses. Question is, what do you do with them?"

She shrugged. "Some I divorce. Others die on me. It's been a sad, sad life, you understand."

"But their bucks help ease the sadness."

Her nostrils flared, and her eyes narrowed. "That wasn't a nice thing to say."

"How nice is it to point that thing at me? And in my own house."

"How nice was it to go down to Portland and start digging in my daughter's and my business?"

I glanced at Dad. The hurt and fear in his eyes clamped a vise on my heart. "Oh, let's just call it a future stepdaughter's curiosity. I do have my dad's interests at heart."

"Isn't that interesting?" Her smile was nasty. "That's just what I told Deanna. Like any good daughter, your will leaves all your belongings to Hale, doesn't it?"

And just like that everything clicked into place—at least, everything about her incomprehensible attraction to a quiet, serious, anything-but-wealthy small-town pastor with little in the bank.

I dropped into the rocker. Bella moved her sneakered toe a fraction of an inch to touch my foot. I met her gaze, and the love I saw there warmed every corner of my heart.

"Hey there, Bella. How're the Balis?"

"My babies are fine, even though their mama turned out to be a lousy substitute for Jessica Fletcher, as you can see."

"Hush there." I reached out and took her hand. "I'm just sorry I dragged you into all this. It isn't your fight." I turned to Madeleine. "It was always about me, wasn't it?"

"Not you personally. It's just that lovely inheritance of yours that's too good to pass up."

"Oh, so I'm to believe that getting rid of me isn't personal."

"I'm so glad you understand." She walked to Dad's side. "Now, Hale dear. You understand I have plans for Haley. And then you and I are going to hurry up our wedding date. There's no reason to wait, like you said in church that Sunday."

Dad barely reacted. He blinked and tightened his lips.

Out of the corner of my eye, I caught the passing of a shadow on the other side of the front window. Could it be Dutch? Lila and her Smurfs? I prayed and watched Madeleine's every move.

I wasn't going down easy.

"If you look in my handbag," Madeleine said, "you'll find an airline ticket, Haley. You have two choices. One, you sign an affidavit gifting your wealth to your father and take a long, long vacation in Argentina. A vacation that'll last the rest of your natural life, you understand. And you're so young, with such a long life ahead of you yet."

I shook my head. "You can't—"

"Ah-ah-ah . . ." Madeleine said. "If you balk at life in South America, then you can choose option two. You and I can take a short drive up to Deanna's home. All sorts of nasty accidents can happen on those sharp cliff edges. Which, of course, would shorten that life of yours considerably."

She turned to Dad. "And Hale? If you love your daughter as much as you say you do, I'm sure you don't want her to take that second option, right?"

Dad gave one single, hard shake of his head, his eyes fixed on me.

Madeleine smiled. "I'm sorry to say, Haley won't be coming back to Wilmont in either case. Oh, yes. Haley, dear. If you take option two, then your father will become despondent over his loss. He'll be unable to go on without his beloved daughter, and leave a new will when he passes too. So what's it going to be? A flight to Argentina or a drive to Deedee's estate?"

I caught my breath, set the fear, the horror aside. She'd said it twice. A drive to Deedee's estate. Did that mean that Madeleine didn't know?

"Does Deedee expect my unwilling company?" I asked.

"No, but my daughter knows what to do. She's a quick learner, and she's done very well for herself."

"So her marriage to Stewart is the culmination of Deedee's education."

"Yes, dear, in a way it is. Now if she does as she's been taught, she'll be set for life."

"And does that teaching include Stewart's imminent disappearance?"

"I don't think he'll disappear. He'll just experience a . . . change of circumstances."

She didn't have a clue. "So tell me. How did Deedee land such a great catch?"

"Have you seen my daughter? She's beautiful."

"Hmm . . . but I'm sure Stewart has known other beauties."

"Ah . . . but Deedee's smarter than the rest. She knows how to make sure a man's secrets stay secret."

Dumb time again. "Oh, you mean the abortion business."

Madeleine stiffened and stared at me.

I averted my gaze and saw the matching looks of revulsion burst out on Dad's and Bella's faces. Again that shadowy motion showed through the window at their backs. I prayed some more.

Deedee's proud mama stepped closer to me. "What are you trying to say, Haley?"

To get that gun farther from Dad and Bella, I stood. "Oh, that it must not have been too hard for Deedee to get Stewart to sign on the dotted line. Not if she threatened to blurt out to the world all about his butcher sideline."

"Well, that did help."

Hmm . . . not exactly what I'd expected. "That helped, huh? What other tool did she use to tighten the screws on the guy?"

"There's no need to burden yourself with our business, dear. Besides, it's time to make your choice. Smart girls can save their skins. Especially when they know when to keep their mouths shut. Among other things."

Again that kaleidoscope in my brain began to click images, phrases, thoughts, and memories in rapid-fire, random bursts. A dark cloud descended, and a feeling of dread filled my gut, my throat.

Oh, Dutch! Where are you?

More to the point, where was Midas? No matter how friendly my pooch, I doubt even he would put up with the threat I faced.

The threats KC had faced.

Poor child.

I stepped closer to Madeleine. "She was going to tell, wasn't she?"

She wouldn't meet my gaze. "What are you talking about?"

"KC. She was going to talk, and you couldn't let her. She could tear down this new life Deedee had made for herself. And you wouldn't stand for it. So you gave her the Coumadin."

"I don't know what you're talking about."

"Oh, Madeleine. That's where you're wrong. It might have taken me longer than I like to get it, but I get it now." I blew out a hard sigh. "KC was going to tell, not only about Stewart's late-term abortions but about Stewart's even dirtier little secret."

Madeleine's hands began to shake. She waved the gun, and

her nicey-nice expression disappeared. "Get going, Haley. I guess you've made your decision. Get in the car—now."

"Sure, Madeleine. I'll get in my car. And I'll drive us to the Marshall mansion. I'll bet there are still a bunch of cops there, gathering evidence. I'm sure they'll be happy to trade your pretty little gun for a pair of handcuffs that match Deedee's."

She laughed nervously. "So you think your scare tactics will get you out of this. Forget it. You should have stuck with your decorating schemes. Let's go. Deedee is waiting."

"Deedee's cooling her heels at the Wilmont jail." When she shook her head, I continued. "And so's Stewart. As far as I can see, your only hope to avoid a death sentence is to testify against your son-in-law. The authorities have a real thing for getting child molesters turned killers."

Dad and Bella gasped.

I had enough of a head of steam that I just went on, aimed straight at the most disgusting conclusion. "Especially one who aborted his own child to keep the fourteen-year-old he impregnated from blowing the lid on his games."

Bali H'ai leaped in through the open window to my side. "Meeeeeeoow!"

Madeleine whirled.

Behind me the front door swung in.

Before me Madeleine spun back around, shook. My high kick hit its target. She dropped the gun.

Dutch walked around me, picked it up, and pointed it at her. It all took five seconds or less.

Moments later Lila and her giant Smurfs broke the stunned silence. I collapsed into the rocker, tears pouring down my face. Midas bounded in the open door and stuck his head under my hand. I gave him an automatic scratch.

I'd figured it out.

I knew where KC's baby was.

And I felt worse than I had when I didn't know.

Dutch came to my side, knelt, wrapped his arms around me, and let me weep, let me grieve. Three dead children, two of them victims of crime.

The Smurfs did their thing.

Dad and Bella, long-time good friends, turned to each other and sought to comfort when comfort wasn't easy to find.

Sin left a pall on all of us. Evil always does.

Epilogue

Three long hours later, Lila and her Smurfs took off. I breathed a sigh of relief. Dutch reached out across the sofa cushion between us and squeezed my hand.

"Long, horrible day," he said.

"Amen."

"It's over now."

"Only in some ways. In others . . . well, it'll never be over for Lori and Ron."

He gave me a long, sustained look. "Will it ever be over for you?"

I shook my head. I didn't speak; I couldn't. Something deep inside me urged me to tell him why, to tell him what had happened to me five years ago. I knew I would. I just didn't know if I could do it right then. I hesitated, and the moment was lost.

His cell phone rang.

I grinned. He'd programmed it with a most appropriate song. The notes to "If I Had a Hammer" chimed out.

He frowned—sort of—over his smile. "This is Merrill."

He listened for a few moments, nodded.

His grin grew.

His green eyes sparkled.

"It just so happens," he finally said, mischief all over his handsome face, "that she's right here. I'm fine with the offer, but you'd better talk to her."

Intrigued, I took his phone. "Yes?"

"Haley?" Tedd asked. "How come you're with Dutch—again? Is there something going on between you two?"

"Yep!" When she gasped, I went on. "We're in the creep-catching business, didn't you know?"

Silence. "You got Marshall?"

"And his wife and mother-in-law. I'll tell you all about it at Mickey Dee's tomorrow for dinner, okay?"

A reluctant "Okay" was her response, followed by, "Are you out of the designer business, then?"

"Of course not! Why would you ask that?"

"Well, because my office is looking pretty sad, and I want you and Dutch to do something about it for me."

"You want to hire us to remodel your office?"

"That's what I said. He agreed."

I looked at the smirking contractor at my side. "Shrink lady, you're on!"

She chuckled.

Then I frowned. "Just make sure you're on the up-and-up, Dr. Rodriguez. You know our track record so far. It seems that everywhere Farrell and Merrill go, dead bodies show up too. Promise me it won't happen again."

Dutch's laughter almost drowned out Tedd's sputters. Almost. But not quite.

I began to pray.

Note to the Reader

Very often, when writing fiction, a nugget of information sends an author on the flight of fancy that in time becomes a book. That's what happened when I learned of the antique bottles discovered by divers in Puget Sound off the shores of Edmonds, Washington. Now, while that discovery is real, I took literary license with it and spun this book from there. Obviously, Wilmont exists only in my imagination and on these pages. So, too, do the bottles I describe and Stingray's dive shop. The characters are all fictitious—well, maybe all but one. I'm sure everyone knows the real Midas. He's the quintessential golden retriever, and I know few people who haven't met one of those lovely, loveable creatures. One of them owns me.

Excerpt from
Interior Motives

"No, you can't."

I clenched my fists and blew a disobedient curl off my forehead. "Who says?"

All six foot something of Dutch Merrill bristled. "I do. And I'm the contractor."

"So what? I'm the designer. I say the old, cookie-cutter, builder's-supply-store doors go, and so they go."

"Listen to me, Farrell. I know you want your funky, antique, hand-carved Mexican doors. And I don't question your design sensibilities. But would you just look at those things for a minute?"

I did. I stared at the gorgeous, hundred-plus-year-old mahogany doors with the kind of patina baby-fresh woods envy. "I'm looking, Dutch, and I see the perfect doors for this design—the ones I told you about three weeks ago when they came in to the auction house's warehouse. I even knew before that. The minute I opened the email with photos from Ozzie's shopping trip south of the border, I knew they belonged in Tedd's office."

"And I told you back then your assistant might be spinning his wheels, that the doors might not fit the frames. And that's the deal."

"But look at the doors."

He pounded the offending wood trim in the doorway. "I have. But I have to live in the present. Back when those things were carved, no one thought about codes and standards and all those boring things. That doesn't mean I get to ignore them. I have an inspector to face."

"You're the contractor, right? Figure out how to fit them."

"How? You want me to knock the place down, stick the pieces and parts in a time capsule, and zip us back to nine-teenth-century Mexico?"

"Hey, if that's what it takes, go for it, Orwell."

I stomped out. Okay, I'm not proud of it, but that's just what I did. I stomped like a two-year-old whose mother had whisked her blanky to the wash. But what good is a contractor if he can't do what you need him to do?

True, Dutch works wonders with the budget, comes in on time or earlier, and manages to make ho-hum structures look anything but. Still, I'm the designer, not him.

I want my doors.

Even if they don't fit.

Which is totally unreasonable.

I had to make a U-turn in the hall of Tedd Rodriguez's office. At one of the doorways in question, I paused.

"Um . . . ah, Dutch?"

"What now?"

Oh boy. That growl didn't bode well for my apology. "I don't blame you for being ticked off at me—"

"Ticked off? Can I trade you in for six normal doors?"

My cheeks turned to the hot side of the color wheel. "I doubt you'll get any takers on that bargain. I know I'd pass."

"Huh?"

I tucked a bunch of wild hair behind my ear, then held out my right hand. "Peace? I know I acted like a brat, and I'm sorry. Please forgive me, and please work with me on the doors."

He stared at my hand as if it were the Trojan horse. Poor guy.

"Come on, Dutch. I feel really stupid, and we have to work together on this project. Meet me halfway here, will you?"

"Halfway might be too far." He took my hand, yanked me toward him, and added insult to injury by ruffling my already more than ruffled hair. "I can't change code restrictions, and you know it."

I swatted at his hands but landed no swats. He's taller and quicker.

With one hand I shoved my crazy hair out of my eyes, and with the other I smoothed my taupe T-shirt over the waist of my long denim skirt.

"Okay." I could be gracious. "So replacing the doors is out. And halfway—whatever that might mean—is also out. What can we do with the doors? Even you have to admit they're gorgeous."

Dutch stepped toward the troublesome decorative elements, intense concentration on his rugged face. He ran a hand through his dark hair, then pulled out a measuring tape and applied it to one of the doors. He shook his head.

"I can't see how I can use them, Haley."

"There has to be something you can do. They're perfect for the design and for Tedd."

"Who's bandying my name?" the gorgeous Latina shrink asked, a half smile on her red-lipsticked mouth. "Are you two at it again?"

"Yes—"

"No—"

She laughed. "I guess there's not much the Merrill and Farrell comedy team can agree on, is there?"

Dutch's eyebrows crashed into his hairline. "Comedy team? I don't think so. It's not so much that we disagree as that Haley hasn't learned that not everything is possible. Sometimes things just don't work. Like here."

I ignored his dumb comment. "So you don't hate the doors?"

"Never said I did."

"You just don't see how to replace the old ones with these."

"Well, these are the old ones, the really old ones, but no. I can't hang these instead of standard doors and stick to code."

The word hang caught my attention. Ideas strobed through my head. "What if . . . ? Hey, go with me here, okay? These frames are wider than the doors."

"That's the problem."

Tedd crossed her arms and leaned against the wall, her smile now full-watt bright.

I ignored what I suspected Tedd's smile meant and continued to think out loud. "To stay within code we can't make the doorways narrower."

"Right again—think about Tedd's clients in wheelchairs."

Another look at the wide hall, which opens to the generous waiting room, and one of the million ideas began to jell. "Of course. But what if . . . ?"

I walked to the waiting room, tapped my lips, and thought some more.

Behind me, Tedd's sharp, high-heeled steps followed Dutch's heavier ones. "What if . . . ?" he prodded.

My brain buzzed as if on a Starbucks overdose. "I hadn't planned artwork for the hallway, but what if I use the doors as wall art?"

He gave me one of his "Now you've really lost it" looks.

"Now, wait. Hear me out. We all agree the doors are fabulous. And they're historic treasures someone—us—has to save. So if they can't be used in modern construction, why don't we take advantage of their art value? The carving is magnificent."

Tedd headed back to where I'd stacked the doors. She ran a red-tipped finger over the intricate detail, her smile wider by the second.

Dutch joined her.

I followed, certain of my new vision.

Patience is not one of my stronger virtues, and it didn't show any sign of fortification right then. But I bit my tongue and zipped my lips. I waited them out.

When Dutch gave a soft "Hmm . . ." I knew I'd won the battle. And, to my credit, I didn't crow.

Instead, I said, "Don't you think small, museumlike halogen spots above each door panel, like the ones I had installed around the perimeter of the waiting room, would make for a dramatic display?"

Dutch began to nod. He whipped out his measuring tape again and nodded some more. "Not only are the doors narrower than the openings, but they're also shorter. That means we should have enough space above them for your spotlights to aim just right. Now, I'll still have to figure out a way to hang them without pulling down the walls—"

"Aw, give me a break, Merrill! I can't believe you're about to throw up another roadblock. That should be a piece of cake for you."

"Yeah, like I can leap tall buildings and stop runaway trains, right?"

I blushed again. "Well, maybe you're not quite Superman, but you're pretty handy with hammer and nails. Get with the program, Dutch, the Toolman, Merrill. Give that old-TV-show guy a run for his money."

"More power, huh?"

I faked a punch to his shoulder. "There you go! Chalk one up for the Toolman."

We all laughed, more out of relief at the averted standoff than at my lame excuse for a joke.

"Teddie!" a warbly female voice called from the waiting room. "Are you here, dear?"

Tedd glanced at her watch on her way to the front. "Look at the time! Yes, Darlene. I'm here. Is Jacob with you?"

"Of course, dear. I wouldn't come without him—it's Cissy's day off, remember?"

My curiosity got the better of me—when doesn't it? Since we began the redesign of Tedd's office, I'd met more than a few of her other clients. I say "other" because I'm on the books too. Tedd has helped me deal with personal bogey-men a time or two. So I wanted to get a look at Darlene and Jacob, whoever they were.

Besides, something about the elderly woman's voice tugged at me, so I followed Tedd into the waiting room.

When I walked past Dutch, I had to do some more ignoring, since he muttered, "There goes that nose again. Snoop, snoop, snoop . . ."

It wasn't easy, but I prevailed. Actually, it was my curiosity that won; it dragged me into the waiting room to catch a glimpse of Darlene and Jacob. I let my dignity squawk.

In the large, boring-beige space stood a tall, slender woman who brought to mind lace and tea parties and all the niceties of the late Victorian period. She wore her snow-white hair pulled into a soft Gibson-girl knot at the top of her head, and the lapels of her pale mauve silk suit were embellished with tiny seed pearls. A spectacular strand of more pearls, golden and marble-sized, circled her neck, while the diamonds on her hands sparkled in the weak incandescent light of the table lamps.

At her side a gentleman stood tall and strong, his hair a steely gray, his eyes almost the same color. But something about his gaze struck me as odd. Sadness swept over me, even though I had no idea why.

"Jacob, darling," Darlene said with a pat to one of the overstuffed tan armchairs. "Come sit here while I talk with Teddie. You'll be in the sun, and you know you like that."

The haunting gray eyes turned to Darlene, then to Tedd, to me, and finally back to Darlene. A frown creased Jacob's high forehead.

"Who . . . who are you?"

My stomach sank to my toes. His disorientation spoke loud and clear. Dementia, possibly Alzheimer's. How terribly sad.

With infinite patience Darlene murmured more soothing words. Tedd waited at their side, silent, a soft smile on her lips. I stepped back so as not to disturb Jacob any further—I was a stranger.

I prayed under my breath. I asked for strength for Darlene, clarity for Jacob, wisdom for Tedd.

A tear slid down my cheek.

Dutch's large, warm hand settled on my shoulder, and I surprised myself when I leaned back.

"Tough, isn't it?" he whispered.

"I can't begin to imagine."

Darlene took a magazine from the central coffee table, opened it to a colorful ad, and placed in Jacob's hands.

I glanced at Dutch. "Awesome, isn't she?"

He gave me a crooked grin. "I don't think I could ever come up with that much patience."

"And love . . ."

"For better or for worse . . ."

We watched for long moments until Willa, Tedd's new secretary, stepped out from behind her reception desk and sat next to Jacob. With gentle words she struck up a one-sided conversation with the elderly man.

Only then did Darlene turn to Tedd. "He's had a bad week."

"And you?" Tedd asked.

Darlene shrugged. That's when I noticed that her suit dwarfed her. Either she'd borrowed the outfit, which I doubted, since it seemed so perfect for her, or she'd lost weight—a great deal of weight—since she'd bought it.

Her sigh was more sob than sigh. "I start treatment again next week."

Tedd tried to hide her reaction to Darlene's words, but I'd come to know her pretty well in the last year and a half. The tiny flare of nostrils and the quick blink revealed her shock.

She only nodded. "Want to come in now?"

Darlene stepped into Tedd's counseling office, her shoulders high, her step firm, her demeanor more tragic by the display of courage.

Before the door closed, Tedd asked, "How many chemo sessions will you need this time?"

I looked up at Dutch.

He looked down at me. "The doors are no big deal."

Ginny Aiken, a former newspaper reporter, lives in Pennsylvania with her engineer husband and their three younger sons—the oldest is married and has flown the coop. Born in Havana, Cuba, and raised in Valencia and Caracas, Venezuela, she discovered books at an early age. She wrote her first novel at age fifteen while she trained with the Ballets de Caracas, later to be known as the Venezuelan National Ballet. She burned that tome when she turned a "mature" sixteen. An eclectic list of jobs, including stints as reporter, paralegal, choreographer, language teacher, retail salesperson, wife, mother of four boys, and herder of their numerous and assorted friends, brought her back to books in search of her sanity. She is now the author of twenty-one published works, but she hasn't caught up with that elusive sanity yet.

Mystery with a kick!

Don't miss the beginning of the

Deadly Décor Mysteries